Dear Mystery Reader:

Are you ready for fun, football, and a little bit of murder? Then strap on your helmet as Susan Holtzer turns up the heat on the University of Michigan's gridiron.

Susan Holtzer continues to turn out high-quality mysteries. In addition to receiving numerous critical acclamations and the coveted St. Martin's Malice Domestic award, the Anneke Haagen mystery series has gained a following as fanatical about Holtzer as Michigan fans are about the Maize and Blue.

This time around, Anneke and her police lieutenant boyfriend, Karl, tackle the dirty side of Michigan football. Football has always been intense in Ann Arbor, but during the biggest event of the season it becomes a blood sport. When a dirty alumni group, an NCAA probe, and a vicious killer hit the University of Michigan, it will take more than a Hail Mary pass to unravel a web of secrets, deceit, and murder.

Enjoy!

Yours in crime,

Joe Veltre

Joe Veltre
St. Martin's DEAD LETTER Paperback Mysteries

Other titles from St. Martin's
Dead Letter Mysteries

FLY FISHING CAN BE FATAL by David Leitz
BLACK WATER by Doug Allyn
REVENGE OF THE BARBEQUE QUEENS
by Lou Jane Temple
A MURDER ON THE APPIAN WAY
by Steven Saylor
MURDER MOST BRITISH ed. by Janet Hutchings
LIE DOWN WITH DOGS by Jan Gleiter
THE CLEVELAND CONNECTION by Les Roberts
LONG SHADOWS IN VICTORY by Gregory Bean
BIGGIE AND THE POISONED POLITICIAN
by Nancy Bell
THE TRAIL TO BUDDHA'S MIRROR
by Don Winslow
A VOW OF FIDELITY by Veronica Black
THE SENSATIONAL MUSIC CLUB MYSTERY
by Graham Landrum
THE GOURMET DETECTIVE by Peter King
MANDARIN PLAID by S. J. Rozan
MISSING BONDS by Bruce W. Most
THE KING'S BISHOP by Candace Robb
AGATHA RAISIN AND THE MURDEROUS
MARRIAGE by M. C. Beaton

PRAISE FOR SUSAN HOLTZER AND HER ANNEKE HAAGEN MYSTERIES

Something to Kill For—Winner of the St. Martin's Malice Domestic Contest

"Engaging . . . Anneke is an appealing sleuth, her policeman a perfect foil and their case enjoyable."

—*San Francisco Chronicle*

"A marvelously plotted story . . . A satisfying conclusion."

—*Mostly Murder*

"An entertaining read . . . Anyone who loves garage sales, flea markets, and antique marts will love this mystery . . . An excellent depiction of life in a large university town."

—*Booklist*

"A lot of fun for readers who enjoy bright characters, fast-moving action and a really good plot."

—*Ocala Star-Banner*

"Populated with people who rise above cliches, a protagonist to be admired and a plot that baffles."

—*Deadly Pleasures*

Curly Smoke

"Inviting prose, refreshing characters, and crisp plotting."

—*Library Journal*

"This second installment of a promising series features appealing characters and skillful plotting. Stay tuned for the third episode."

—*Booklist*

Also by Susan Holtzer

Curly Smoke
Something to Kill For

BLEEDING MAIZE AND BLUE

SUSAN HOLTZER

St. Martin's Paperbacks

While many of the locales and physical structures in this book are real places, the characters and events portrayed are entirely works of fiction. Any resemblance to actual events or real persons, living or dead, is purely coincidental.

BLEEDING MAIZE AND BLUE

Library of Congress Catalog Card Number: 96-21367

ISBN: 0-312-96284-3

Printed in the United States of America

St. Martin's Press hardcover edition/September 1996
St. Martin's Paperbacks edition/September 1997

10 9 8 7 6 5 4 3 2 1

When a culture is flawed, its institutions are inevitably flawed as well. But it has always seemed to me that a great university is perhaps less flawed than other institutions, if only because it is one place where admitting to flaws is permitted.

This one's for Michigan—and for the *Daily*.

The character of Zoe Kaplan is dedicated, with love and gratitude, to the memory of Zolton Ferency.

ACKNOWLEDGMENTS

The list of people who helped me with this book is a long one. First and foremost, I want to thank the staff of the *Michigan Daily*, which was gracious in the extreme to a random alumna. Special thanks go to then editor in chief Jessie Halladay, who answered question after question with great patience. And, most especially, to David Friedo, who has made more difference to the *Daily* than perhaps even he realizes.

I also want to thank Craig Keilitz, of the Michigan Athletic Department, for information about NCAA regulations, and about Michigan and college athletics; Professor Carl Berger, for information about the arcana of the University's computer conferencing system; Gary Erickson, of the Marin County (California) coroner's office, for helping me murder my victim properly; and Mason Jones, for vetting my computer information (and without whom I would still be writing on an old Underwood.) All of these people gave me invaluable information; any errors of fact in these pages are mine and mine alone.

ONE

The city room past midnight sizzled and popped as the *Michigan Daily* neared deadline. Harsh fluorescent lights high overhead turned the leaded glass windows black and reflective against the night. At the long row of aging Macintosh computers, student reporters banged out late stories and shouted questions and profane comments across the room. Downstairs in the production room the night editor, a frayed junior in a Crash Worship T-shirt, dragged on her mouse and swore monotonously, casting an occasional venomous glance at the clock.

"No, I'm sorry," the freshman trainee at the news desk was saying into the instrument for the fifth time. "There's no one here from the sports staff. Yes, I'll tell him." The trainee replaced the receiver and called out: "It's the AD himself this time."

"Tough shit," sports editor Gabriel Marcus called back. "It's too late now; he had his chance an hour ago when we phoned him for comment." He picked up the phone that connected him to the production room. "Mary," he spoke to the night editor, "can you give us enough space?"

"I've got you ten inches on page one," she said firmly. "That's the best I can do."

"Okay." Gabriel peered at his own terminal. "I can cut from the gymnastics story to get the rest on breakover." He hung up and punched the number that connected him to the sports night editor downstairs, ignoring the anguished outcry from the author of the gymnastics article.

Someone had "liberated" one of the old oak benches from the downstairs composing room and stationed it under the window behind the sports desk. Sitting on it cross-legged, consciously nonchalant, Zoe Kaplan fielded questions and profane congratulations, watching the clock tick down to her first front-page story. In a rare moment of introspection, she thought, This is one of those times I'll remember for the rest of my life.

"Okay, we're down." The night editor appeared at the top of the back stairwell and sank into a chair in front of the old dumbwaiter shaft.

"Good." Gabriel stretched widely and powered down his terminal. "And thanks, Mary. Sorry for the scramble, but we had to keep it quiet until the last possible moment."

"Worth it." The night editor showed her teeth, a shark's smile. "I love sticking it to the athletic department. I just wish I knew," she said darkly to Zoe, "how the hell you got this. Never mind"—she raised a hand, palm outward—"the fewer people who know, the better. Where the hell is my Coke?" She grumbled away toward the Coke machine and Gabriel swiveled his chair toward the window, propped his feet on the oak bench, and gazed at Zoe.

"Not bad," he said, flexing his fingers.

"Not bad, hell," she retorted. "It's fucking fantastic and you know it."

"It's pretty good. . . . For a sophomore."

"It's only the story of the fucking decade, that's all."

"I always said humility was your most endearing quality, Kaplan," Jeff Bryson said, flopping down on the window seat next to her.

"If I were humble," Zoe retorted, "I'd be perfect, and then all you little people wouldn't adore me the way you do." She gulped Coke and grinned at him. "And you know what's the best part?"

"What?"

"How pissed off the other papers are going to be. Don't you just love thinking about that asshole Dobie walking into the *Free Press* tomorrow morning and seeing the *Daily*?"

"That's a very immature attitude," Gabriel said loftily. They glared at each other with ferocious glee, savoring the high.

"Kaplan, telephone," the trainee called over from the city desk.

"Who is it?" she called back.

"Your roommate."

"Oh, jeez." Zoe dropped her voice and shook her head violently. "Tell her I'm not around," she mouthed. She really was going to have to do something about Paula, but not tonight.

"What a night." Katie Sparrow, gorgeous red hair flaming out around her face, perched on the edge of the desk. "And tomorrow," she said, waving at the assignment sheet posted next to the window, "all I get to do is cover track practice, while you get to have old Foghorn rip out your heart and make you eat it."

"Actually, I wanted to talk to you about tomorrow," Gabriel addressed Zoe.

"They're probably planning a press conference right now," she said. "I can't wait to see what sort of damage control they come up with."

"There's more to it than just writing up what the athletic department gives out," Gabriel pointed out. "Russell Truhorne is going to try like hell to control this story, and he's very, very good at it. That's why I want to lay out the follow-up now." He swiveled back to his desk. "Gather round, children, and let's synchronize watches." Rapidly he laid out assignments—athletic department reaction, press conference, backgrounders. "And we want some local interviews—a couple of ex-jocks, the president of the M-Club, student leaders, that sort of thing."

"I wouldn't mind doing the backgrounder," Jeff Bryson volunteered.

"I'll stick with the athletic department," Zoe declared. Sidebar features could be fun to do, but visibility and reputation came through covering hard news. Sports reporting, after all, is my means, not my goal, she reminded herself.

"You're going to be about as popular over there as an Ohio State flag at a pep rally," Gabriel warned her.

"I know," she agreed hungrily, grinning. "Ro's going to go ballistic." Russell Truhorne, after all, wasn't going to be the interesting one; the athletic director was too good at his job—slick and manipulative, not confrontational. No, the real explosion was going to come from Ralph Roczynski, the head football coach famous for his violent—and carefully choreographed, Zoe was sure—outbursts. She could hardly wait.

"Besides . . ." Gabriel glanced over toward the assignment sheet. "You're supposed to be on that President's Weekend stuff, aren't you?"

"Oh, shit, I forgot all about it." The yearly bash for members of the President's Club—people who'd donated $10,000 or more to the University—had seemed like a great thing to crash when she'd thought about it back in September. Not that she really expected anything but a sarcastic minor feature out of it; she was just automatically attracted to any place, thing, or event that was posted off-limits. On the other hand . . .

"Actually, Gabriel, it all fits together. This whole weekend is sort of a sports special. Karl Genesko is the guest of honor; he's donating two Superbowl rings to the U at Friday night's banquet, and then Saturday they're retiring the number he wore when he played here. In fact," she added, "I think I'll start out with Genesko tomorrow morning. He's done a lot of recruiting for them. That way, I can tie the two stories together."

"Jeez, you're a greedy bitch, Kaplan," Jeff Bryson laughed.

"You got that right," Zoe retorted. "I'll catch the press conference in the afternoon," she said to Gabriel. "No way they'll get their shit together before then. Especially," she chortled, "because they're going to be spending most of the day trying to figure out who leaked the story to us." At this she broke down in a fit of uncontrolled laughter, and Jeff and Katie joined in.

"Maybe." Gabriel tried to maintain the serious demeanor of the senior editor, then gave up in the face of their hilarity. "All right, all right," he choked finally. "We'll play it by ear." He ran his hands through his hair with an air of frustration. "We'll see how things shake out tomorrow and then decide."

"Gabriel, it's my story," Zoe insisted.

"Darlin'," he said evenly, "by tomorrow there's going to be *so much* shit, and it's gonna hit such a *big* fan, that there'll be plenty of it for all of us to play in."

TWO

How the hell did the bitch *get* the story?

Charlie Cassovoy was reeling. He stared down at the *Daily*, at the screaming black headline. If he looked up, he would see the barely concealed sneers of the faces of the other *Detroit News* sportswriters, all those young bright-eyed predator faces that were carefully not looking at him. Bright eyed even at eight o'clock in the morning. Charlie blinked several times, rapidly, trying without much hope to blink away his hangover-induced headache. Normally he shrugged off his hangovers as the acceptable cost of getting drunk, but today it seemed to hurt more than usual.

He felt the old sickness that always attacked him when he saw a great story that someone else had broken. Only this time it was twice as bad, three or four times as bad. He could feel bile rise in his throat.

"Hey, Cassovoy." Sports editor Max Delaney looked like he'd just eaten something nasty—but then, he always did. "Didn't you used to have *con*-tacts?" he asked. Nastily. Delaney had those same bright predator eyes. Charlie could feel the killers circling, seeking weakness. He blinked again. Never let them see you bleed.

"This crap?" He folded the *Daily* and dropped it in the wastebasket next to his desk. After thirty years working for the same crummy paper you'd think they'd give him an office of his own. "Shit, they don't have anything," he said. "No who or what, no facts at all. Hell, the whole story could've been a one-sentence headline." Thinking: What good are contacts when some bitch can use her pussy to get whatever she wants?

"Well, it's one hell of a sentence. And it's one sentence more than you've brought in in the last twenty years."

"Hey, breaking news isn't my job, Delaney," Charlie counterattacked. "I'm a columnist, remember? It's the rest of these clowns who're supposed to get the news—if they can recognize it."

"Oh, yeah, that's right. You got your Big Story once, didn't you?" Delaney etched sarcastic capital letters onto the words. "When was that, Charlie? Some time around World War I, wasn't it?"

"See any other Pulitzers around this place, Delaney?"

"How does it feel to have done one thing in your life and know you'll never do anything else, Charlie?"

"Better than never having done anything at all," Charlie snarled. He sat down heavily at his desk and began opening his mail, keeping his face a blank. It would be disastrous to let Delaney know how close to the bone his last shot had come.

The Pulitzer, of course, had been in 1957—and he was one of the youngest recipients ever, he reminded himself. He'd been covering high school sports for the *Toledo Blade* when he accidentally overheard a conversation between a high school football coach and one of his former players who had moved on to a nearby college. When Charlie heard the words "seven-point spread" followed by the words "big payday," he promptly called the NCAA. The subsequent investigation led to one of the biggest gambling and game-throwing scandals in college sports history and made Charlie Cassovoy a household name—for about fifteen minutes.

Still, the fifteen minutes had been enough to land him a high-profile job on the *Detroit News*, and for a while he figured he'd died and gone to heaven. He must have been about 35, covering one more boring Detroit Lions game, when it first dawned on him that the penultimate moment of his life had already happened. That all the rest of his life was downhill on a slippery slope to nowhere.

That was when he started drinking in earnest, because he could recapture the feeling best when he was drunk. What was it the jocks called it these days? Fire in the belly—the intense desire to be the best, to be a winner. Every now and then, Charlie remembered what it was like to have been a winner.

Right now he needed a drink; at least that might help the hangover-induced headache. But he didn't dare go into one of the Jefferson Street bars at eight o'clock in the morning. He was too fucking famous.

The irony of it wasn't lost on him. Twenty-five years ago, when he'd just won the Pulitzer (a thing virtually unheard-of for a sportswriter), nobody outside the newspaper business knew who the hell he was. Now, when all he ever wrote were diatribes, everyone in town knew his name.

It was when he started blowing stories, forgetting interviews, and antagonizing local teams, that they kicked him upstairs and gave him a weekly column. For a while he was relieved, then angry, then bitter. Oddly, it was only when his generalized malice began to spill over into his writing that people started to notice his column. Somehow, he tapped into the well of half-subconscious resentment that so many average fans feel for their putative heroes, the resentment of the ordinary working-class joe for the young and the strong and the wealthy, fortune's favorites.

He took on all of them. He vilified players for demanding huge salaries and team owners for refusing to pay enough to build a winning team. He attacked referees as incompetent and players who challenged a call as crybabies. When an athlete agreed to an interview, Charlie printed whatever would make him look most foolish, greedy or unpleasant. If an athlete refused to be interviewed, as many of them began to do, he crucified them for "forgetting the fans who pay for their Porsches."

Within five years, he was a legend in the Detroit sports world. His column, "The Voice of the Fan," now ran twice a week and was second in readership only to the woman who wrote weekly about her sex life. His narrow, dyspeptic face, with the rimless bifocals perched on his nose, adorned the sides of Detroit buses and grimaced from billboards advertising the *News.* It should have been enough.

It should have been me, he thought as he dropped junk mail into the wastebasket atop the *Daily.* I should've been the one to bring down those Ann Arbor bastards. His mouth twisted; the only people he despised more than college students in general were Michigan students—arrogant little turds who thought they were God's gift just because their rich daddies could buy them Michigan degrees. Even Michigan jocks gave you that same sideways look, when they thought you weren't looking, like they were sniggering at the label on your J. C. Penney shirt.

He reached for the phone, thinking: Contacts? Wait'll they see what *real* contacts can do.

His first call was to the Michigan Sports Information Office, where a young assistant PIO believed Charlie would help him land a reporting job on the *News.* Charlie was experienced enough to avoid the specific question; instead, he asked things like: "Any players miss practice today?" and "I bet some of the big-shot alumni have really been burning up the phone lines, huh?"

After that, he took a couple of calls and made three more, and when he finally hung up he sat and stared at the phone for a while. Nothing specific yet, of course, but it was early days. And there were a couple of suggestive things. . . . He stood and picked up his briefcase, thinking: This time it's not gonna get away from me.

Thinking: How the hell *did* the bitch get the story?

THREE

"How the *hell* did she find out about it?" Assistant Athletic Director Frank Novak raged, pacing his office. "*Nobody* knew they were meeting. There was no one else in the room but Russell and Greenaway. Even Russell's secretary didn't know who he was meeting with. Hell, even *I* didn't know. It's impossible!" He glared at the crumpled copy of the *Daily* lying on his desk.

Wendy Coleman, Novak's student assistant, gritted her teeth. She'd been hearing the same refrain for the last half hour, and she was sick of it. She was also worried. If the story were true, she badly wanted to know which player was involved. Or more accurately, which player wasn't—specifically Kyle Farmer. Unfortunately, the story didn't say; for all its huge, trumpeting banner headline, it didn't give a whole lot of information. She picked up her own copy of the paper and quickly read through the story again.

NCAA TO INVESTIGATE 'M' FOOTBALL RECRUITING

Investigator warns Truhorne
To expect full-scale probe

By ZOE KAPLAN

The *Daily* has learned that the National Collegiate Athletic Association will shortly announce a wide-ranging probe of the University's football recruiting practices, focusing particularly on alumni and booster activities.

NCAA investigator Alvin Greenaway told Athletic Director Russell Truhorne yesterday he had received information that at least one, and possibly more, Michigan alumni had given "illegal inducements" to present or former 'M' football players. Greenaway did not reveal the identities of either the players or the alumni in question. He also did not reveal the source of his information.

Greenaway, himself a Michigan alumnus and former member of the 'M' tennis team from 1964 to 1966, warned Truhorne that the investigation could not be stopped. He pointed out that the violations in question represented a major infraction that, if proved, would unquestionably lead to severe punishment. Such punishment could include NCAA probation, loss of scholarships, a ban on television appearances and post-season bowl games (and the accompanying loss of TV revenue), and possibly even the dreaded "death penalty." He suggested, however, that potential penalties would be lessened if Michigan were to launch its own investigation and uncover and punish the infractions itself.

> In a private meeting lasting more than an hour, Greenaway told Truhorne that he would initiate the investigative process as soon as he returned to NCAA headquarters in Overland Park, Kansas, early next week. He also said that because he was a Michigan alumnus, he himself would not be handling the investigation.
>
> Contacted at his home last night, head football coach Ralph "Ro" Roczynski maintained that he knew nothing about a pending investigation and vigorously denied any recruiting violations. "They can investigate everything from our travel vouchers to the paper in the can," he shouted, "but they won't find a goddam thing we did that's illegal."

The rest of the story was mainly background, detailing NCAA investigation procedures and recapping various recent penalties handed out to other schools for recruiting infractions. Next to the text was a photograph of Truhorne and an old, blurry one of Greenaway, in Michigan tennis whites, apparently dug out of old archives.

Wendy sighed. She wished she could talk to Kyle, but she didn't think she'd be able to locate him. Besides, if she didn't get Frank Novak back on track, this day was going to be even more of a debacle than it was already shaping up to be.

"Remember, you have to meet with that alumni committee at eleven o'clock this morning," she warned him.

"Oh, God, I can't." He looked appalled. "What am I going to say to them? Wendy, you'd better call them and cancel. They're alumni; they'll understand."

"They probably would, of course. But they went to a lot of trouble to set up this meeting. And the committee includes Eleanor Sullivan and Daniel Najarian. Remember," she said brightly, like a kindergarten teacher, "they only want to talk about procedures, not specifics. And it's just a private meeting, no press or anything like that."

"I suppose you're right." Novak rubbed his eyes, dislodging his black-rimmed glasses. "God, what *are* we going to tell the press?"

What do you mean "we," white man? Wendy thought, stifling a snort. Like Russell Truhorne would let you near that podium. Still, beneath her contempt she felt a small pang of sympathy for the big, untidy man. The feeling annoyed her; she wasn't accustomed to feeling sympathy for well-paid middle-aged white men.

She'd been surprised when he hired her in the first place, a twenty-two-year-old black sophomore—and a girl—out of the Detroit projects. She decided that he wanted a black chick in the office to impress the brothers coming through on recruiting trips, and she expected to be offered up as a special bonus to some hotshot high school no-neck or sleazy alum. But for someone working her way through school, it was too good a job to pass up. She made a point of finding out exactly how to file a sexual harrassment complaint, took the job, and waited.

It never happened. Novak hired her, alternately overworked and ignored her, and generally took her for granted. If she were honest, she had to admit he didn't treat her any differently from anyone else.

Oh, he was a racist, of course, one of those "we did it, why can't they" types. But his racism, and his sexism, seemed confined to the institutional attitudes of all white men. On a personal, one-on-one level, he truly didn't seem to care what color a person's skin was, as long as their blood ran clear maize and blue.

If only he weren't such a pompous ass.

"Frank, we need the number of recruiting contacts for the last four years—all Michigan staff." Colin Matthews, the Sports Information Director, shoved open the door and entered without ceremony. He was dressed, like all athletic department staff, in a businesslike dark suit, but with it he wore his trademark tie, hand-painted with a huge, snarling wolverine. "Yeah, I know." He intercepted Frank's dubious glance at the wolverine. "But if I *don't* wear it they'll ask why, and that would make it worse." He waved a hand, dismissing the tie. "I also need a copy of that mailing we sent out to all the alumni clubs last year—you know the one I mean."

"The one warning them against any personal contact with high school athletes." Frank nodded crisply. "Right." He sat down behind his desk and began making notes. "You'll probably also want a copy of our most recent NCAA report for backgrounder. And what about the compliance audit?"

"No, but let me have copies of all our recruiting brochures."

"And I assume," Frank pursed his lips in thought, "you'll want the complete paper trail on the specific player who's named in the accusation. As soon as they bother to tell us who it is," he finished acidly. He made another note, feeling better now that he had something specific to do. Minor tasks, maybe, but meaningful nonetheless. One part of the important whole.

In the division of labor within the athletic department, Frank Novak was the one who did the shitwork. Frank was perfectly aware of this; in fact, he was mildly proud of it. Shitwork was all the thousands of details that kept any huge enterprise—from a university to a corporation to an army—running smoothly. And Frank knew he was good at it.

He had come to terms with his own limitations early in life. Even as an undergraduate he'd had no great ambitions, no adolescent vision. He lacked any remotest qualities of leadership or charisma. What he did have was an endless capacity for minor or repetitive (some would say boring) detail, a habit of precision, and a willingness to do any task that needed doing regardless of its status implications. He was, in sum, the perfect subordinate, and he was perfectly comfortable in the role.

He would have been a happy man at, say, Eastern Kentucky, or Sacramento State. Not that he was *un*happy; but the high-octane quality of the Michigan operation kept him perpetually on edge; there were so many things that could go wrong, and the stakes were so high. On the other hand, he could no more have worked for another school than he could have grown another head.

He'd grown up as an Ann Arbor kid, but he'd been a *west side* Ann Arbor kid, in the days when the west side was for townies. Kids who lived on the west side had fathers who worked at Hoover Ball Bearing or Argus—both gone now—or, if they worked for the University, wore blue work shirts to plant department jobs, instead of corduroy jackets to classrooms. Or, as in Frank's case, had no fathers at all.

Lester Novak had gone patriotically off to war against Germany and never returned. Rose Novak, who had been secretly glad to see him go, used her government pension to buy a small house, got a secretarial job with the University, and spent every nonworking moment until the day she died in a futile chase after Grand Master points in bridge tournaments. She kept Frank fed and clothed, never mistreated him, and was relieved when he left.

Frank found his family in Michigan Stadium.

In those days, before Michigan football (and college football everywhere) exploded into a multi-million-dollar enterprise, before every game was an automatic sellout, local kids were allowed free into empty end-zone seats after half-time. Frank Novak saw the second half of every Michigan game from third grade through the end of high school.

He himself hadn't a single athletic bone in his body, and in truth it wasn't the athleticism that attracted him; nor was it the spectacle, although he appreciated those elements of it. What captivated Frank was the sheer, heady *belongingness.* When the crowd rose to its feet, roaring, like a single organism, and Frank stood and cheered and shouted along with them, he became part of something magical, not just one small, solitary boy but a fragment of something infinitely wonderful.

If he were graduating from high school today, Frank knew, there was no way he'd ever be accepted to Michigan—or be able to afford it if he were. Luckily for him, in 1955 Michigan was far easier to get into; it was also far cheaper. If you lived at home, in fact, a Michigan education was within reach of most Ann Arbor kids.

He enrolled without any great trouble, wangled himself a job as a student assistant in what was then a vastly smaller, simpler, and more casual athletic department, and simply stayed.

Because, even after he married a local girl; even after he raised two sons—regardless, this was his family.

"Oh, and I'd better have that budget analysis you did during the summer, too," Matthews said.

"Let me do a slightly different version for you," Frank suggested. "I can do a breakout of recruiting costs as a factor of total budget, and of football budget."

"Great," Matthews enthused. "If we can't dazzle them with footwork *or* baffle them with bullshit, maybe we can numb them with numbers."

"Where is—" Frank stopped at the tinny beep of the interoffice phone and waited as Wendy picked up the receiver, listened for a moment, and mouthed "Truhorne."

"Yes, Russ?"

"Frank, I need you to do something for me." The athletic director's voice, even over the phone, was crisp and authoritative.

"Anything, of course."

"Among other things—" Russell Truhorne managed to project rueful amusement in the midst of catastrophe "—the TV people want to try out some new equipment at the game Saturday, and they need to bring in another trailer and arrange for additional wiring. Unfortunately, they didn't bother to inform us until now. I'd like you to take care of it this morning, if that's all right."

"Yes, of course." Frank nodded his head vigorously at the unseeing telephone. "I'll work it out with them."

"Thanks, Frank," Truhorne said warmly. "I knew I could count on you."

Wendy, who had been listening in, was making frantic semaphore signals that Frank had ignored. "What about the alumni committee?" she reminded him when he hung up.

"Frank, I'm going to need that material within a couple of hours," Matthews warned.

"Oh, hell." Frank ran a hand over his head, making his already unruly hair stand out from his head in clumps. "Well, look," he said after a moment, "the TV people will just have to wait. The alumni are more important."

"They're both important," Wendy pointed out. "After all, they both mean money."

"You're right. Okay, how about this—do you think you can put together the items Colin wants?"

"I think so," she agreed, pleased. "All except those budget breakouts."

"I can do those when I get back." He thought rapidly. "I'll go over to the stadium now and deal with the TV problem. You call the people on the alumni committee and ask them to meet me at the president's box at the stadium instead of in the conference room."

"Sure, that should work." Her face cleared. "It might also impress them enough to chill them out a little."

"I'll be back at noon." Matthews waved a hand and left, but Frank and Wendy were too absorbed in their scheduling to do more than nod.

"I wish we could get someone from the coaching staff there to sit in," Frank gnawed his lower lip, "but I suppose they're all busy. Besides . . ." Wendy knew what he was thinking; coaches were notoriously hard to control. "I know." Frank snapped his fingers. "Find out if Karl Genesko can join us."

Sometimes the old guy actually surprises me, Wendy thought, nodding agreement. She penciled in "Alumni" in the eleven o'clock slot on Novak's calendar and picked up the phone.

FOUR

"Daniel, I hope I didn't wake you." Richard Killian spoke quickly into the telephone, the obligatory words almost perfunctory. "Have you seen this morning's *Daily*?"

"Yes." Daniel Najarian sounded even grimmer than Richard felt. "I knew it would come to this sooner or later."

"Knew what would come to this?" Richard's voice spiked with anxiety. "You mean you know who's responsible?" Damn, that was a stupid thing to say. Richard wanted to take back the words the instant they left his mouth. This was Daniel Najarian, he reminded himself, taking a deep breath.

He and Najarian were putative equals in Ann Arbor, both of them active and successful Michigan alumni. But like the old joke went, some alumni were more equal than others. He'd met Daniel Najarian, of course, at various alumni functions. But Najarian, with his genius and his millions, was a head-table kind of guy, whereas Richard was merely one of any number of active alumni. That, Richard planned, was going to change—but only if he handled this latest crisis correctly.

"No, I do not know who is responsible," Najarian snapped. "What I mean is that, given the insane football fixation among a certain portion of Michigan alumni, a scandal was bound to happen eventually."

"Daniel, cheating is a risk in any competitive endeavor." Richard fought back the inclination to make soothing noises, to avoid arguing with the great man. "And competition is meaningless if you don't care about it."

"College football as it is currently organized is *intrinsically* meaningless," Najarian declared. "It provides true competition only to an elite handful of participants, and artificially contrived pseudo-competition to the masses."

Good, Richard thought. He's enjoying it. This is the sort of thing he wants from people.

Charm, he knew, didn't work on Daniel Najarian, and charm was Richard's most potent weapon. Najarian was one of those rare creatures who legitimately enjoyed arguing. Virtually alone among those who insisted they loathed sycophants, Najarian actually meant it. He only respected you if you argued with him; only if you openly disagreed with him could he fully believe you weren't after him for his money or his status.

Richard wasn't sure how he knew all these things. In truth, he didn't so much *know* them as *understand* them, at some deep intuitive level. It was this intuition that was the secret, the linchpin of his charm, which was quite real.

"Well, we've argued this before." Richard laughed lightly. "The question is, where do we stand now?"

"We don't stand anywhere until this mess is cleared up." Najarian sounded uncharacteristically gloomy. "If we announced a major academic recruitment drive now, we'd be laughed out of town."

"But an NCAA investigation could drag on for months. Or even years," Richard protested, his voice spiking with anxiety. He could see his great opportunity slipping away, sliding down a greasy slope of scandal.

For Richard Killian, this was big-time stuff, the opportunity of a lifetime. He had hardly been able to believe his luck when, a couple of months ago, Najarian had called him at his home in San Francisco and asked him to be part of his committee.

What he planned to do, Najarian explained, was to donate a four-million-dollar matching grant to the University, for the purpose of establishing a student recruiting drive unlike anything ever done before. The University, he said, would search out the brightest, most academically gifted high school students, all over the country, and sell them on the merits of attending the University of Michigan. With the endowment they would set up, there would be scholarship money, there would be guaranteed summer jobs in their fields of study, there would even be travel grants. It was time, he said acerbically, that the University put as much effort into finding intellectually talented students as it did recruiting the physically talented.

Richard had had to stifle the urge to gulp, Why me? But of course, he'd been active in student recruiting on the West Coast for a long time. Most people assume colleges only recruit athletes, but in fact most major universities recruit other students as well, using alumni whenever possible. Richard had done all the diddly-shit things colleges do—college fairs, promotional mailings, speeches to high school assemblies—because he believed in the University, and because he enjoyed it, and also because it was good business. But there'd never been anything like the drive Najarian was proposing. It would be an absolutely brilliant thing for the University.

It would also be a brilliant thing for Richard Killian. The restaurant he owned in San Francisco would be just the beginning; with this kind of visibility, he could begin to think about a franchise chain of Maize and Blue sports bars in every major city in the country. Richard knew the idea was a winner; all he needed was that first big push. Daniel Najarian was going to give it to him.

"It might work, at that," his wife Caroline had agreed the morning Najarian's call had come. "A lot of people get really silly about that rah-rah alumni stuff. If you can position yourself as a kind of super-alumnus, you could make a major media splash." She picked up her briefcase. "I'll be home late tonight. I think Manfred Williams is ready to take the plunge on that new mutual fund. Oh, and by the way," she riffled through a sheaf of phone messages, "the cleaner called. They said your red-and-black silk shirt had to be returned for spot cleaning. It won't be ready for your trip."

"It doesn't matter. I don't want to wear red this weekend anyway. We're playing Wisconsin."

"Good Lord." She looked at him with mild contempt. "Do these people really care about that sort of thing?"

"Well, I wouldn't be ostracized or anything," he replied, "but it wouldn't feel right. Would you wear a red dress to a Cal-Stanford football weekend?"

"I wouldn't *go* to a Cal-Stanford football weekend," she said caustically. "Just because I got my degree from Berkeley doesn't mean I have to sit around guzzling beer, shouting slogans, and watching a batch of no-neck idiots pummeling each other on a football field."

"You really don't figure you owe Berkeley anything, do you?" he asked curiously.

"Owe them? No, why should I? I paid for my education, and I pay damned high taxes to keep the place going."

"How sad for you," he had said to her, meaning it.

He thought about the conversation now, searching for a response to Daniel Najarian. This was too big an opportunity, for Michigan, and for himself, to let it get away.

"Look, Daniel, this could all be a mistake," Richard said persuasively. "And even if there is an investigation, it isn't as if anyone on the committee has anything to do with it."

"Are you so sure of that?" Najarian asked coldly. "After all, Eleanor Sullivan has been involved in football recruiting for years. So has Jeffrey Person. So, Richard, have you."

"For that matter," Richard replied, stung, "so have you, Daniel. Just because you focus on the academic whiz kids, do you think it doesn't count? After all, you've always got a couple of jocks working in your lab every summer. Do you really think intellectual ability can be assumed to preclude dishonesty?"

"Touché," Najarian said softly. "And now, having made my point for me so lucidly, you understand why we cannot proceed as planned."

Oh, shit. Screwed. Richard laughed openly. "I walked into that one, didn't I? Look, Daniel, we've got this meeting scheduled with Frank Novak this morning. Why don't we go ahead with it for the moment, and see how things shake out over the next few days? For all we know, the whole thing is a crock. The story in the *Daily* is so vague they could just have picked up some weird rumor."

"Yes, that's possible," Najarian agreed grudgingly. "All right, we'll proceed as planned for the moment. But remember, I haven't made a formal commitment of the money yet."

"I'd hardly forget four big ones, Daniel." Richard laughed amiably and hung up, then sat and swore at the telephone for several colorful minutes. He was *not* going to let this opportunity get away, certainly not over a lousy football recruiting violation.

FIVE

Mornings were already getting cold. Anneke Haagen pulled the heavy dark-green drapes and felt the draft pouring in with the October sun, finding unseen crevices in the old oak window frames. She added new storm windows to her mental list of new-house chores, down there in the "winterizing" category with furnace inspection and firewood. And a chimney sweep—the living room fireplace looked like it hadn't been cleaned out since the Coolidge administration.

From next door, in the tiny fourth bedroom they'd turned into Karl's dressing room, she could just hear the closet door close, the sound muffled through thick plaster walls. Hurriedly she did a last mirror check, straightening a wisp of short, gray-flecked hair. She straightened her charcoal silk pants, running a finger along the waistband. The finger stuck along the side, where she felt a small roll of flesh she was sure hadn't been there a few weeks ago. The pants were definitely tight, she realized with dismay.

"Are you ready?" Karl Genesko's six-foot-five, 250-pound frame filled the doorway.

"Just about," she answered, flustered by his sudden appearance. She turned away from the mirror self-consciously. "We need to do something about storm windows," she said, hoping he hadn't seen her examining herself.

"Don't we want the fixed storm-and-screen combinations?" he asked. They discussed storm windows, weatherstripping, and the merits of triple glazing on the way downstairs, subjects which can fill any possible conversational gap among midwesterners. At the foot of the oak staircase they separated briefly, going to their respective offices to collect briefcases and other paraphernalia for the day ahead.

It was one of the things Anneke had first appreciated about the big old house—*two* extra ground-floor rooms, offering enough space (and especially enough privacy) for two adults who'd each lived alone for a long time before coming together.

They had met at a time when she was coming off a failed marriage followed by a spectacularly bad relationship; when she'd wanted nothing more than an independent, well-ordered, and most of all emotion-free life. She had resisted involvement with a kind of imbecile terror; Karl was the one who insisted on commitment. But even when she finally agreed, it was to everything but marriage.

"If that's truly the way you want it," he said, "I won't pressure you. But, you know, marriage doesn't absolutely have to be claustrophobic. You're going into a relationship, not a prison."

"I know that, but . . . no, that's not it," she said with a sudden flash of insight. "It's the other way around."

"I see." As usual, to her relief, he understood her at once. "You're not leaving an escape hatch for yourself. You're leaving one for me." He was too intelligent to batter her with protestations of undying devotion; instead, he simply nodded. "All right, we'll play it your way—'everything but marriage.' "

A week later he called her at her office. "Can you meet me this afternoon at two o'clock?"

"I think so. Why?"

"I'll tell you when I see you." He gave her an unfamiliar address on Olivia and hung up before she could press for information.

She pulled her Firebird up to the curb in front of a big, comfortable-looking house on a street lined with other big, comfortable-looking houses, marveling that so much of Ann Arbor's Burns Park neighborhood had survived the construction feeding frenzy of the late fifties and early sixties. Its choice location, barely half a mile from campus, was the very element that put it at risk; too many blocks like this one—Oakland, Prospect, even parts of Cambridge—had become student slums, their fine old houses viciously subdivided into rabbit-warren apartments. Still, somehow most of the area had survived, remaining the sort of quintessential university neighborhood that hardly exists anymore outside nostalgic television sitcoms. The houses and yards were well kept, but not *too* well kept (which would have signaled a politically incorrect level of concern for appearance); the front yards were green without the putting-green perfection of suburbia; most of the cars at the curb or in driveways were defiantly small and battered.

When Anneke got out of the car, Karl was already standing on the sidewalk waiting for her, looking—for him—almost impatient. He held a set of keys ready in his hand, and when he unlocked the door and motioned her inside, the gesture was almost a flourish.

The house was empty, yet it felt . . . welcoming, Anneke decided. Airy, spacious rooms off both sides of the large center hallway; ten-foot ceilings soaring overhead; golden oak woodwork, its varnish darkened with age but at least, thank God, not painted over. She stood still for a moment, analyzing the ambience. A good house, solid and mature and comfortable.

"What do you think of it?" Karl asked.

"It's wonderful." She glanced upward toward the head of the wide staircase. "How many bedrooms?"

"Four, but one of them is barely the size of a closet."

"Then that's what we'll use it for," she declared, making an instant decision. "We both have too many clothes anyway." A thought struck her. "Can we get a long-term lease? I don't want to have to move again in a year."

"It's not for rent," he said. "It's for sale."

"You mean you're going to *buy* it?"

"No." He shook his head, his dark eyes on her face. "*We're* going to buy it. Jointly. That is," he added, watching her, "if you really meant what you said about 'everything but marriage.' "

"We're . . ." The instant of pure panic was followed, to her own surprise, by sheer amusement. "You son-of-a-bitch," she laughed up at him.

"Well, possibly," he replied, smiling. "After all, these days real estate is a good deal harder to get out of than marriage."

It took time, of course, to get the house prepared—repainting, recarpeting (the upstairs had been electric-blue shag throughout), the inevitable plumbing (Burns Park homeowners are customarily advised by their realtors to keep a plumber on retainer). Refinishing the woodwork, they decided with disappointment, would have to wait, but by the time they moved in, the major work was complete. Still, after two months in residence, Anneke's to-do list continued to get longer instead of shorter.

Her own office, at least, was finished and ready. Originally the formal dining room, it was white and gray and spare, so minimalist, Karl had noted, that it was almost invisible. But this morning she had no time to draw tranquility from its quiet brightness. She scrabbled through the papers on her desk, hunting for the printout from last night's work session; by the time she found it, Karl was standing in the double doorway waiting for her.

"Just let me check my calendar." She dug the weekly printout from her briefcase. "Oh hell, I forgot—we need to call about the garage roof."

"And an automatic garage-door opener," Karl added.

"And we still need to get rid of those things in the garage storage closet." The previous owners had kindly abandoned a dozen or so rusted cans of used motor oil and other assorted toxins, which neither the garbage pickup nor the city dump would accept. She scribbled a note on the calendar page, one eye on the list while the other checked her watch for the time.

"How busy are you today?" he asked, putting a hand on her arm.

"The usual—twenty-seven different bits and pieces. Why?"

"Look, why don't we each spend an hour at work, then take the rest of the day off and get some of the more pressing things done?" He looked at her seriously. "If all of this is bothering you so much, let's take a whole day and just do it—at least the most important things. Knowing you, I don't think you'll be comfortable until you feel you have it under control."

"Is that my problem?" she asked sharply. "That I'm a control addict?"

"A bit." He smiled at her. "Everyone is, to some extent. Once you feel in control, you'll be able to forget about the house and enjoy the weekend."

"Well, I could turn the Willow Company project over to Calvin. It's mostly a LAN setup anyway. And I suppose I could put off those tax forms. Oh, all right, why don't we?" She shoved the calendar back into her briefcase. "We ought to be able to get the storms and the garage door business taken care of, and I think Michael Rappoport knows a good chimney sweep. And why don't we make a full-scale hardware store run?" She reached into her briefcase and withdrew a dark blue folder printed in gilt, with the words *President's Weekend* centered under the University of Michigan seal. "What's the schedule for the weekend? Will we have any time to get to the recycling center?"

"No." He took the thick brochure from her hand. "We're going to run all the errands we can squeeze in today, but then I want you to relax and enjoy yourself—otherwise the weekend will just turn into one more chore."

"I suppose you're right," she admitted ruefully. "It's just . . ." She waved an arm, encompassing the house.

"You don't have to do it all at once, you know."

"Maybe not," she retorted, "but you won't be so casual the first morning you have to scrape an inch of ice off your windshield. Or break a leg on that loose brick on the front steps. Or get scalded in the shower because the dishwasher started up."

"Anneke, a perfectly ordinary family lived in this house, exactly the way it is, for the last ten years," he pointed out with annoying reasonableness. "It won't collapse around our heads if we don't do everything immediately."

"I suppose I am obsessing, aren't I?" She was struck by the literal accuracy of the word.

"Creating a home is a process that never gets 'finished,' " he said.

Creating a home. She hadn't thought of it in those terms before. "The house . . ."

"The house is only one part of it."

But of course the house was the more easily manageable part. The house was concrete, tangible; when you refinished oak floors, you had nice, glowing floorboards to show for it—a visible result, a task accomplished. With a house, you could make lists, check off things done. A *home* was more complicated, fraught with emotional content.

"All right, fun and games it is," she declared. "What's the drill?"

"Why don't I drop you at your office for an hour or so, and you can rearrange schedules so you can take the day off. I'll come back and pick you up at ten, and we can go on from there."

"Fine. And if we have time," she suggested, trying to get into the spirit of things, "we can drive out to that garden center on Jackson Road and have a picnic lunch at Farmer Grant's."

"Good." He had his hand on the doorknob when the telephone rang.

"It's yours." They'd each kept their previous telephone numbers when they'd moved. Karl strode across the hall to his office, and Anneke made one last check of her briefcase before she followed. When she reached his door, she saw him glaring at the telephone, his mouth a tight line of anger.

"Yes, of course . . . Yes, I'll be there . . . Right . . . No, I'll pick up a paper on the way." He set the receiver into its cradle with a careful emphasis that was more revealing than any slam would have been.

"What is it?" Anneke asked. "Is it a murder?" Although Karl was nominal head of homicide investigation for the Ann Arbor Police Department, he spent most of his time on administrative operations; in truth, there were few homicides to investigate in Ann Arbor.

"Not unless I commit it," he said tightly, only half-joking.

"For heaven's sake, what is it?" Anneke repeated, now thoroughly alarmed.

"They've just announced a full-scale NCAA investigation of Michigan football recruiting. Or rather," he corrected himself, "the *Michigan Daily* just announced it. Apparently, the NC bloody double A hasn't bothered to officially inform us yet."

"But . . ." Anneke stared at him, questions tumbling over each other in her head. "Who was that on the phone?" she asked finally.

"Frank Novak's assistant. Frank's one of Russ Truhorne's Assistant AD's," he explained to her blank look. "He wants me to sit in on a meeting this morning."

"The M Club?" The group, composed of former M lettermen, would be wild over this.

"No. Seems there's a plan in the works to establish a huge scholarship fund and recruiting drive for 'the best and the brightest.' Nonathletes, of course." His voice was sarcastic. "They were planning to meet with Frank this morning to pick his brains about recruiting procedures, only now they're screaming blue murder."

"But what can you tell them?"

"Not a thing." He smiled briefly. "I think Frank just wants me there for backup. What's more," he went on, "this probably won't be the last of it, either. With the President's Weekend starting Friday, every big-time alumnus we've got will be in town."

"Oh, God, not this weekend." Anneke's stomach contracted.

"Yes, that too." Karl kept his voice down with visible effort. "But that's the least of it."

"What's the specific charge?"

"I don't know, and from what Frank said he doesn't either."

"What a mess," she said, beginning to process the implications. "I take it they don't know who it is who's involved, either?"

"So you're doing it, too." Karl stared at her.

"Doing what?" she asked, confused.

"One headline—one accusation—and we're guilty. Every one of those enraged alumni did the same thing—calling not to find out *if*, but to find out *who.*"

"But . . . I suppose you're right," she admitted. "My instant impulse is to say that if they're investigating, they must know something. Still," she continued thoughtfully, "the NCAA *doesn't* investigate unless it has some sort of information to start with, does it?"

"Maybe, maybe not. They're the NCAA—they do what they damn well please." Anneke could almost feel the waves of anger emanating from him. "Let's get out of here," he said tightly.

"Well, so much for our day off," she said with a shaky attempt at humor.

"Oh, hell." He stopped with his hand on the doorknob. "I'm sorry. I forgot all about it."

"That's all right," she said quickly.

"No, it isn't. And anyway, once we calm down these screaming alumni, there isn't going to be anything for me to do about this. Look," he said, "the meeting's at eleven o'clock. Why don't you drop me at City Hall, I'll get a cab to the stadium, and you can meet me there when the meeting's over? We'll still have the whole afternoon."

"The stadium?"

"Right. They're going to meet in the president's box, up under the pressbox. Probably because being in the stadium tends to shut people up." There was almost a smile on his face. "Besides," and this time he did smile, "this way you get to drive."

It was one of the small adjustments they were still working out. Anneke had traded her beloved little Alfa Romeo for the Firebird because Karl simply couldn't fit in the tiny sports car. But even so, she found that when they rode together, it was usually in Karl's Land Rover, with Karl at the wheel.

Once in the Firebird heading downtown, Karl didn't seem disposed to talk about the NCAA, and anyway, there wasn't much to say until they had more data. Anneke forced herself to relax, leaning back against the seat and trying to put work and remodeling and the NCAA out of her mind. It was, after all, gorgeous, glorious October; when midwesterners move elsewhere, fall is homesick time. Ann Arbor dazzled in the early-morning sunshine, crisp and bright and crystalline, the tree-lined Burns Park streets shedding red and gold in a blaze of fall color. "Snow shovels," she said aloud, snapping her fingers.

"We signed up for that snow removal service, remember?"

"They only do sidewalks, not the driveway or the front walk." She steered the big black car into the stutter of morning traffic on Hill Street, braking to avoid a decrepit red Honda backing blindly out of a driveway.

"Well, let's get a snowblower then. Put it on your hardware store list and we'll check them out this afternoon—and put hedge clippers on the list, too. And mulch for those rhododendrons."

"All right, all right." She forced a smile. "You know, you're beginning to sound positively . . . domesticated."

"I suppose I am," he admitted. "I'm enjoying it." As she turned left onto Washtenaw, Anneke thought, with something like surprise: He really does look happy. Now why surprise? she asked herself. Because I really don't, after all, expect it to work out?

"You know," he said, "this is the first house I've ever owned."

"You're joking."

"No. When I was married, neither of us wanted the responsibility. And a condo always seemed more practical anyway—football players are on the road so much."

"Why now?" It had never occurred to her to ask before.

"I think," he answered after a short pause, "for the solidity of it, the permanence."

"I'm not sure I believe in permanence," she responded. "Like the Jim Morrison biography says—'no one here gets out alive.' "

"But we create what islands of stability we can," he said gently.

"I suppose." She was silent for a moment, remembering her last house, burned to the ground in a conflagration that had taken everything she owned. In the six months since, until they moved into the Burns Park house, she'd lived in a furnished cottage, buying virtually nothing except office essentials and clothing to replace her destroyed wardrobe. She'd been a serious collector of art deco, but now when she looked at a beautiful piece it no longer seemed to excite her. "For heaven's sake," she said finally, steering around a slow-moving Volvo, "let's talk about something cheerful. What's the schedule for the weekend?"

"Well, Friday there are the various seminars—didn't you want to go to the Virtual Reality session?"

"Yes; I've been wanting to hear what Henry Baker's doing," she replied, referring to a computer science professor who'd won a MacArthur Fellowship the year before. "Although I'm afraid he's going to water it down."

"Not necessarily. As I understand it, the faculty take these President's Weekend seminars fairly seriously. After all," he said, grinning, "these are Michigan alumni they're talking to, not the unwashed masses. Is that the only one you're going to?"

"I'm not sure. There's a session on the Old English Dictionary project I may do if I have the time."

"If it interests you, you should make the time," he said sternly. "Anyway," he continued, "Friday night there's the banquet—"

"Where you're the guest of honor."

"Yes, and there's a President's Reception before it. Then Saturday there's the pregame brunch, and the game. And of course there'll be various pregame and postgame parties."

"And you're to be the star turn during halftime. You know, it does sound like fun." She completed the loop around one-way streets, swooped into the City Hall parking lot, and braked at the front door. "All right, Lieutenant, I promise to put aside gloom, doom, and household chores and help you celebrate all weekend."

"Good." He released his seat belt. "I'll meet you under the press-box at about eleven-thirty."

SIX

Despite her promise, as she drove back toward campus and pulled the Firebird into its slot in the Maynard Street parking structure, Anneke's thoughts focused on the NCAA investigation. And as she walked to her office, she discovered, somewhat to her surprise, that her paramount emotion was anger. In fact, she was as angry in her own way as Karl. Only, where he was angry at the investigation's effect on Michigan, she was mostly angry at its effect on him. For all his outward nonchalance, he'd been looking forward to the ceremonies of this weekend. But now the long-planned tribute to Karl Genesko, All-American—complete with commemorative film, testimonial dinner, presentation of two Super Bowl rings to the University, and finally, at half-time of Saturday's game, the retirement of Number 54—would be at best a side event, at worst a mockery. Karl, after all, was an active recruiter for Michigan.

"Damn and bloody hell," she said aloud, drawing a startled glance from a passing student.

The weekend was the least of it, Karl had said. Well, maybe, but she'd still like ten minutes alone with the bastard who'd done it.

Whoever he was. And whatever "it" was. She discovered another emotion weltering around amid the anger, and identified it, this time without surprise, as curiosity.

This morning, sunlight even penetrated the dirty skylight of the Nickels Arcade, picking out the windows of the tiny shops lining each side. She plucked a copy of the *Daily* from a rack next to the small post office and blinked at the text. The screaming black headline was easy enough to read, but the rest of it was too small. Swearing, she opened her briefcase and withdrew her new reading glasses with loathing. Shoving them on, she read quickly through the first few paragraphs before tucking the paper under her arm and climbing the battered stairs to the second floor. There she pushed open the old, glass-paned door bearing the gilt legend "A/H, Inc., Computer Solutions," and walked into pandemonium.

"Universities shouldn't be in the business of training football players anyway." Marcia Rosenthal stood in the center of the crowded front office, waving her coffee mug for emphasis.

"Why not?" Ken Scheede, Anneke's office manager, challenged. "One of the purposes of a university is preparing people for jobs, isn't it? If we train writers and doctors and accountants, why not football or basketball players?"

"Scheede, that is so low density. Because football players don't need a college education, that's why," Marcia asserted triumphantly, the effect ruined slightly as coffee slopped over the side of her mug.

"Sure they do. They need the same things other professionals do—high-level training in their chosen field and a liberal education to give it context. Just like a kid with talent in art or in math."

"Even so," Marcia backpedaled and attacked from another direction, "there's one big difference—the kid with the math talent doesn't get a four-year free ride, complete with training table. That kid has to pay his own way."

"Which, if you're a minority, chances are you can't do." That was Calvin Streeter, a tall, gangling black sophomore who'd walked into her office six months ago with a chip on his shoulder and a beautiful touch with C programming. "Which is why kids grow up in the inner cities thinking athletic ability is the only way they can succeed. The college sports establishment perpetuates the stereotype that blacks can only succeed if they're jocks."

Football has never been Politically Correct, a fact that produces serious schizophrenia in the Ann Arbor psyche each fall. For some, it's a source of vast pride that a great university can also mount a great football program; for others, an equal source of embarrassment. So this was an old argument, one that had been going on since the sixties, radical activists on one end of the spectrum, traditionalists on the other, everyone else perched uneasily at various points in between.

"Well, maybe this'll actually do some good," Marcia said. "I mean, if even Michigan can't do it right, it's got to show what a hopeless mess the whole thing is."

"Hang on a minute," Anneke spoke finally. "Listen to what you just said. 'If even Michigan can't get it right.' Do you hear the breathtaking example of Michigan arrogance in that?"

"I guess." Marcia looked uncertain. "Why?"

"Because," Anneke said, "that arrogance is part of the fabric of this whole University. We all have it, even the students who bitch about the place all the time—it's woven into us from the first day we get here. Like those bumper stickers that say 'Arrogance is bliss.' That's what's really at risk here."

So?" Marcia responded. "Maybe they can use a little reality testing."

"You won't think so when you go out into the job market, and that Michigan degree doesn't have quite the gloss it does now," Ken leaped in. "Or when alumni aren't quite so anxious to help out Michigan grads, because they just don't feel the same way about the place anymore. Look, for some schools NCAA probation would just be a minor embarrassment—either they're scum schools to start with or they aren't into football the way we are. But Michigan has too much ego involvement in doing it by the numbers and still winning."

"Well, it's still just football," Marcia said, shrugging. "It doesn't really have anything to do with me."

"If that were true," Anneke rejoined, "we wouldn't all be talking about it. Even if you're not a football fan—even if you hate football—you can't live in Ann Arbor and ignore it. Everyone in the city is going to be affected by this," she said slowly, realizing it fully for the first time, "even if they're not connected to the U at all."

The argument wound down, and they sorted through the day's assignments, working out the complex timetable to accommodate the class schedules of student programmers, the only ones she hired.

"What's on the agenda?" she asked Ken.

"Four more requests for bids." He pointed to a pile of papers on her desk. Anneke examined them briefly and made a face.

"More networking. If I never see the initials L-A-N again, I'll die happy."

"Yeah, I know. But those two are both previous customers. And the other two are Internet projects. I wouldn't mind working on the Folk Music Society thing."

"What are they after?"

"They want to set up a Web home page on the Internet."

"All right. I suppose so. I've got that database application to work on, and the Gay History project, but I can handle one more job, I think. And we can put Marcia on the two LANs. How's the City Hall program coming?"

"We're in the debugging stages. Are you sure you can take on another project?" he asked dubiously.

"It's either that or turn down a customer that we'll never get back," she replied. "I can push back the Gay History deadline a few weeks—they're not in a tearing hurry."

"Well, if you're sure . . ."

"I'm sure." Well, she was nearly sure, anyway. What she was really sure of was that business was too important to pass up. A/H was busy and successful and she was determined to keep it that way.

They discussed work for a few more moments, and when they were done Anneke turned to the *Daily* and looked again at the NCAA story. None of her young staff, Anneke noted, had disputed the accuracy of the report; they took it for granted that something illegal had occurred. So had she, of course, until Karl called her on it—and in fact, at gut level she still did.

She spread out the *Daily* on her desk and reread the story with growing dissatisfaction. What was wrong with it, she decided, was not what it said but what it didn't say. Why was it so vague? Surely the investigator—Greenaway—had told Truhorne more than was reported. Perhaps the reporter hadn't gotten that part of the story? But why not?

For that matter, the source of the story itself was unduly mysterious. Nothing was attributed; just: "The *Daily* has learned." Anneke leaned back and stared at the headline.

How on earth *had* they gotten the story?

She turned to the computer, opened her current project management file, and stared at the Compaq's screen for a while. Most of the major projects were allocated to staff and more or less under control, but there wasn't much room to maneuver. In addition to programming projects, she herself had a deadly batch of chores scheduled—government paperwork, record keeping, hardware testing and installation. How the hell had she gotten bogged down like this?

Well, that's what business is all about, she told herself firmly. Fun and games were all very well, but keeping A/H going was the most important thing. The notion of fun and games reminded her—there was a game she'd written a few years ago, totally obsolete now but still, she thought, conceptually sound. Redesigned and rewritten, it would make a spectacular multimedia game, different from anything out there now. Even in its current primitive incarnation, it had a virtual-reality feel to it, and if she reprogrammed it to take advantage of contemporary graphics capabilities . . . she'd need a source for the graphics, of course . . . perhaps live-action video mixed with computer animation, like Roger Rabbit . . . replace the old keyboard operations with a totally mouse-driven interface . . .

She came to with a start to see Ken standing at her desk looking at her curiously.

"Everything all right?" he asked.

"Yes," she answered, refocusing on reality. "Yes, of course," she repeated. "Everything's fine." She returned her attention firmly to the screen in front of her. "I'll be working here until around eleven. After that, you can use the Compaq for your debugging."

"You know, we could use additional staff," he suggested.

"Where would we put them?" She looked around the room, already cluttered with four desks and half a dozen file cabinets. There was another, smaller office to the rear, housing the Sun workstation and more file cabinets.

"We could get a bigger place. There's a four-room office down the hall coming vacant next month."

"It's a possibility. But we'd need more equipment, also. I don't know, that sort of expansion can be risky."

"Yes, but think of the potential." He waved a hand. "Not only would we be able to take on more work, we could also move into bigger projects."

"I don't really want bigger projects," she said. "It's too hard to control, with nothing but part-time staff."

"Well, yes, but . . ."

"Look, Ken, let's talk about this later, all right? I've got to get out of here by eleven." She stared at the project manager screen. Not enough time this morning to really get anything done on the database application; anyway, she'd better finish up those personnel forms for the state. She reached for the mouse, only dimly aware of Ken's retreating form.

SEVEN

"I'm not going to stand out here waiting much longer," Daniel Najarian warned, not troubling to hide his impatience. He glared impartially at the other three members of his committee and at the young, dark-skinned woman standing uncomfortably with them.

"He'll be here any moment, I promise," Wendy Coleman said for the third time. "I'm sorry I can't let you into the President's Box, but Mr. Novak has the key."

"Oh, lighten up, Daniel." Eleanor Sullivan lounged against a dark-blue-painted metal post under the stadium press box, one hand in the pocket of her Levi's jacket, the other holding a cigarette. "Whatever's holding Frank up, it has to be important—you know how compulsive he is. Or maybe you don't—you do profess to have such contempt for the athletic department, don't you?" She shook long gray hair out of her eyes in a gesture Daniel considered too young for her advanced years.

"Not for the athletic department," Daniel corrected her, more out of the habit of precision than because he cared. "For college athletics in its current form at Michigan."

"Oh, yes. Right." Eleanor's smoke-roughened voice was sarcastic. "I forgot. You do at least give the athletic department credit for knowing its job, don't you?"

"I thought so, at least." Daniel looked pointedly at his watch.

"Relax." Eleanor blew a smoke ring and smiled, a genuinely friendly smile. "He'll be along soon. Frank Novak would never stand up a group like this."

"Yeah, I've got to give you points for political correctness, anyway." Jeffrey Person, his mocking smile flashing white against nearly black skin, held up one hand and ticked off categories. "Two white men, one woman, one black. Two midwest, one southeast, one west coast. Why, you'd almost think you planned it that way."

"What I planned may now be irrelevant in any case," Daniel snapped. "I'm not sure I want to go ahead with it under these circumstances."

"Oh, you'll go ahead with it," Eleanor said placidly. "You're too heavily committed to back out now."

"I'm not committed at all," Daniel rejoined. "So far this whole committee is purely exploratory."

"I don't mean a formal commitment," Eleanor responded. "I'm talking about the psychological commitment you've made to yourself."

"I also know when to cut my losses, be they financial *or* psychological," Daniel said, acknowledging to himself that she was probably right. But only up to a point. The list of risks he was unwilling to take wasn't a long one, but looking foolish was on it.

The thing about Daniel Najarian was that he was a genius. Not the ordinary Ann Arbor 120-to-140-IQ kind, but the real thing. His IQ, for those who believed in that sort of thing, was so far off the scale that no one bothered to measure it after his third birthday. He was reading the *New York Times* at age three; composing tolerable concertos at age six; solving quadratic equations at age eight.

By the time he was twenty-three he had a B.A., a Ph.D., and had completed medical school at Michigan. By the time he was thirty, he was the director of one of the premiere biomedical research institutes in the world, and the holder of five patents that virtually revolutionized the production of pharmaceuticals. (Unlike so many scientists, he was very nearly as business-smart as he was science-smart.) By the time he was forty, he was so rich that his wealth had taken on a life of its own.

When the money began to pile up at a rate fast enough to alarm his accountant, he looked around for a suitable charitable enterprise, and settled on the University. For one thing, he'd enjoyed his time there; for another, he believed in the notion of elite education and hoped to nudge Michigan further in that direction. And besides, the University offered people to argue with, people who weren't cowed by his intellect or his money. It was the one place where he was neither the Big Boss nor the Resident Genius.

His philanthropy was as idiosyncratic as his work, given not through conventional channels but directly to individual units or researchers, and not necessarily to hard-science fields. He wasn't sure himself how he selected his beneficiaries. Sometimes a particular project captured his interest, or a particular individual. Once, he'd brought, or bought, a young filmmaker from Stanford with the promise of a million-dollar, no-strings grant. On another occasion, he'd been so impressed with the work of a young Norwegian architect that he'd donated a campus building for him to design.

He became more or less famous on campus and among Michigan alumni, known as a kind of kamikaze donor who swooped down on unsuspecting departments and showered them with unexpected largesse. His picture appeared regularly in the *Daily* and in the *University Record;* he spoke at convocations; he attended small private dinners at the presidential mansion. He was careful not to wonder how many of his Michigan friendships would evaporate if his fortune did likewise; he hoped not all of them would, and knew he could never know for sure.

People of average intelligence comfort themselves with the fond belief that geniuses are usually social misfits. This is, of course, untrue. Daniel Najarian was socially adept, and aware, enough to maintain both cordial professional relationships and a fair number of close friendships, among them, in fact, Eleanor Sullivan.

He even enjoyed sports—in their place. He had become interested in football as a fourteen-year-old college freshman, calculating more or less correctly that it would provide him with a social connection to other, older students. He discovered, somewhat to his surprise, that he actually appreciated the game, both for its chessboard complexity as well as its calculated savagery. Besides, it was the one interest he was able to share with the more "normal" populace.

He also understood that athletics were an integral part of Michigan's curiously schizophrenic reputation. Whenever the football team lost, he spent the following day fielding barbs from coworkers (whose own schools' teams, of course, never even made the newspapers). He kept an occasional eye on high school sports in the Chicago area and was pleased when he was able to recommend a local athlete whom he thought might have the combined ability and intelligence to succeed at Michigan.

On the other hand, since he also believed firmly that a world-class university had no business squandering its scarce intellectual resources on the training of professional athletes, he was aware of a discomforting level of cognitive dissonance. He knew this was one cause of his current anger. Still, an NCAA scandal would be a shamefully humiliating blow to the University—and to him personally.

"We can hardly launch a huge student recruitment drive," he declared, "when the University is involved in a major scandal. We'd be laughingstocks."

"Not necessarily." Richard Killian spoke for the first time, a shade of diffidence in his voice. "Look, I've done a lot of student recruiting on the west coast," he forged ahead, "and the truth is, the kind of students you're looking for aren't likely to care about athletics one way or the other."

"Perhaps not," Daniel said stiffly, "but they *are* likely to care that an institution is in utter disgrace."

"Not unless it affects the whole fabric of the place," Richard maintained. "One alumnus screwing up really won't matter that much. Look," he persisted in the face of Daniel's open skepticism, "you asked me to be on this committee because I have a lot of experience recruiting students. I'm telling you what I know from that experience."

"And believe it or not," Jeffrey Person interjected with a sardonic smile, "there are some skinny little black kids who don't give a shine about sports, either."

"Race isn't an issue here, Jeffrey," Daniel said.

"Oh, no? I suppose I was asked to be on this committee because of my sparkling personality? Or was it my good looks? Come off it, Daniel. You know the University won't dare let you set up this scholarship fund unless you can prove it'll recruit minorities, too. That's what I'm here for, and we both know it."

"I never denied it," Daniel replied with a tight smile. "But there are a large number of other African American alumni I could have asked instead. I asked you—I asked all of you—because of your experience recruiting, even if only recruiting athletes."

"You know, you're not inventing nonathletic recruiting here," Richard Killian said, smiling in his turn. "The alumni club in northern California already works like hell recruiting bright kids for Michigan. We set up booths at college fairs, we send out mailings to honor society lists, we talk up Michigan every chance we get."

"I'm sure you do." Daniel hoped he sounded polite rather than condescending. "But with the money this scholarship program will offer, we can go after the very best students everywhere. Merit scholars. Westinghouse Science Competition winners. Young writers and artists. The best young minds in the country. We're going to recruit for intellect the way the athletic department recruits for athletes."

"Only without the NCAA telling you what you can and can't do," Eleanor said.

"Luckily," Daniel replied, "those sorts of controls aren't necessary outside the athletic milieu. It's unfortunate that they are necessary within it." He glared out toward the fifty-yard line. "Football has a great deal to answer for at Michigan."

"I seem to recall a couple of football players had summer jobs at your lab, didn't they?" Jeffrey Person asked with feigned innocence.

"So do half a dozen other Michigan students who've never seen the inside of the stadium," Daniel snapped.

"Yes, but didn't Jack Crenshaw work for you for two summers while he was still in high school? *Before* he ever came to Michigan?"

"Jack Crenshaw was, and is, a brilliant student."

"Of *course* he was. And the fact that he was also two hundred eighty pounds and the fastest offensive tackle in the state of Illinois didn't have a thing to do with it."

The Crenshaw business had been a mistake, of course, Daniel conceded, but only to himself. But Crenshaw had been perfect for Michigan, brains and brawn combined, living evidence that the ugly compromises weren't necessary even when Daniel knew they were. Cognitive dissonance, he thought, was not merely an uncomfortable mental state, but a potentially dangerous one as well.

"You're not suggesting, I hope," he spoke softly to Jeffrey, "that I, or any of us here, is the culpable party in this scandal?"

"No-o-o, I don't think so, actually," Jeffrey replied, appearing to take the question seriously. "I think we'd all have too much to lose—'the bubble reputation' and all that."

"Yes, I agree." Daniel was careful not to show surprise at the apposite quotation.

"I can't even imagine risking it," Richard said with an exaggerated shudder. Daniel thought he sounded tense.

"Would it be that great a risk for you personally?" he asked curiously. "After all, no offense intended, but a restaurant owner isn't really in the same category as an attorney or a scientist or a former Regent." He waved a hand at the others. "There is, after all, no public trust involved."

"You think not?" Richard sounded mildly angry. "Let me tell you about the Maize and Blue. It's a restaurant and sports bar, a lot like a dozen other restaurants and sports bars in San Francisco. What makes it special is five years of very carefully crafted public relations—and *that's* based on the Michigan connection. Every Michigan alumnus who comes to the City stops by the Maize and Blue. Sportswriters looking for a Michigan story know they might find it at the Maize and Blue. Coaches drop by for free drinks when they're in town; former players come by for a nostalgia fix; former marching band members drop in and play a few riffs. We even," he said with pride, "made Herb Caen's column a few times. Do I have to tell you what this scandal could do to me?" He paused. "And yes," he added, "high school coaches show up from time to time. And sometimes they bring videotapes."

"Has it ever occurred to you to wonder why we do it?" Jeffrey Person asked after a moment, cocking his head.

"Because it's Michigan," Richard said, still sounding angry. "Because it's something we have that we can be proud of. Is that such a bad thing—to want something to be proud of?"

"Not if it's real," Jeffrey answered.

"I thought it was," Richard replied bitterly.

EIGHT

Anneke walked to the parking structure, gunned the Firebird down the ramp and headed toward the stadium, running the slalom of slow-moving cars on William and accelerating down Main Street with a satisfying burst of speed. She tried to put work out of her mind, forcing herself to relax and concentrate instead on the explosions of fall color along the streets.

Michigan Stadium sits on the corner of Main Street and Stadium Boulevard, more or less in the center of Ann Arbor. Behind it, other pieces of the huge Michigan athletic complex sprawl down toward the railroad tracks, but across Main Street lie primarily residential neighborhoods. A behemoth among football stadiums, 101,501 and counting, it somehow contrives not to loom too menacingly over its neighbors. Partly this is due to the broad strip of grass and trees along the Main Street side, partly by the fact that the huge oval bowl is actually built into a hollow, so that more than half its bulk is below street level.

Or perhaps it is simply so much a part of the local landscape that Ann Arborites hardly notice it anymore.

The dark-blue-painted chain-link fence around the stadium perimeter is fully locked only at night. Anneke parked on Snyder, crossed Main and walked along the fence until she found an open gate at the north end. She came into the stadium under the upper tier of seats and proceeded along the concrete walkway, her footsteps echoing off the metal superstructure overhead, past shuttered concession stands and bits of equipment stashed or stowed in the Wednesday silence awaiting the Saturday frenzy.

No, not total silence. In the distance, she could hear occasional rumbles, the clanking of metal, voices raised. Two or three figures appeared and disappeared on mysterious errands. During football season, Michigan Stadium never slept.

She reached the area under the press box and turned and came out into the stands. The entry was about two-thirds of the way up from the field itself, which glowed brilliant green in the morning sun. The rows of dark-blue benches fell away vertiginously at her feet.

But instead of the empty silence she expected, she found herself instead in the midst of a gaggle of people who seemed to be milling about like irritated bumblebees.

". . . lack of consideration on top of everything," a compact, powerfully built man in an expensive business suit was saying.

"He really will be here as soon as soon as he possibly can," said a young woman with delicate features and skin the color of rich espresso.

"Oh, chill out, Daniel," a wiry, good-looking African American man said, directing his annoyance toward the expensively dressed man. "You're not the only one with other business on campus, you know—I've got an important appointment myself this afternoon."

"It's hardly the same thing," the man called Daniel said offensively.

"Oh, really? Believe it or not, Daniel, our lives are as important to us as yours is to you. And some of us even have social goals that go beyond making money."

"Is that shorthand for another student protest?" Daniel asked sharply. "What are you up to, Jeffrey? I hope you're not planning anything that will cause trouble on campus."

"Not the sort of trouble you mean." The man called Jeffrey spoke lightly, but with an undercurrent of something else.

"That's enough." The speaker was a short, compact gray-haired woman in blue jeans and denim jacket. "Both of you, behave yourselves. However offended you are that Frank didn't crawl on his knees to meet with you, Daniel, there's no point in taking it out on everyone else." She nodded toward the young African American woman.

"I really do apologize." The young woman contrived to look politely regretful. "As I'm sure you can imagine, the entire athletic department is in crisis mode. Mr. Novak felt sure that he could count on all of you to care more about Michigan than about your own egos."

It was a direct hit. "I guess we deserved that," a good-looking thirty-something man said, grinning ruefully.

"I'm sure both Mr. Novak and Mr. Genesko will be here at any moment," the young woman said. "They were only supposed to need a few minutes with the television people, but you know how television can be." So that's where Karl is, Anneke registered the information. The young woman smiled, encouraging the others to share her amusement at television people.

"Frank gone into hiding?" A slight, paunchy man in a sagging brown suit emerged from the entryway and peered at them through rimless glasses. He panted slightly as he approached the group and dropped his battered briefcase on one of the benches with an audible thud. "You guys find out who's been pissing in your high-priced soup yet?" Anneke noted with amusement that the well-dressed group seemed to withdraw from the newcomer.

"Hello, Mr. Cassovoy," the young woman said warily. "The press conference is this afternoon; I'm sorry, but the department won't have anything for the newspapers until then." Her voice pressed down slightly on the word *newspapers*, and the rest of the group went instantly silent. Although no one seemed to move,

Anneke had the sense that they had somehow closed ranks. No one looked directly at the newcomer.

No, in fact one person did. On the other side of the aisle was a girl in jeans and a bulky red sweater, her long curly black hair falling around her face. A black bookbag lay on the bench next to her, and a notebook was open on her lap. She was staring at the man named Cassovoy with undisguised curiosity. Now why would a random student be that interested in a badly dressed, middle-aged, thoroughly unprepossessing reporter?

As she thought the last word, memory clicked in. And as it did, the girl looked directly at her, and with a small grin followed by a shrug shoved the notebook into her bookbag and stood up.

NINE

Bloody hell, Zoe thought, doing her best to grin cheerfully toward the older woman. So much for anonymity. Although whatever's going on here doesn't sound too exciting, she admitted to herself; just some sort of alumni committee. And Genesko isn't going to give me thing one anyway. Still, she was annoyed; if this was Investigative Reporting 101, she'd just flunked.

Besides, I wonder what she's doing here? At one level, at least, Zoe felt pleased with herself for recognizing the woman, out of context like this—every journalist needed a good memory for faces. Anneke Haagen, local computer consultant, who'd spent a day at the *Daily* last spring looking over their computer setup, when the board was thinking of upgrading.

Zoe examined the tall, slim figure covertly as she arranged papers in her bookbag, buying time—well, she's tall to me, anyway, she laughed at herself. Gray silk pants and pink-and-gray striped shirt under a charcoal wool jacket; great sense of style—drop-dead elegant without any of that overdressed Bloomfield Hillbilly look. I hope I look that good at her age. Shit, I wish I looked that good now.

Not that I'm *too* bad, she told herself firmly, practicing self-esteem skills. I mean, when you live in East Quad you just naturally go all grunge or people think you're a dork. I may not be willowy, but I can do professional-looking when I need to. She pushed at the wild mane of curly black hair that surrounded her face. If I put my hair up and put on makeup like I did in high school. Still, she recognized reality when she saw it—I won't look like that when I'm over forty; I'll look like my mother.

Zoe felt the usual mixture of admiration and resentment that her mother always produced. Knowing the ambivalence was normal (she and her mother had both read *Mothers and Daughters* during the summer), she wondered briefly what sort of resentments she'd feel if she'd had a "normal" mother, instead of Berniece Kaplan, Radical Mom—a woman who listed her occupation on her income tax return as "activist."

Bernie Kaplan, née Cohen, had been born into a UAW family, one whose persona was forever defined by the fact that her father had been "on the bridge." The phrase requires no further elaboration in Michigan; the image of Walter Reuther, facing down the guns and the goons of General Motors in Flint, is part of the state's collective unconscious, as rooted in the Michigan psyche as Washington crossing the Delaware. Everywhere, to have been there confers honor. Even years later, when she had become a bitter, acrimonious enemy of the UAW over its role in Michigan politics, Bernie Kaplan would not say a bad word about Walter Reuther.

At the University of Michigan (the first in her family to go to college) Bernie connected with Ann Arbor's radical base—radical in ways her UAW parents neither fathomed nor approved. Then, when she graduated with a degree in political science (a year late, after taking time off to work for George McGovern's presidential campaign), she startled both her parents and her radical friends by marrying Martin Kaplan and moving to—"can you imagine?"—the upscale, vaguely liberal Detroit suburb of Birmingham.

"Liberal," Berniece had scoffed. "A city full of love-me liberals." And she warbled the lines from the Phil Ochs song—"love me, love me, lo-ove me, I'm a liberal." Then she set about putting her formidable political skills to work.

"Don't you ever want a real job?" Zoe had asked her mother plaintively when she was fourteen. Everyone else's mothers seemed to have jobs by then, mostly real estate or catering, but Carol's mother was even going to law school.

"Why would I want a job? Your father's law practice makes all the money we need." Berniece looked at her daughter shrewdly. "Zoe, I don't need money to validate the work I do—that's *their* value system, not mine. I was a feminist before you were born, but I'm damned if I'll buy into the capitalist scoring system. I think she who dies with the most *accomplishments* wins. Besides," she added with determined honesty, "I have a lot more fun this way."

Looking back on her childhood, Zoe marveled at the steady stream of politicians, activists, and social cause gurus who streamed through the big brick house in the old downtown section of Birmingham. They all came, the important and the merely self-important, because Bernie Kaplan, pain-in-the-ass though she might be, would work her butt off once she committed to a campaign. They came because, over the years, her name on a petition or a brochure came to mean something.

"I drive them crazy," Berniece said, laughing. "I won't take a political job, I won't run for office, I've never even asked for a favor—and it makes them nuts that they can't figure out what I want." She shook her head in disgust. "These are the people who are supposed to be running the country, but if I told them that all I really want is a just society, they'd have me committed."

To the child Zoe, of course, the Very Important Persons were only important if her mother thought they were. And few of them survived the scrutiny of what Martin Kaplan called "Berniece's shit detector." (Nothing put a politician on the Kaplan shit list faster than trying to end-run Bernie by appealing to Martin "man-to-man.") Zoe learned to take no one at face value—she understood the concept of the hidden agenda before she understood the multiplication table.

She could have turned out cynical, of course. Well, I suppose I am, in a way, she admitted—unlike her mother, she seemed to have been born an observer rather than an activist. But against the venality, the self-aggrandizement, the pomposity, Bernie Kaplan always managed to find a few gems. "If I didn't believe there were *some* good people out there, I wouldn't bother at all," she told Zoe. "Think of it as an application of William James's *Essays in Pragmatism*—you'll read him in college. If you believe that there are good people in the world and you're wrong, you lose nothing in the end. Whereas if you believe that everyone is evil, and you're wrong, you *gain* nothing. So you may as well believe in some decency somewhere, because your own life works better that way."

How many mothers discuss philosophical treatises with their teenage daughters? I guess there are really only a couple of things I can complain about, Zoe conceded. I do get real tired of hearing, "Oh, you're *Bernie's* daughter!" And I do wish to hell, she thought, looking at Anneke enviously, that she'd been three or four inches taller.

"You know who I am, don't you." Zoe hoisted her bookbag onto her shoulder and stood up. Might as well try the straightforward approach.

"Yes, I think so." Anneke smiled at the girl. "I did an estimate for some new computer installations for the *Daily* last spring; I remember seeing you."

"I know; I remember you. But I'm surprised you recognize me—after all, I was just a freshman trainee writing headlines at the sports desk."

"I'm not sure why, myself." Anneke appraised her for a moment. "I guess I noticed you because I'm still surprised to see a woman sportswriter. And also, you have a very . . . memorable look, for some reason. I think it's your eyes."

"Memorable?" Momentarily diverted, Zoe wondered if that was a good or bad thing. Being memorable might not be so great for an investigative reporter; still, she felt foolishly complimented by the idea. And she'd always had a sneaking pride in her eyes, definitely her best feature—a brilliant coppery gold that made a startling contrast to her black hair. "Well, you've got me," she said finally. "I'm Zoe Kaplan."

"Anneke Haagen." To Zoe's surprise, Anneke held out her hand in a formal gesture that it took her a moment to reciprocate.

"I'm glad to meet you, although I wish it weren't here." Zoe looked a challenge at her. "Are you going to blow my cover?"

"Good lord, no. Why would I? Are you here covering their meeting?"

"Sort of," Zoe equivocated. "What're they meeting about, anyway?"

"Even if I knew, I think you should ask them," Anneke replied carefully.

"Well, it was worth a try," Zoe said cheerfully. "Actually, I'm here because I was trying to track down Karl Genesko for a quote, but he's off somewhere with Novak. On the other hand, I think there's *something* interesting going on here. I just can't quite figure out what it is. But it doesn't have anything to do with the NCAA business, I'm pretty sure of that. I guess I'll follow up on it later."

"Who are they all?" Anneke asked. "Do you know?"

"Well, the black woman is Wendy Coleman, Frank Novak's assistant. She's also Kyle Farmer's squeeze, by the way." She didn't bother to identify Kyle Farmer—anyone who didn't know the name of Michigan's premier running back and Heisman Trophy candidate wasn't worth talking to anyway. "The others are all hotshot alumni. I've been sitting here listening to them bitch for the last fifteen minutes. Let's see—I assume you recognize Eleanor Sullivan." Zoe gestured at the sixtyish woman in denims, wreathed in cigarette smoke, and Anneke nodded. Everyone in Ann Arbor knew the legendary Eleanor Sullivan, who, among other public activities, had served sixteen years on the University Board of Regents. She was nearing seventy now, but her round face, with its snub nose and pale blue eyes, was as combative as ever, and her trademark long gray hair hung straight down her back to well below her shoulder blades.

"The guy who looks like a Mafia don," Zoe indicated the squarish, powerfully built man in the dark suit, "is the great Dr. Daniel Najarian."

"Oh, of course. I should have recognized him too." Najarian should have been ugly. He had a heavy forehead, large nose, and deep-set brown eyes under brows that met in the middle. But there was such intelligence in his face that after a few moments it erased the effect of his physical features.

"Sure. Najarian Biomedical Laboratories, more money that God, and gives a ton of it to the U."

"Didn't someone call him the Godfather of Michigan Philanthropy?"

"Yeah." Zoe giggled. "In the *Daily*, in fact. And did we catch some heat for that one." She pointed again. "The hot-looking stud in the black leather jacket is Richard Killian, some sort of restaurant owner from San Francisco. Used to be a *Daily* editor, actually." Killian had a shock of black hair that fell forward—artfully?—over his forehead, brilliant blue eyes, and a perpetually cheerful expression that didn't seem to darken even in the midst of argument. Under the buttery leather of his jacket he wore softly tailored black pants and a dark blue silk shirt buttoned at the neck without a tie.

"The black guy is Jeffrey Person. Lawyer from Miami. He was a cornerback for Michigan about ten years ago." Person's complexion was dark enough that the no-longer-politically-correct adjective fit. He had a smooth, handsome face with finely-chiseled features, and he wore a conventionally expensive business suit that covered but didn't disguise his athletic, well-muscled body. "I think he's involved in sports law—if I had to guess, I'd guess he's planning to turn agent."

She started to ask Anneke what she was doing here—she certainly didn't look like the rah-rah type—but her attention was caught by the sight of two workmen in the center of the field. They were refurbishing the big maize-and-blue Block-M that straddled the fifty-yard line, and she found herself wondering, not for the first time, what it must feel like to stand out there on Saturday afternoon, in the biggest college football stadium in the world, surrounded by more than 100,000 nameless faces, battered by the roars of 100,000 throats. Did you absorb energy from it? Shrink from it? Blot it out?

"It's impossible not to be a little awed, isn't it?" Anneke commented.

"But you have to get over that, or you can't function."

"They call Michigan Stadium the twelfth man. Not the fans—the stadium itself."

"I know. I've stood here before trying to understand what they feel, and I can't." Zoe shook her head in frustration. "Because if you can't understand what it *feels* like, you can't describe it properly."

"That's true." Anneke nodded. "It's one of the biggest problems most women have understanding sports—because most of us have never had the experience of putting our egos on the line in such a public way."

"That's the real key, isn't it?" Zoe pursued the thought. "It isn't that women aren't competitive . . ."

"God knows," Anneke interjected acidly.

"Yeah, right." They shared a moment of laughter. "Oh, we're competitive enough," Zoe continued, "but at least when we crash and burn it's not in front of crowds of people."

"But I think that's a *dis*advantage," Anneke demurred. "I've always thought the best thing boys learn from team sports is precisely that—how to cope with public humiliation. How to *risk* public humiliation. Do you remember a Minnesota defensive end named Jim Marshall?"

"You mean the guy who recovered a fumble for the Vikings and ran it sixty yards the wrong way?" Zoe laughed. "Who doesn't? It's made every football blooper reel ever made."

"And Chris Webber, calling a time-out the team didn't have, costing Michigan the NCAA basketball championship. And a dozen others you can name. I think there's a critical learning experience in situations like that."

"You mean boys learn to suck it up and we don't." Zoe considered the thought. "So they can come in here, and look up at 100,000 screaming lunatics, and say 'fuck you, I'm just gonna play my game and you can kiss my ass if you don't like it'."

"Something like that." Anneke laughed. "But it also means," she added more seriously, "that they can walk into a classroom, or a boardroom, and do the same thing."

"I never thought of that," Zoe said. "Oh good, here comes Novak." They both turned toward the northwest corner of the stands, where Frank Novak was edging his way hurriedly in their direction between the rows of benches. Still no Genesko though, Zoe thought irritably. That guy over there sure wasn't him—and what the hell was he doing, anyway?

The unidentified figure in the stands was directly behind the north goalpost, moving downward with jerky steps and carrying, preposterously, a big blue-and-gold Michigan banner held high in front of him. He looked weird, Zoe laughed to herself. He was carrying the banner, on its long pole, like a marching band flagbearer, his arms straight out from his body, the end of the post braced against his stomach.

Why on earth . . . ? Zoe didn't finish the thought. As she watched, the figure staggered on the last step, seemed to waver, and then, all by itself in the empty stadium, pitched soundlessly over the low brick wall surrounding the field, to lie facedown and unmoving on the bright green grass.

TEN

"My God . . ." Anneke moved first, starting down toward the field. But even before Zoe could begin to follow her, another figure emerged from the tunnel on the east side of the stadium and sprinted down the field.

"Jeez, that's Genesko!" Zoe was momentarily transfixed by the sight of Karl Genesko, All-American, pounding downfield. "Wow, he can still run, can't he? Come on." She scrambled down the steps without waiting for Anneke to follow, clambered over the brick wall and raced toward the end zone.

She did fifty yards in what she thought was probably creditable time for a five-foot-two woman carrying a five-pound book bag. But when she stopped breathlessly just under the goalpost, Genesko was already kneeling by the figure, and Frank Novak was standing next to him wringing his hands like an old woman.

"Holy shit," she breathed when she had a clear view of the man on the ground. Ignoring Novak's glare, she mentally cataloged as much as she could before they inevitably shooed her away. The figure was a man—about forty, Zoe calculated rapidly. Limp brown hair with a receding hairline, navy blue windbreaker, khakis, gray running shoes. His hands were still wrapped tightly around the four-foot flagpole.

The other end of the pole was sunk deep into his stomach.

He lay on his side, curled into a semifetal position, the pole lying sideways to his body. Pale blue eyes, open and staring; surprisingly little blood; an appalling stench.

All these things she noted rapidly, already arranging them into descriptive paragraphs in her head. She added in Genesko's face, tight and angry looking. Now she needed to find out who the guy on the ground was, what he was doing here.

"Move away, please." Daniel Najarian shouldered past Zoe and knelt next to Genesko, who stood up and moved aside without argument. Zoe watched raptly; she'd never expected to see the great Dr. Najarian in action.

"Is he dead?" Charlie Cassovoy shoved his way past her and she swore to herself. Shit, she'd forgotten there was another reporter around. The rest of the alumni group had also followed, and now stood in a hushed semicircle, staring. "Is he?" Cassovoy demanded.

"Yes, he's dead." Najarian stood up, wiping his hands on a handkerchief. His ugly/interesting face was stern. Frank Novak looked sick, Zoe noted, as did Charlie Cassovoy. She felt a brief surge of satisfaction—her first dead body, and she hadn't even blinked.

"But that's a . . . you mean he was stabbed with a *Michigan banner*?" The voice belonged to Richard Killian, who sounded more surprised than upset. Behind her, Zoe heard murmurs of horror, but when she glanced over her shoulder she noted expressions that ranged from pity to avid fascination.

"Would you all please—" Genesko was interrupted by the arrival of a small, stocky man in the dark blue uniform of campus security.

"Jesus." The word was more prayer than expletive. The man, who had a dark Latino face, looked down at the body and crossed himself with a gesture that appeared automatic; his eyes were wide but he appeared otherwise controlled. "If you people will stay put, I'll call the police."

"I am the police." Genesko removed his wallet from inside his jacket and flipped it open; Zoe could see the glint of sun on the metal shield. "How many security people do you have here?"

"In the stadium? I'm not sure. Three guys, maybe."

"All right." Genesko nodded briefly. "Use everyone you can find. First, before you do anything else, have every gate in the fence locked; no one to go in or out. Then call the police dispatcher—" he rattled off the phone number "—and tell them what happened; they'll know the drill. After you do those things, please round up every person inside the fence who isn't employed here and ask them to take a seat here in the stadium. Ask stadium personnel and television people to remain at their work locations until we speak to them. Especially the TV people—please tell them they are not to enter the stadium itself for any reason. That's all. Quickly, please." His voice, which was perfectly low and unhurried, had the effect of a whip crack. The security guard disappeared at a trot, and Genesko turned back to the group clustered in the end zone.

"I have to ask all of you to please take seats in the stands. Mr. Novak will go with you, and I'll be along to talk to you myself, as soon as possible."

"If you don't mind, I'd prefer to go back to the hotel," Daniel Najarian said. "There are business matters I must attend to."

"Of course," Genesko agreed. "Just as soon as possible, I assure you."

It almost worked, Zoe thought, amused; probably would have, with a slower crowd. But these folks, however pompous they might be, were too sharp.

"You can't keep us here," Richard Killian objected, and Zoe could feel the group tighten in incipient rebellion. These weren't people who accepted authority unquestioningly.

"Ladies and gentlemen." This time Genesko's voice was raised. He moved aside so that the body was clearly visible. "I think you must all realize that we're dealing with a murder here. And therefore, I assume you understand that there are certain procedures we *must* follow."

"Excuse me, Karl." Eleanor Sullivan's voice was so low that, paradoxically, it commanded everyone's attention. Her face was tightly controlled, but Zoe thought she detected a flicker of worry. "Do you know who he is?"

"Yes." Genesko spoke directly to her. "Frank recognized him." His eyes swept the group. "He is, or was, an NCAA investigator named Alvin Greenaway."

In the dead silence that greeted Genesko's announcement, Zoe heard someone whisper: "Oh, shit, that tears it."

After that, no one protested further when they were herded into seats on the ten-yard line. Zoe, sticking close to Anneke, let herself be led along with the rest, marveling at her luck. She maneuvered for a seat a little to the side of the others, purposely positioning herself so she could see and hear as much as possible. She kept one eye on Genesko, but even so she only picked up the raised eyebrow, accompanied by a small shrug, because for a confused moment she thought it was directed at herself. Then she realized the gesture was intended for the woman next to her.

"Is he yours?" She looked at Anneke with added respect.

"In a manner of speaking," Anneke answered with a smile.

"Not too shabby. He's still got a great bod, doesn't he?"

"As a matter of fact, he does." This time Anneke laughed outright. "But don't ask for any more details because you won't get them."

"But then how'll I ever learn anything?" Zoe asked in mock innocence. "Oh, well. Y'know, I used to have a real thing for football players when I was a kid," she confided. "In fact, my first crush was on John Elway."

"Don't let Karl hear you say that," Anneke chided. "That's what he calls 'quarterback idolatry.' "

"Yeah, I can imagine. *Real* football people know that *DE*-fense wins football games," Zoe intoned, dropping her voice to a gravelly baritone.

"Right. Anyway, now you can have your pick of the whole Michigan team, offense or defense."

"Shit, no," Zoe replied sharply. "Just the opposite. I won't date *any* jocks—it'd compromise my objectivity."

"I never thought of that." Zoe was pleased that Anneke seemed to accept her statement at face value; in her experience, most older people were like, isn't she cute, she sounds just like a real reporter. But this woman was okay.

"Do you know what they're doing?" Zoe pointed toward the end zone, now swarming with police.

"Not really. Examining everything, photographing, collecting evidence."

"I wish we were close enough to see," Zoe complained.

"There really isn't much *to* see, I don't think."

"Still . . ." Zoe subsided, and for a while she watched the distant activity in silence. Then she tried eavesdropping (these were suspects, after all), but there was precious little to hear; the small assembly mostly sat silent, glum and waiting. They mostly sat well apart from each other, in fact, spread out across several rows of the hard wooden benches. On the other side of the stadium she could see another group of people forming in the stands. A uniformed policeman stood in front of them, but Zoe had no idea who any of them were.

"Damn. I wish I could hear what's going on over there," she said fretfully. But the group on the other side of the field was no more animated than her own, and after a few minutes they began to leave. Then, for what seemed like hours (but was in fact, by Zoe's watch, less than twenty minutes), nothing else happened. Just when she thought she would scream from boredom, the huge figure of Karl Genesko at last detached itself from the activity in the end zone and approached the stands. Finally, some action.

"Thank you all for waiting," Genesko said pleasantly (like we had a choice, Zoe snorted to herself). "I'm Lieutenant Karl Genesko, as most of you know, and this is Sergeant Bradley Weinmann." He indicated a youngish man standing next to him with notebook and pen. "I'd like to get preliminary statements from each of you while you're together, so you can check each other's memories. I realize there was a good deal of coming and going while you all waited, and perhaps this way we can get a clearer picture of everyone's movements. If you'll please identify yourselves for the record, and let us know where you're staying in Ann Arbor? Dr. Najarian?"

"Daniel Najarian, Winnetka, Illinois." Najarian had the air of a man accustomed to respectful attention. He sat erect but relaxed on the uncomfortable bench, neither slumping nor fidgeting. "I'll be staying at the Carlton Hotel through the weekend."

"Can you tell me what time you arrived at the stadium?"

"At approximately ten minutes before eleven. I walked around for a short time before I came over to the president's box. I believe I reached the box almost exactly at eleven. You were just arriving, as I recall."

"Was anyone else here?"

"I did not happen to notice anyone when I first entered the stadium." Najarian's voice was, if anything, even more precise. "When I reached the box, Mrs. Sullivan was already there, seated on a bench just below the overhang. And before you ask, I did not see Alvin Greenaway at any time—not that I would have recognized him prior to this. In fact, I saw no one else I can identify, although," his tone was thoughtful, "there were of course a number of people apparently going about their lawful business."

"Did you remain in the stands during the entire time you waited for Mr. Novak?"

"Actually, no. Shortly after you went to find Mr. Novak, I left briefly. Mrs. Sullivan, in fact, accompanied me part of the way. I assume we were both on the same errand."

" 'Same errand'," Eleanor Sullivan mimicked. Her face, although carefully made up, was lined and wrinkled, an elderly face; but her long gray hair and casual style, coupled with her expression of alert interest, made her seem younger. "If you mean we both had to go to the john, Daniel, why don't you say so? Anyway," she said to Genesko, "that's what *my* errand was."

"Thank you, Eleanor." Genesko smiled openly. "I take it that means you only walked together as far as the rest rooms?"

"We didn't go in together, if that's what you mean." She had the raspy voice of the longtime smoker. "Since I'm far too old to squat over a urinal, yes, we separated. And I was gone for a fair length of time, too—it took me a while to find an open ladies' room. So you see," she spread her hands, "neither of us has an alibi."

God, what great stuff, Zoe crowed to herself, scribbling as fast as she could. She had her notebook open inside her bookbag, and with her left hand thrust inside she was taking notes as invisibly as she could manage, praying she wouldn't be noticed. A few rows down she saw Charlie Cassovoy scrabbling for something in his briefcase, and felt a flash of envy when she saw the outlines of a laptop computer. Well, reporting was more than technology. She'd just scrawled a question to herself—why Genesko and Sullivan on first-name terms?—as Eleanor Sullivan spoke the word *alibi*.

There was a kind of stir among the assembled group, although no one spoke aloud. The word hung in the air; Eleanor Sullivan, Zoe thought, looked suspiciously pleased with herself.

"Did either of you," Genesko continued without comment, "see anyone during the time you were behind the stands?"

"No." They spoke together. "I assume, Lieutenant," Najarian went on, "that you know the purpose of this meeting?"

"Yes." Genesko nodded. "Mr. Novak filled me in earlier."

"May I ask you, please, to treat it as confidential." The words were a statement just short of a demand. Genesko nodded again.

"To the extent that I can, certainly." He turned to Richard Killian, who identified himself as a restaurateur from San Francisco; he'd arrived "pretty nearly" right at eleven o'clock.

"I don't really understand why you're questioning *us*," he asked. "I mean, we were all here together when Greenaway . . . well, don't we all alibi each other?"

"I'm afraid not," Genesko replied. "We can't tell yet exactly when Mr. Greenaway was stabbed."

"Well, yes, but we were together here for at least fifteen minutes," Killian persisted.

"Shall I answer that, Lieutenant?" Daniel Najarian went on without waiting for a response. "Alvin Greenaway could have been stabbed as much as half an hour before he came down those stairs."

"You mean he could have been staggering around under the stands all the time we were . . ." Killian looked briefly sick.

"Probably not," Najarian said consideringly. "If I had to theorize, I'd say it was more likely that he was unconscious for a time."

There was a queasy silence before Genesko resumed his questioning. "Did you remain here from the time you arrived, Mr. Killian?"

"No. Once I realized Mr. Novak was going to be late," Killian said, once more cheerful, "I wandered around the stadium, just sort of looking around." He hadn't seen Greenaway either. "I was just playing alumnus. You know, stirring up old memories." He smiled disarmingly and spread his hands.

Uh-oh, Zoe thought, Persona #7B, Boyish Charm. Bernie's shit detector would be clanging off the scale. Yet even as she cynically catalogued him, Zoe realized she was smiling in response. Well, what the hell, at least his type is fun to be around.

ELEVEN

That's what I was doing, too, Jeffrey Person reminded himself. Just wandering around rekindling old memories, that's all. As he waited his turn with Genesko, he gazed down at the brilliant green of the field and watched memories unroll with no fondness whatsoever.

He'd spent four years on that field—four years as a third-rate, third-string cornerback, having his ass chewed out daily by an acerbic (and ambitious) assistant coach. The Great God Ro, after all, couldn't be bothered with some raggedy-ass benchwarmer.

Jeffrey Person could never decide if he loved Michigan or hated it, just as he could never decide if he loved football or hated it. Sometimes he'd think about how he'd been used and exploited down on that field, alternately bullied and ignored, and he'd feel like tearing down the whole place, brick by fucking brick. Sometimes, when he thought about how far he'd come from his mama's shack in the Florida backwoods, he felt a wave of something almost like warmth for the enterprise, and the place, that had given him the chance to make it happen.

Not that they did it for him, Jeffrey thought acidly. He'd just been one of a hundred or so serfs laboring in the fields for the massa, bringing in big bucks for the greater glory of the plantation. As far as they were concerned, he'd been just another warm body willing to beat himself up for the price of a college education, the football equivalent of cannon fodder.

Ro wasn't even the one who'd recruited him. That had been another assistant coach, sweating like a pig in the steamy Florida heat while rather desultorily extolling Michigan's grandeur. The recruiter hadn't seemed to care very much whether the boy Jeffrey, in ragged jeans with his bare feet tucked under him, decided to come to Michigan or not. Jeffrey knew he was only there as a favor to his high school coach, because Coach Murphy had sent Michigan half a dozen first-rate players over the years.

Nor did Jeffrey have any intention of taking this guy up on his halfhearted offer. He certainly wasn't going to go north, to frigid winters and strange accents and hostile white faces. Not when he had a couple of perfectly good offers to small Southern schools.

But small Southern schools weren't good enough for Mama.

"Are you crazy?" she sputtered when he told her his plans. "You got a shot at a big-time Michigan college degree and you think you're gonna pass it up? Not while I draw breath you won't."

"Mama, that guy didn't even really want me," Jeffrey protested. "You could see it. Why should I go somewhere they don't want me?"

"To learn how," she shot back at him. "Because that's what it's like being a black man in this country. Unless you want to spend the rest of your life in the backwoods, you're gonna learn how to walk into any room in this country, whether they want you there or not. Now you sign that letter, and *I'll* take it into town and mail it."

He still wasn't sure she'd been right; there was a lot to be said for an education among other African Americans. But he knew that wasn't what had been on his mind at the time. He recognized now, the man looking back at the boy, that he'd mostly been scared, flat-out terrified of Michigan. And only partly of the strangeness. He'd also been terrified of failure.

Not failure in the classroom. That had always come easily to him; he understood without conceit how intelligent he was. No, what frightened him was Michigan football, the big-time, all-consuming nature of it. Jeffrey knew what no one else suspected—that he would never really be a Michigan-caliber football player. Because, however hard he tried, he could simply never convince himself that winning a football game really *mattered*.

Locker-room pep talks—now called "motivational speeches"—had always left him feeling flat, almost cheated. The other players would whoop and holler and pound on each other, and Jeffrey would whoop with the rest, hoping that if he went through the motions, the feeling would follow. But always, one part of his mind stood aloof, mildly amused, wondering how one could place so much importance on so trivial an endeavor.

Half-consciously, he continued to fake emotion he didn't feel. Because football might not be important intrinsically, but for a black backwoods Florida boy with no prospects whatsoever, it constituted the most important element of his life. Football was his ticket to ride.

Football had gotten him out of the shantytown, had gotten him a first-class college degree, had paved his way to and through law school. And football was by God going to get him to the next level.

He turned casually and surveyed the others in the stands with him, careful not to catch Eleanor Sullivan's eye. Good, he thought; she was equally oblivious of him. And then: What a mess.

He returned his attention to Genesko, examining the big man with curiosity. Genesko had been one of the naturals—big, fast, strong, *dedicated*. Jeffrey had seen films of him playing, and now he mentally superimposed the Karl Genesko game face onto the calm, controlled man in front of him. He'd been controlled as a player, too; no snarling, no posing or hot-dogging, just taut, expectant readiness that was infinitely more effective. It was the eyes mostly, Jeffrey recalled, the eyes that were never still, flicking back and forth across the field to pick up the most infinitesimal movement.

Somehow, Karl Genesko had managed to convince himself that,

for sixty minutes a week, there was nothing in the world more important than winning a football game. Jeffrey, caught between respect and a mild contempt, wondered how he had managed it. Certainly he was no intellectual lightweight; Jeffrey reminded himself that Genesko had been famous for the intelligence of his playing style. The reminder was also a warning that it would be a fatal error to underestimate the man.

"You're Jeffrey Person?" Genesko had finally reached him.

"That's right. I'm an attorney in Miami."

"You were a cornerback about ten years ago, weren't you?"

"Yes." Jeffrey felt a flicker of surprise. "Do you memorize every scrub who ever played for Michigan?"

"Not all of them." Genesko grinned. "I saw you get into an Ohio State game one year, going up against Cris Carter."

"Shee-it." Jeffrey leaned back and returned the grin. "That sumbitch was *big* for a wide receiver."

"He was that. He could hit, too." Jeffrey thought the expression on Genesko's face was one of remembered pleasure, and he recalled that Karl Genesko was also one of those players who purely loved to *hit*. It was something else he'd never fully understood, another of his personal deficiencies. It was also something else to keep in mind, the fact that Genesko loved to hit.

"Are you also at the Carlton?" Genesko continued.

"Yeah. That's where the President's Club blocked out rooms."

"Would you describe your movements for the record?"

"Right." Careful, Jeffrey cautioned himself. "I got here a few minutes before eleven. You know," he smiled disarmingly, "I wanted to walk around for a while, soak it all in. Got to the box here about five after. Daniel and Eleanor were already here."

"Thank you. I take it that once you got here, you didn't leave?"

"Nope." Jeffrey shook his head. "Ms. Coleman showed up a couple of minutes later, and when she said Novak was on the way I assumed he'd be along pretty quick." He grinned again. "I never figured Frank Novak to be operating on CPT."

He was gratified when Genesko smiled in response. "I suppose that's true. While you were walking around before you got to the press box, did you see anyone?"

"Just the usual. None of these folks—" he indicated the assembled group "—and not Alvin Greenaway, either, as far as I know. All I saw were groundskeepers, TV people, et cetera. At least," he said carefully, "that's what they all seemed to be."

TWELVE

That is the problem, isn't it? Anneke asked herself, turning it over in her mind. She herself had seen a number of people when she arrived, anonymous figures in anonymous clothing moving around the stadium on mysterious errands she hadn't even bothered to wonder about. Had one of them been Alvin Greenaway? Or one of the people gathered here? She hadn't the smallest idea.

"Hell, if the prez himself wandered by in jeans and a Michigan sweatshirt no one would notice in this place," Zoe muttered, echoing her thoughts.

"I know," Anneke whispered back.

"So what's the point of all this, do you think? A fishing expedition?"

"I'm sure he knows what he's doing," Anneke said repressively.

"Hey, don't get bent out of shape," Zoe grinned. "I figure he does, too. That's why I'm asking."

In spite of herself, Anneke smiled. The girl radiated such cheerful energy that it was impossible not to feel her own spirits rise in response. But before she could reply, Karl picked up the questioning again.

"Ms. Coleman? For the record, would you describe your movements?"

"I got here early." The young woman paused and looked across the stadium. "About . . . maybe a quarter to eleven. I checked with Mr. Novak over at the TV trailers, and they were still hassling about camera stunts or something. You know, set up cameras on the goalposts, or the quarterback's helmet, crap like that." She paused again, looking flustered. "Anyway," she hurried on, "Mr. Novak asked me to come here to the box, to keep the . . . to apologize to the alumni for him and ask them to wait for him."

"Thank goodness you showed up," Novak said. "I don't know what I'd have done without you."

"You didn't ask her to meet you here, then?" Genesko asked.

"No-o-o," Novak replied slowly. "At least, I don't think I did. Did I?" he appealed to Wendy.

"Yes you did, Mr. Novak," she said quickly. "Don't you remember? You wanted me to take notes."

"I don't remember, but this whole morning has been such a disaster I'm surprised I can remember my own name." He ran his hands through his thinning hair.

Genesko didn't pursue the issue. Instead, he asked Wendy: "About what time did you get to the box here?"

"Right about eleven o'clock." She sounded surer now. "Ms. Sullivan was already here."

"What route did you take from the TV trailers to the box?"

"Just straight through. I came in at that entry aisle over there." She pointed to the northwest corner of the stands.

"Thank you." Karl looked at her thoughtfully before redirecting his gaze. "Mr. Cassovoy?"

Two rows below, the rumpled sportswriter looked up with a start. "Yeah? Right. You know who I am—Charlie Cassovoy, *Detroit News.*" He pronounced it *Dee*-troit, accent on the first syllable.

Looking down at him from above, Anneke could see the top of his head, where a scraggly tonsure of hair surrounded an expanse of pinkish scalp.

"Would you tell me please how you came to be here?"

"Just following up leads." His face wore an unpleasantly smug expression. "A little bird told me this was where the action was."

"Like we'll think he's got some sort of Deep Throat in the athletic department," Zoe sneered in Anneke's ear. "He thinks he's hot shit because he won a Pulitzer about a hundred years ago." Anneke smothered an answering grin.

"What time did you arrive?" Karl continued.

"Just a couple of minutes before the guy took his dive over the wall. When I got here everyone was standing around yammering. I looked for Frank but he wasn't here. He showed up just before . . . you know. So did you, from the other side."

"Yeah, from the . . ." Zoe let the sentence die off. Anneke looked at her, and felt the blood drain from her face as she realized what the girl had been about to say. "Hey, take it easy. It was just a random idea," she said, forgetting that she hadn't actually voiced it.

But it wasn't random, Anneke realized. Other people were going to note the same point, the one that hadn't occurred to Anneke until this moment: Where had Karl himself been, during the half hour before Alvin Greenaway's sudden appearance?

She ran the scene through her memory, seeing Karl charging across and downfield just seconds after Greenaway's collapse. The recollection was vivid—despite the situation, she'd experienced a frisson of déjà vu excitement at the sight of Karl running across a football field. Running *across* . . . But if he'd been with the TV people, he and Frank Novak should both have been at the *northwest* corner of the stadium complex, where the TV trailers and other facilities were always located.

She shook her head. Nonsense; he'd probably been with Novak the entire time. They could have been working out camera setups over by the locker rooms, or checking electrical cables, or . . . She didn't pursue the thought, because Charlie Cassovoy was speaking again.

"And by the way, what about Novak? Aren't you gonna question him too?"

"I wasn't anywhere near here!" Novak said hotly. "First I was in the director's trailer, and then I was around behind the clubhouse tunnel, and then I was back around the electrical shop."

"Which, as it happens, is under the stands," Cassovoy pointed out.

"Mr. Cassovoy," Karl interrupted sharply. "I assure you we intend to follow up on everyone's movements." He held everyone's eyes briefly before his gaze moved on.

"Uh-oh," Zoe whispered, and Anneke heard gleeful anticipation in her voice. "It's showtime."

"And you are . . . ?" Karl asked her.

"Zoe Kaplan." She took an audible breath. "I'm a student living in East Quad. I'm also a *Michigan Daily* reporter."

"You!" Frank Novak leaped to his feet and spun around. "It's her!" he squawked.

"I see." Karl ignored Novak; Anneke could have sworn the look on his face was amusement. "And were you also looking for Mr. Novak?"

"Actually," Zoe answered boldly, "I was looking for you." When Karl raised an eyebrow in question, she said, "I was looking for comments from alumni."

"Ask her how she found out!" Novak shouted. "Make her tell you who the spy is!"

But instead Karl asked, "What time did you arrive?"

"About a quarter to eleven. See, I wanted to catch you before the meeting. I knew there was no way I'd get near you once it started."

"So you were here *before* Ms. Sullivan?"

"Yeah, but no one really noticed me. I mean, all they see is a student. And a *girl.*" She gave the word a sarcastic twist, and received an answering smile. "She was the only one who spotted me." Zoe jerked her head at Anneke. Karl's face held a complicated expression that Anneke didn't even want to decipher. He stared at both of them for a few moments.

"For the record, Ms. Kaplan," he said finally, and Anneke knew he was choosing his words with care, "will you tell us your source for this morning's article in the *Daily*?"

"For the record, Lieutenant," Zoe answered, "I cannot reveal my source."

"You're not going to let her get away with that," Novak yelped furiously. "She's a Michigan student, and she'd better start behaving like one. The *Daily* is a student newspaper; it's supposed to be supporting the University, not tearing it down."

Instead of responding, Zoe smiled brightly and drew her notebook from her bookbag. Placing it visibly on her lap, she carefully wrote down Novak's words, while Anneke desperately gulped back incipient giggles.

"Don't you dare print what I'm saying!" Novak gobbled. "Make her stop!" he shouted at Karl.

Karl also looked like he was choking back laughter, Anneke thought. But his voice, when he spoke, sounded exasperated.

"Mr. Novak, please. Ms. Kaplan, do you have anything more to add at the moment?"

"No, sir." Anneke was sure Zoe hadn't missed the implication of the last three words.

Clearly Novak hadn't either. "This isn't over yet, young lady. You aren't going to get away with this by pretending you're a real reporter."

"She *is* a real reporter." To Anneke's surprise, it was Richard Killian who barked the words at Novak. "The *Daily*, Mr. Novak, is a real newspaper, not a mouthpiece of the University. And Ms. Kaplan has the identical First Amendment rights as the *New York Times*. Don't you dare," he said to Zoe, "tell them the name of your source."

"Richard, don't be ridiculous," Najarian snapped. "Just because you spent a couple of years on a student newspaper, you are not Walter Cronkite. This is a murder investigation, not a cheating scandal. Of course she has to tell them everything she knows."

"I don't care if we're talking about cannibalism or high treason," Killian snapped. "There is no more critical journalistic principle than source confidentiality."

"He's right," Charlie Cassovoy interjected. "The little lady doesn't have to say a word." He gave Zoe a conspiratorial wink. "You hang in there, honey."

Suddenly they all seemed to be talking at once. Anneke heard the words "Supreme Court"—that was Jeffrey Person—and the words "what bullshit," from (she thought) Eleanor Sullivan, along with references to "girl sportswriters" and "image of the University."

"Ladies and gentlemen, please." Karl's voice rose above the babble. "If you please?" When the multiple arguments subsided, he said, "Thank you for your patience. Since most of you are staying at the Carlton, it would be most efficient to interview you there this evening, if you have no objection."

"What about them?" Jeffrey Person pointed across the stadium, where the other small group was dispersing. He sounded more curious than challenging.

"They've also been interviewed," Karl replied. Then, when Person continued to peer at him, he said, "There were a few tourists who simply wandered in to look at the stadium."

"I see." Person gave a quick nod.

"Thank you all," Karl said again. "We'll be in touch with each of you this evening."

Anneke remained seated as everyone else scattered, visibly anxious to escape. Zoe shoved her notebook back into her bookbag, her dark gold eyes sparkling with excitement. "I'm outa here," she announced.

"What are you going to write?" Anneke kept the question casual with an effort.

"Only what I saw and heard. Truly." Zoe put her hand over her heart; the gesture was serious rather than flip, and Anneke found herself touched by the girl's earnestness. Careful, she warned herself; remember she thinks of herself first and foremost as a reporter.

"Ms. Kaplan?" Karl had approached so noiselessly that both women jumped. "I'd like to speak with you this afternoon, please."

It was a statement, not a question. After a moment, Zoe said, "Sure. I've got to cover the press conference at three o'clock . . . how about five, at the *Daily*?"

"Fine. I'll meet you there."

"Okay. Oh, and will you come too?" she asked Anneke.

"Me? But . . . " Anneke shook her head, nonplussed. "I don't think that's a good idea."

"Please?" Zoe seemed entirely serious. "I really want you there."

"If you think you can use me as a buffer, it won't work, you know," Anneke warned her.

"I'm not doing that," Zoe protested hotly. "I don't use my friends."

"No, I don't think you do," Anneke said slowly, looking at her. She turned to Karl. "If you don't mind?"

"Not in the least." His expression was bland.

"All right," she capitulated.

"Good. See you then." Zoe grabbed her bookbag and trotted away up the stairs. Anneke looked at Karl.

But all he said was, "So much for the hardware store."

THIRTEEN

"Crime stories belong to the City Desk," City Editor Faye Leonard was saying for the third time.

"But this is a *sports* story," Gabriel Marcus pointed out, in a voice of polite reasonableness, also for the third time. "Besides, she was *there.*"

"But she has no experience covering crime stories. She hardly has any experience covering *any*thing, for Christ sake."

"She was good enough to break the NCAA story."

"That was blind, dumb luck, and you know it."

I wish they'd stop talking about me like I'm not here, Zoe thought. Her jaw was beginning to ache with the effort of keeping her mouth shut, but she knew she had to let Gabriel run with this particular ball.

They were crammed into a tiny, windowless room carved out of the *Daily* city room, on the second floor of the old brick building at 420 Maynard. The ugly gray metal desks overflowed with piles of paper of various kinds—newspaper, notebooks, copy paper, napkins used and unused, pizza boxes empty and half-empty. Sheesh, how do these guys breathe in here, Zoe wondered.

"David, it's a flat-out matter of contacts." Gabriel was speaking now to the editor in chief himself, David Carmichael. "We have the contacts in the athletic department, and on the football team, and that's where this story is."

"But you *don't* have the police contacts," Faye countered.

"Does the investigating officer and his girlfriend count?" Zoe interrupted sweetly, playing her trump card.

"His girlfriend?" David asked, easily diverted as he always was.

"Right. She's a friend of mine," Zoe replied.

"Besides," Gabriel, seeing their advantage, pursued the line of argument, "she also knows all the suspects—she spent the whole morning with them."

"Yeah," Zoe followed his lead, "and since they've already seen me around, they won't think of me as press and clam up."

"Just because she can recognize a few alumni doesn't mean she can cover a murder investigation." Faye wasn't giving up without a fight. "I mean, what does she know about things like police procedure?"

"Get real, Faye," Gabriel snorted. "How many murder investigations have *you* covered? They're not exactly a staple of Ann Arbor journalism, after all."

"Even so . . ."

"David, you know . . ."

They were both talking at once now, fighting for the editor's attention. He looks like he'd rather be hiding in the belfry, Zoe sneered to herself, watching the pained expression on David Carmichael's face. He'd been elected editor in the first place as a compromise between a talented but politically conservative candidate, and an ambitious moderate who was also an administration suck-up. David Carmichael had no apparent politics, which seemed to make him the ideal choice until people realized, too late, that he actually had no opinions whatsoever.

He didn't have one now, either. Gabriel played his final card.

"Look, David, the bottom line is that we're already on top of it. Zoe is writing the murder itself—I mean, she was there, after all—and she's already scheduled to cover Truhorne's press conference this afternoon. Jeff Bryson has appointments to interview Kyle Farmer and a couple of other football players after practice today, and Katie Sparrow has a call in to the NCAA office for information on the investigation and background on Greenaway. Of course, I can call them all off, but . . . " He spread his hands.

"Well, as long as you've already got the wheels in motion," David said, looking relieved.

"In other words," Faye snarled furiously, "they stole it, so they get to keep it."

"You can't steal what's yours to begin with."

The yammering continued for a few minutes longer, but they all knew that once David did actually make a decision about something, nothing short of a nuclear blast would change it. Still, after Faye had blown out in a rage, he continued to worry at it.

"She is awfully inexperienced," he said. "Look, Gabriel, I want you to honcho this thing."

"Absolutely," Gabriel agreed. "I'd intended to from the beginning."

"And I want you to report to me regularly, keep me fully informed every step of the way. I want the police and the administration to know that this is being handled from the very top."

"No problem," Gabriel nodded again. "Don't worry about it, David. I've got a good staff; we'll handle it right." He paused, two beats. "Now," he said, "what about the issue of revealing our source?"

"I guess," David said slowly, "we really should . . . "

"Reveal a source?" Gabriel raised an eyebrow.

"Well, maybe we can run it by Professor Acheson, in the law school," David temporized.

"Look," Gabriel finally took pity on the beleaguered editor, "normally I'd never give a source to the cops. But in this case, the usual reasons for protecting a source don't really apply." He looked at Zoe and she grimaced.

"Damn, I suppose you're right. It's just that I was hoping for more later on. And you know Genesko's going to tell his buddies in the AD's office."

"Probably," Gabriel agreed. "But think how we'd look if we refused to cooperate and they found out anyway."

"Yeah. We'd look like real shits. Oh, well."

"Good," David let out his breath in a gust of relief. "Then I'll leave it to you."

"Does Jeff really have interview appointments with Farmer and those other players?" Zoe asked as they climbed the slate stairs to the city room.

"He will have," Gabriel replied, grinning.

"And the NCAA call?"

"Ditto."

"You are too wicked," Zoe said admiringly. She checked her wristwatch. "Oh, shit, I better get moving—I've only got half an hour before the press conference."

The press conference began as shambles and went downhill from there.

It had been scheduled originally for one of the fourth-floor meeting rooms in the Union, but when Zoe arrived she discovered it had been reassigned to the ballroom on the third floor. She trotted up the wide central staircase, hearing the muted roar from above even before she crested the stairs.

There were at least a hundred people milling around in the big open space outside the ballroom doors, but the noise seemed to be coming equally from within and without. She struggled through the crowd to the door, using her bookbag as a battering ram, only to be stopped by a blue-uniformed security guard with a disgusted look on his face.

"Sorry, kid, no students allowed. Press only." He voice was a bored monotone, as though he'd been repeating the same words for the last half hour, which Zoe assumed he had.

"Down, Cerberus." She gave him her best bright-little-girl

smile. "I am press." She dug into her bookbag and located her wallet in its bottom recesses. "Here, see?" She flipped it open to her *Daily* press card and kept the smile firmly on her face while the guard examined the card suspiciously.

"Yeah, okay, go on in." He sounded even more disgusted than he looked.

Zoe brushed past him through the doors and stepped into a madhouse of shouting, arguing, gesticulating humanity. Rows of folding chairs were arranged down the center of the room, but virtually no one was sitting in them. Even so, there was no lack of total floor space in the huge ballroom, but everyone was pressing forward in one direction, toward the end of the room at which a table and five empty chairs were arranged like waiting sentinels.

So this was what a media feeding frenzy was like. Zoe flung herself gleefully into the maelstrom, using her bookbag to force a path between two large men engaged in a shouting match, squeezing under the outstretched arms of a cameraman and narrowly avoiding being clipped by a microphone in the hands of an overdressed woman with improbably blond hair and far too much gold jewelry.

Fucking television, Zoe swore silently as she tripped over a fat cable and nearly went down on her knees. She spotted the logos of at least a dozen TV operations, including local stations from Detroit, Lansing, and Toledo, national networks, cable networks, and even a couple of the sleazy tabloid shows.

Across the room, she got a brief, reassuring glimpse of a *Daily* photographer battling his way toward the table, before he was swallowed up in the mob. Well, he'd probably get something; photographers were all a little crazy anyway. Then she too was swept forward as the door behind the table opened, figures in business suits emerged, and the crowd of shouting media people surged forward.

And after all that, the press conference itself was an anticlimax. Oh, the TV people probably got what they were after, Zoe sneered; a couple of minutes of "film at eleven" and some talking heads. But for print media, it was all bullshit.

Russell Truhorne, flanked by Ro and PIO's from both the athletic department and the administration, read his statement, a masterpiece of obfuscation laced with equal parts innocence, concern, and cooperation. He touched briefly on his friendship with Alvin Greenaway, neither denying it nor emphasizing it, and expressed total faith that the Ann Arbor police department would bring Greenaway's killer to justice. The Michigan Athletic Department, Truhorne assured them all, was extremely upset about events of the last two days, and would of course cooperate fully with the NCAA, with the police, with the media.

The questioning afterward, dominated by the TV people, was even more feeble. Truhorne didn't know, he said, what the specific NCAA charges would be. He had no idea who might have wanted Greenaway dead, or why (although he did manage to suggest, with elegant subtlety, that the police were searching for a lone mugger). He knew nothing about the progress of investigations, either NCAA or police. He did admit, to Zoe's delight, that the *Daily* story was "more or less" accurate, but other than that, Russell Truhorne gave a first-rate imitation of a man who didn't know anything about anything.

Only when the questioning turned to Ro was anything really quotable said, and even Ro kept a firm grip on his famous temper.

"Do I know what the NCAA charges are?" He repeated a TV reporter's question slowly, savoring it. "Did you get here late, son?"

"No." The reporter looked confused.

"So you heard Mr. Truhorne say he didn't know what the charges would be?" Ro waited, forcing the reporter to answer with a nod before he continued. "Do you really think," his voice rose as only a football coach's voice could, "that I might know the answer to that question and *not tell the athletic director*?" He paused to make sure everyone had gotten it. "Now, does anyone out there have a *sensible* question?"

"Do you think that NCAA regulations are too stringent?" That was Jacko Clarke from Channel 3 in Detroit, who always wore

Michigan State green on his Friday night telecast, asking a question for which he already knew the answer.

"I think they're necessary to protect the student athlete."

"I think they're a crock."

Truhorne and Ro spoke together, the harsh coach's voice overriding the smooth one.

"You're talking about kids who don't have rich daddies sending them a big check for walking-around money every week." Ro took the ball and ran with it. "Kids who can't afford clothes, or dates, or movies. Kids who can't even go out for a hamburger with their friends because they haven't got two dimes to rub together." Ro's voice rose, and Zoe could hear the honest anguish he felt. "I've had kids who couldn't even afford *shoes*, for Chrissakes. And the NCAA tells us we can't even buy them a Coke at McDonald's."

"You seem to really care about your players." The speaker was a man Zoe had never seen before, standing next to a cameraman wielding a minicam. His voice oozed sincerity—well, it oozed, anyway, Zoe thought. "I suppose you wouldn't be human if you didn't think about bending the rules sometimes."

The room stilled. The sports reporters in the audience, the ones familiar with Ro, held their breath in delighted anticipation, waiting for the explosion that would make the whole dreary press conference worthwhile.

It didn't come. Instead, to their vast surprise, Ro chuckled.

"Nice try, asshole." He looked around the room, picking out a few sportswriters he recognized and favored them with a genuine smile, inviting them to join in his contempt for the TV reporter. Several of them, especially the print boys, laughed with him. Ro milked the moment briefly, and then turned serious once more.

"Because there are a lot of people here who don't know anything about college sports, or about me, let me say a couple of things for the record. Did I ever give or lend a player money, even for an emergency? I did not, not once. There's an emergency loan fund for that sort of thing, available to every student on campus. On the other hand, do I think I should be able to? Of *course* I do. How come a journalism professor—" he glared at them all impartially—"can do a favor for a student, and I can't? How come an art student can sell his paintings while he's in school, but a football player can't even sell a goddamn T-shirt?" He waited as if expecting an answer; when none came he turned to Truhorne and whispered audibly, "Are we done here?" Then, without waiting for a response, he stood up and walked out. The press conference was effectively over.

FOURTEEN

She could have gone to the hardware store on her own, Anneke scolded herself as she pulled into the City Hall parking lot. But it was to have been as much excursion as shopping trip; Karl had looked forward to browsing, to examining and planning and selecting, and she hadn't wanted to usurp his obvious pleasure in the process.

Well, she could at least have gone back to her office and spent the afternoon working. But having given herself the day off, she would have felt cheated if she'd spent the day designing peer-to-peer networks.

In the end, after sitting irresolute in her car for a while, she'd gone to Zingerman's, where she sat at one of the wooden picnic tables on the outdoor patio, eating a bagel with scallion cream cheese and mindlessly watching the belligerent sparrows. Not your average birds, Zingerman's sparrows; today they were entertainingly aggressive, strutting and flapping from table to table, squabbling for chunks of black rye bread, snatching food right off the plates of unwary diners. No indecision here; the sparrows had no trouble knowing exactly what they wanted and going straight for it.

When she tired of the sparrow theater she drove back downtown and wandered through the antique shops scattered on the streets between Main and Division, finding nothing that piqued her interest.

At Zingerman's, at first, she'd thought about the murder, first as human tragedy and then as intellectual puzzle. But she quickly discovered, to her guilty dismay, that her chief reaction was one of resentment over the collapse of her day's outing. After that, she tried not to think about it at all. In fact, I spent the day drowning worms, she admitted to herself, smiling slightly at the phrase. It was a favorite of her son-in-law, the fisherman's definition of futility. I ought to call them, she thought, see how the baby's doing. Maybe go out to Boulder for a visit.

The thought brought her up short. How could she even consider leaving, with all the things going on in her life? But before she could analyze the question further, Karl opened the passenger door and slid into the seat next to her, with the graceful economy of motion that always surprised her.

"You taste like chocolate," he said when he had kissed her. "Got any more?"

"Here." She dug into her briefcase, laughing, and handed him the small white bag. "I can't keep any secrets from you, can I?"

"Yeah, the world's greatest detective, that's me," he growled, extracting a stick of chocolate-covered orange peel.

"You mean you haven't made an arrest yet? Gee, and you've already been at it . . . what? Four hours?"

"Right. And that's three more than the average TV cop takes." He jerked his head toward the Huron side of the parking lot, and Anneke saw with a start that it was parked absolutely solid with TV trucks, a forest of white dishes perched atop vans emblazoned with monograms, eyeballs, and other insignia.

"My God, so many?"

"I think we've got everyone here but the BBC and TV-Moscow."

"It never occurred to me." She spotted a van from ESPN, another from *Hard Copy*. "Why on earth?"

"Michigan football is always big news, and now they've got a murder, a couple of big names, and the scent of scandal." He made a face. "It's a natural."

"Big names? That includes you, doesn't it?" Anneke felt her stomach twist.

"As far as the TV boys are concerned, I'm part of the mix, certainly." He paused and took another chocolate from the bag. "Eventually," he added, "they're going to figure out that I ought to be a suspect instead of the investigating officer."

"That's ridiculous." She heard her voice rise with dread. She turned the ignition key and backed out of the parking spot, scowling. "For one thing," she said as she pulled out onto Fourth Avenue, "once you find out what exactly Greenaway was investigating, that should help focus the investigation."

"It might." Karl tightened his seat belt as she veered left onto William. "Except we called NCAA headquarters in Overland Park, and we spoke to Greenaway's superiors. And they haven't got one single clue about what Greenaway was up to."

"What? That's impossible, isn't it? I mean, NCAA investigators aren't self-starters. Without authorization? I don't get it."

"Neither do they." He spread his hands. "According to them—and I don't think they'd lie about *this*," he interjected acidly, "Greenaway wasn't on assignment, he was on *vacation*. He was in Ann Arbor visiting his daughter."

"Then somebody *here* . . ." She made the logical leap, and he followed her train of thought.

"Right. He comes to Ann Arbor for purely personal reasons, yet the day after he arrives he tells Russ Truhorne there's going to be an investigation. Which means someone here in town told him something he knew would force an investigation. Which is why," he concluded, "we have *got* to find out who the *Daily*'s source is."

"What about written notes? Didn't he at least keep a record of his conversations?"

"Not that we found." He shrugged.

"Are you absolutely sure," Anneke said slowly, "that the investigation was the motive for murder?"

"Not one hundred percent positive, no. But we've pretty well ruled out a random mugging—his watch and wallet were untouched, and the weapon isn't the sort of thing a mugger would use. As for personal motives, his daughter was in class all morning and there's no one else we know of in town who knew him personally except Russ Truhorne."

"Still . . . " Anneke maneuvered the Firebird into a parking spot on Maynard and cut the engine. "Would anyone really *kill* over a recruiting violation? I mean, it's not an actual crime, after all—not something someone would go to jail for."

"No, but think of the possible costs," Karl answered. "To begin with, for anyone on the coaching staff or in the athletic department, it means the end of their career—not just here, but at any decent school in the country. For a player, it means the end of his college playing career, the loss of his scholarship, conceivably the potential loss of either millions in income, or a college degree, depending on why he's at Michigan."

"All right, but you can't make the same sort of case against alumni, surely?"

"Sure you can. Some of these guys have an enormous ego involvement in their alumni status—hanging out with the football team or bragging about Michigan football back home can be the most important thing in their lives. Believe me, I've seen them hanging around the team. And then, some of them use their alumni ties for business networking, too. It can be a major source of customers, clients, even friends. If they're publicly identified as the reason Michigan football got hit with a major NCAA penalty, they'd be ostracized. And yes, I think there are people who would kill over that."

"I suppose you're right. Disgrace can be a powerful motive."

"Exactly. If it were me, a disclosure like that would finish my career." He spoke casually, but Anneke knew he was right.

"Well, it isn't you," she declared, throwing open the car door with more force than she intended.

"No, actually, it isn't." He grinned at her. "Now let's go see what we can squeeze out of your new friend."

FIFTEEN

"Lieutenant Genesko, what do you know about the *Michigan Daily*?"

The speaker was a good-looking youth with curly reddish hair and a serious expression overlaying what Anneke felt was a naturally cheerful face. Zoe had introduced him as sports editor Gabriel Marcus. He and Zoe sat opposite Karl and Anneke at one end of a big conference table in a sort of library on the second floor of 420 Maynard. The wood-paneled room was lined with shelves on which stood rank after rank of huge, folio-sized bound volumes of past newspapers.

The Student Publications Building itself sits on a small lot a block from the main campus. It is an old-fashioned brick-and-stone structure, with leaded glass windows, a heavy carved oak doorway, and a slate roof topped by a small cupola that *Daily* people refer to as the belfry. From the outside, it is the sort of building that engenders warm fuzzy feelings in sentimentally inclined alumni. Inside, however, the fine old building is shabby and worn, marred by scarred woodwork, chipped slate, and ill-conceived alterations.

"Not a great deal." Karl answered Gabriel's question politely. "Other than the fact that it's the University of Michigan student newspaper."

"Well, even that's only partly right, depending on semantics." Gabriel rolled a pencil between his fingers. "See, the *Michigan Daily* isn't your average student newspaper. It was founded in 1890 by a group of Michigan students, but it was an independent venture, *not* a University one. It was totally self-supporting from the very beginning. We do *not* get funding from the University. Even this building is *ours.*" He looked around the room, filled with late-afternoon sunlight, and the fondness in his face was evident. "I know it's got 'Student Publications' carved in the lintel out front, but it was built entirely with funds generated by the *Daily* itself."

"I see." Karl nodded. "So you don't see yourself as a student newspaper?"

"Sure we do. But we see ourselves as—we *are*—an *independent* student newspaper. What we are *not* is a *University* newspaper. That's why the masthead reads 'One hundred six years of editorial freedom.' " He pursed his lips, then grinned suddenly and waved a hand at the shelves of bound volumes. "If you're interested, I can show you reports of a dozen pitched battles with the administration over that very issue. And by the way—" the grin disappeared "—the *Daily* never lost *any* of them."

"I believe I take your point," Karl said. So did Anneke—Gabriel was, in effect, warning him not to attempt to apply administration pressure against them.

"Now, given our status as an independent newspaper," Gabriel continued, "you understand that we have exactly the same First Amendment rights as any other newspaper. Including the right not to reveal the source of any story we print."

"I see." Karl's face remained impassive; he expected this, Anneke thought unhappily. "Then you still refuse to tell me the source of your story?" he asked Zoe.

"On the contrary." It was Gabriel who answered. "In *this particular case,*" he said carefully, "we're happy to be able to cooperate with the police." Even Karl, who rarely gave anything away, looked surprised. Anneke, catching Zoe's eye, saw the girl grinning widely, and Gabriel's mouth was twitching as though he, too, were holding back laughter. What on earth are these children up to? Anneke wondered. "The trouble is," Gabriel spread his hands, "it's not really going to help you."

"Well, why don't we wait and see." Karl pulled a notebook and pen from the inside pocket of his jacket. "Let me ask you a few questions, Ms. Kaplan."

But Zoe shook her head. "It'll be better if I show you instead of telling you," she said, standing up. "Come on."

"Ms. Kaplan," Karl sighed audibly, "is all this really necessary? Where are we going?"

"Call me Zoe. We're going to the Union. Really, you'll understand much better this way."

She refused to say another word, although she gave Anneke a reassuring grin before leading them down the stairs and outside. The odd little procession trooped down Maynard, and Zoe paused briefly to spin the 15-foot-high Rosenthal cube in the center of Regents Plaza before turning in at the side entrance to the Michigan Union. She led them up one flight of stairs to the main floor, and then up again. On the second floor she turned down a long corridor, heavily paneled in dark wood.

"There," she said, pointing at the blank wall.

"I beg your pardon?" Karl said.

"Right there. That's my source." She pointed again, and this time Anneke saw, down near the floor, a small square of metal grillwork painted dark brown to match the paneling.

"Are you telling me," Karl said slowly, "that you overheard the conversation between Russell Truhorne and Alvin Greenaway through a heating duct?"

"You got it. I told you it wouldn't help."

There were several moments of total silence while all four of them stared at the grate, and then Karl threw back his head and laughed aloud. Anneke could feel the whoosh of released tension in the two students. Despite her disappointment—she'd had real hopes that this would provide a concrete lead—she found herself joining in the general laughter.

"So this is why you agreed to reveal your 'source,' " Karl said finally.

"That's right," Gabriel answered. "Since it wasn't a question of protecting an individual, we decided it would be silly to start a war over it."

"Besides," Zoe added, "I'd've felt like a total dork if I made a big-deal Freedom-of-the-Press issue over it, and then people found out I was 'protecting' a heating duct."

"Well," Karl said, "it certainly looks like you're right about this not being much help. But I still need to ask both of you a few questions."

"Sure," Zoe agreed amicably. "But do you mind if we go back to the *Daily* to do it? This place just doesn't seem real . . . private." And laughing once more, she trotted toward the stairs.

Back at the *Daily* library, Karl once again took out his notebook and pen and looked at Zoe seriously. "You realize that the question of 'source' has really only been backed up a step. What I have to ask you now is who told you Truhorne and Greenaway would be meeting there in the first place?"

"No one did," Zoe answered promptly.

"Ms. Kaplan . . . "

"No, honestly. Look, this is what happened. I was doing a story on basketball season ticket sales." She wrinkled her nose in disgust. "There's been a lot of arguing about who gets first pick, how seats are assigned, and like that. So I went over to Truhorne's office to get a quick quote—you know, add some life to the story—only his secretary says he's in this big important meeting and can't be disturbed."

"Did she tell you who he was meeting with?"

"Shit, no. In fact, that's what got me going—she was acting real freaky. I said I'd wait, and she said he wasn't in his office, and I asked where he was—I figured I'd wait around outside the door and catch him when he came out—and she wouldn't tell me that either. That's when I saw the words *Michigan Union* and a room number on her memo pad," Zoe concluded triumphantly.

"So you went over to the Union. But you didn't wait outside the door?"

"Uh-uh. See, by this time I was beginning to figure out that something was going on that they didn't want anyone to know about."

"Which of course made you feel you *had* to know about it."

"Right." Zoe beamed at him, ignoring the irony in his voice. "I mean, if they don't want you to know about something, it's usually because it's worth knowing, you know?"

"I'm afraid I do know," Karl said dryly. "Can you tell me, though, how you knew about the heating duct?"

"Well, I didn't, exactly, at least not about that specific heating duct. But the Union heating duct thing is sort of *Daily* folklore."

"I don't follow you."

"It goes back to the fifties," Gabriel interjected. "A *Daily* sports reporter found out that they were having a special meeting of the Board in Control of Intercollegiate Athletics, only they wouldn't give out any information about it. The reporter was prowling around trying to find out what was going on, and he happened to stumble on a heating duct that connected to the meeting room. He was able to overhear the entire meeting, at which the Board secretly decided to fire the football coach."[1]

"Great story," Zoe added admiringly. "Almost as good as mine."

"Yes. Well." Karl paused. "Ms. Kaplan . . . "

"Please, call me Zoe," she said again.

"All right, Zoe, can you tell me how much of the meeting you

[1]See "Report Elliott Coach," *The Michigan Daily*, Nov. 14, 1958, page 1.

actually overheard? Most of it, do you think?"

"I'd guess I heard almost all of it. I'm pretty sure they were just starting when I got there."

"And Greenaway definitely didn't say who was the focus of the investigation?"

"Hell, if he had you'd've read about it in this morning's *Daily*, believe me."

"I suppose so. Did Greenaway reveal who his *informant* was?"

"No, sorry." Zoe shook her head. "In fact, Truhorne asked him that a couple of times—he was really pissed—but Greenaway wouldn't say. You know," she added slowly, "Greenaway seemed like a good old guy. Pretty straight. He *wasn't* trying to engineer a cover-up, you know, just giving Truhorne some advance warning. I got the feeling he was almost as upset about the whole thing as Truhorne was, but he told Truhorne he was going to play it by the book, and he sounded to me like he meant it."

There was a moment of silence. We've forgotten Alvin Greenaway himself, Anneke realized—Greenaway as a person rather than as a dead body, or as a golem of the NCAA.

"You know," Zoe broke the silence, "you can get all this from Truhorne himself, can't you?" She looked at Karl with bright-eyed curiosity. "Or are you using my statement to check up on his?"

"Perhaps I'm using his statement to check up on yours." Anneke saw the glint of humor in Karl's eye; apparently so did Zoe, who laughed aloud.

"Touché," she said cheerfully. "Okay, look." She pulled out a reporter's notebook and pen. "I've given you everything I had, right? Now will you answer a couple of questions for me?"

"A couple, yes. If I can," he replied cautiously.

"Greenaway really was killed with a Michigan flag? Do you know where the flag came from?"

"It apparently came from one of the concession booths underneath the northwest corner of the stands—it seems to be one of a cluster that decorated the booth."

"Is that where the actual stabbing took place?"

"We think so, yes. We found bloodstains behind the counter, although we need to confirm that the blood belonged to Alvin Greenaway."

"Can we get a photograph?" Gabriel put in.

"From a distance only. The area has been cordoned off by the police."

"Do you know *when* the actual stabbing took place?" Zoe asked. "I mean, did it have to be right before he came down the steps, or could it have been a while before?"

"He could have been stabbed some time before he appeared, but we don't know what that time frame is yet."

"If the possible time's more than, say, twenty minutes, it could have been anyone there," Zoe mused aloud. "Where's the body right now?"

"The county coroner's office is performing the autopsy. We expect to have preliminary results within twenty-four hours."

"Sheesh, this isn't what I want." Zoe tossed her pad on the table. "Look, do you really think he was killed because of the NCAA investigation?"

"It seems the most likely motive, but we're not ruling out others yet." He looked at her for a moment. "I can tell you this—first, his wallet and wristwatch were not taken. Second, his briefcase was found in a storeroom a few hundred feet from the concession stand. And finally, there was a notebook lying next to the briefcase, with several pages apparently ripped out."

"Wow. Thanks." Zoe scribbled in her own notebook. "So someone was looking for something he'd written down," Zoe theorized, "and apparently found it." She paused consideringly. "Which is why you're focusing on the happy little group that was in the stadium at the time?"

"We're questioning them, and others. Remember, the stadium isn't a locked room. Anyone could have walked in and walked out without being noticed."

"Yeah, but . . . I suppose." Zoe looked at him. "One more question—how do you know Eleanor Sullivan?"

"I don't think it's appropriate for me to answer personal questions at this time."

Zoe looked disappointed, but she didn't press the issue. "Okay, thanks," she said finally. Then, as Karl and Anneke stood up, she said, "There is one more thing I'd like to ask—a favor. Look," she said in a rush, "I know you've got a lot of good buds in the athletic department, but could you not tell anyone about the heating duct thing?"

Karl smiled slightly. "Well, I can't make any firm promise, but I'll do my best."

SIXTEEN

Once they were outside, Anneke said, "You won't, will you?"

"Tell the people in the athletic department about the heating duct?" He laughed. "No, I won't. I may have to tell the prosecutor's office, though, and I can't answer for them."

"Well, maybe you can just tell them it was a case of eavesdropping, without going into detail. They're nice kids; I like them." Particularly Zoe, she thought; she had felt one of those instant sparks of understanding with the girl, that rare feeling that suggested the possibility of real friendship. The difference in their ages was relevant but not determining—cross-generational friendships were not that unusual in Ann Arbor. Here, age seemed to affect only the manner of friendship, not the quality.

"I'll do my best," Karl agreed. She unlocked the car doors and he slid into the passenger seat, buckling his seat belt with one hand. "At least," he added, "now we know why she wanted you there."

"What do you mean?" Anneke, reaching for the ignition, stopped and looked at him.

"Just that I think she knew I'd be more likely to keep her secret, with you there to back her up."

"What a nasty thing to say." She snapped the ignition and jerked the Firebird forward with even more than her usual speed. Her chest was tight with an emotion that might have been anger or might have been fear. Fear of what? she wondered, and could find no answer. She wished suddenly that she were alone in the big car—that she could aim it in some unknown direction and simply drive, as fast and as far as the Firebird could take her.

"I never meant to suggest," he said quietly when they stopped at the light at William and State—why is this light *always* red, Anneke fumed—"that Zoe was simply using you. Friends do turn to each other for support, after all."

"I suppose you're right. Sorry," she said ungraciously, all her emotion evaporating in an instant. She felt suddenly weary and ashamed. What was it about relationships, she wondered, even simple friendships, that made them so . . . *fraught*?

"Damn," he said in an undertone, and then, to her, "Look, I have to go out to the Carlton next; they've set us up with a temporary office there. But even detectives have to eat. Why don't you drive me out there and have dinner with me? Brad's meeting me there; he can drop me at home when we're done."

"Do you know," she said conversationally, "that I've gained nearly ten pounds since we moved in together?" They were heading down South U toward home; now, without comment, she turned left on Hill and continued toward Washtenaw. "No, it's not about vanity," she insisted, examining him for nonexistent signs of amusement. "It's about . . . do you remember what my refrigerator used to look like?"

This time he did smile. "I remember you once quoted some comedian when you described it. You said the only things in your refrigerator were mustard, mayonnaise, chutney, and a dozen other kinds of condiments—that you didn't have any food, you just had stuff to put *on* food if you ever got any."

Despite herself, she chuckled. "Exactly. But you see," she continued more seriously, "that was by choice; it wasn't about dieting, or about laziness, either. It was simply the way I preferred to organize my eating habits. I used to eat at random, whatever I felt like whenever I felt hungry. Now there are . . .*meals.*" Even as she spoke, she heard the words with dismay. Dear God, she thought unhappily, am I really sitting here complaining because *he* cooks three-course meals, or takes me out to the best restaurants?

"In other words," Karl nodded, "your own preferences have been overridden. And of course, it isn't just meals, is it?"

"I never realized it before," she answered him obliquely, "but at heart I may really be a loner. I'm not used to having to . . . consult someone else's interests. Even when I was married, Tim and I led essentially separate lives."

"And is that what you want?" His voice held no hint of emotion.

"No!" The protest was immediate, unthinking. "No, it isn't."

"Well, then." He put a hand on her arm. "Tell me this. What would you do if you had two programs that crashed your computer every time you ran them together?"

She didn't answer at once. It's not that simple, she wanted to say, but the metaphor was sufficiently apt to start her mind working on it. It also made her realize that she'd been operating on emotion rather than intellect; still, the problem was one of emotion, after all. *Could* you apply pure logic to emotions?

"The first thing you do," she said finally, "is make sure each program works properly by itself."

"And assuming they do?" he prodded.

"Then the easiest solution," she said severely, "is to sequester each of them and run them individually, or even on separate machines. All right, all right, I'll admit the easiest solution isn't usually the most rewarding. But do you have any idea how maddening, how absolutely brain jarring troubleshooting a system can be?"

"Not precisely. I do know you're phenomenally good at it. Now," he said as she turned the car into the Carlton's parking lot, "why don't we get some dinner—salmon for me, salad for you?"

The Carlton Hotel was a series of four long two-story buildings arranged in a square around an open-air courtyard. The restaurant was at the back of the lobby, defined only by a low platform and red velvet ropes. It was more than half full, and most of the diners, Anneke noted, carried some sort of maize-and-blue stigmata. She mulled over the notion of troubleshooting a relationship. Well, at least she could begin to take responsibility for her own eating habits, she thought as she waited for her salad.

But the salad, when it arrived, filled a bowl the size of a young bathtub, an obscene mountain of food thickly coated with pasty white dressing. Anneke stared at it with dismay for a moment, and then suddenly the sheer absurdity of it kicked in.

"You see what I mean?" She pointed at the offending mass, overcome with laughter. "It's hopeless. It's a conspiracy," she choked out between giggles. "I'm going to weigh 200 pounds, and you're going to trade me in for some cheerleader."

"Probably three of them." He laughed with her.

"Oh, good." She gasped for breath. "Before you kick me out, I can network them together for you—three dumb terminals to one host." At which point she broke down totally.

When she finally got herself under control, she realized that Karl had somehow summoned the waiter, who stood next to the table with the carefully blank expression of someone confronting a possible lunatic.

"Would you please take that away," Karl said to him, "and bring the lady . . . ?" He looked questioningly at Anneke.

"A shrimp cocktail and a cup of black bean soup," she said at once. "And do you have any croissants?"

"Certainly," the waiter said. He hesitated as if about to ask a question, then apparently thought better of it and removed the huge bowl of salad without further comment.

"It's only a 'meal' if I think of it in those terms, isn't it?" she pondered out loud when he had gone.

"Isn't a lot of debugging," Karl asked, "primarily a matter of a different way of seeing?"

"Oh, eat your salmon," she said, laughing as she reached for a bread stick.

They were just starting their coffee when Karl raised his head and directed a smile toward the lobby. Anneke turned, expecting Brad Weinmann, but instead saw the short, stocky figure of Eleanor Sullivan crossing toward them. She still wore blue jeans and running shoes, but she had changed into a brightly-embroidered white shirt and big, chunky turquoise earrings half-hidden beneath her hair.

"Don't let me bother you during your dinner," she said when she reached the table. "I imagine you won't get much peace until this is solved."

"Don't be silly, Eleanor, you could never be a bother." Karl's voice was warm with welcome as he stood and rather ceremoniously seated her. "Have you had dinner?"

"I grabbed a bite a while ago, thanks."

"Coffee, then?"

"Decaf." She made a face. "Piece of advice—don't get old. It sucks. But if you don't mind . . . ?" She pulled a pack of cigarettes and a lighter from her patchwork leather purse.

"Of course not." Karl motioned for the waiter and ordered a pot of decaf, then said formally: "Eleanor, I'd like you to meet Anneke Haagen. Anneke, I'm sure you recognize Eleanor Sullivan."

"You were at the stadium today too, weren't you?" Eleanor's pale blue eyes, filtered by large wire-rimmed glasses and hazed by cigarette smoke, fixed on Anneke sharply before turning to Karl. "Suspect or personal?"

"Oh, very definitely personal."

"Good. It's about time." She patted his hand. "Is that the ring you're keeping?"

"Yes. It was the first, and besides, it's marginally less ugly than the other two." He held up his hand to display the Super Bowl ring, a massive chunk of gold set with a single diamond surrounded, on various sides, by the words *Pittsburgh Steelers, World Champions, 1974, Superbowl IX*, the scores not only of the Super Bowl game itself (Pittsburgh 16, Minnesota 6) but of the Steelers' AFC play-off victories, and, finally and unbelievably, an engraved outline of the Vince Lombardi Trophy itself.

"You know, even I never figured you for three Super Bowl rings," Eleanor said, laughing. "You were one of my better guesses." She grinned widely at Anneke's politely quizzical expression.

"Eleanor and her husband provide summer jobs in their law firm for a few football players every year." Karl came to Anneke's rescue, matching Eleanor's grin. "I was lucky enough to be one of them. How is James, by the way?" he asked Eleanor.

"Up to his buns in that Marybrooke fraud case. But he'll be here for the dinner Friday night—he wouldn't miss the Karl Genesko testimonial. When Karl hit campus," Eleanor turned to Anneke, "he was six foot five and had to fill his pockets with rocks to hit two hundred pounds. I figured a good-sized tight end could just about blow him over, but I also thought he had potential. Inner potential. We've got a state-of-the-art gym in our office, and he spent every hour he wasn't working building himself an NFL body."

"Is that allowed?" Anneke asked dubiously.

"You mean, does the National Collegiate Slavery Association allow it? Gaaagh!" Eleanor made a noise like an angry espresso machine. "Oh, we checked it out. That gym is 'employee welfare.' Every one of our people is encouraged to use it; surprising how many actually do. So the NCSA couldn't do a thing. Like everyone else in this country, they won't be happy until we're all reduced to absolute equality of mediocrity." She glared at Anneke. "Unfortunately for them, we've always been able to find a few kids who don't want to be *mediocre.*"

"Eleanor's never been a big believer in egalitarianism," Karl commented.

"That's one reason I love sports." She dragged on her cigarette. "It's one of the few areas left where superior ability is visible and quantifiable—where you can't pretend everyone's as good as everyone else."

"It just occurred to me," Karl said. "Wasn't Jeffrey Person one of yours?"

"You bet he was. One of our best. Wouldn't surprise me if he becomes a Supreme Court justice. Or NFL commissioner." She stubbed out her cigarette and looked Karl in the eye. "Time to talk about the mess we're in?"

"Eleanor, just what *have* you been up to?" Karl asked quietly.

"Up to?" she asked with transparent innocence. "Karl, Daniel's committee is only talking about *academic* recruiting." She shook her head. "I promise you I've never in my entire life had anything to do with 'illegal inducements.' "

"I never for an instant thought you did," Karl replied. "You have too much ego involvement in beating the NCAA at their own game. On the other hand . . . "

"Look, Karl, you need to clear this up fast, before it turns into a snake in your hands. Don't waste time on side issues."

"Eleanor—," he said, then: "Look, I have to go. I'll want to interview you more formally in a few minutes."

"Well, it beats sitting around the police station with the drunks and hookers. How come we're gettin' coddled like this—because we're all deep-pockets alumni?"

"It's not coddling, it's common sense. We call it lulling suspects into a false sense of security," he replied, smiling.

"I don't think, actually, that that's a joke," Eleanor said shrewdly.

"You're right. It isn't." He raised a hand in the direction of the lobby, and Anneke saw Brad Weinmann nod in response. To her surprise, she also spotted Zoe crossing the lobby toward the restaurant. Zoe saw her at the same moment, and smiled and waved to her.

"I may be home late," Karl told Anneke, standing. "Eleanor, please stay out of trouble?"

As if Karl's departure were a signal, Zoe stepped onto the platform and threaded her way between tables.

"Hi," she said. "I didn't expect to see you here." She spoke to Anneke, but her eyes flicked almost unconsciously toward Eleanor.

"I just drove out with Karl to have dinner," Anneke replied. "Eleanor, this is Zoe Kaplan. She's with the *Daily.*" She was intrigued by the notion of Zoe and Eleanor face to face, but she felt a responsibility to remind Eleanor of the girl's purpose.

"I'd hardly forget, after that scene in the stadium." Eleanor's pale blue eyes were bright with interest. "Pull up a chair. Still keeping your mouth shut about your source?"

"It's all taken care of." Zoe dropped her bookbag on the floor and sat down eagerly. "Do you mind if I ask you a few questions?"

"Reporter-type questions, on the record? Sure, shoot."

"Well, first of all, did you ever know Alvin Greenaway?"

Eleanor burst out laughing. "You really cut to the chase, don't you? No, I didn't; never heard of him until your article this morning."

"But you have been fighting the NCAA for a number of years."

"Sure I have—that's all on the record. But my quarrel's not with the operation of the thing—or at least not entirely. It's about the whole fabric of it. Look," she leaned back, drawing on her cigarette, "the NCAA isn't an *agency*, it's a member organization. The assholes at Overland Park don't make policy—the assholes from the member institutions do that."

"I know you've been active in recruiting football players for Michigan," Zoe said, then paused before continuing carefully: "Do you think there have been instances of illegal recruiting at Michigan?"

"Oh, hell, of course there have." Eleanor rubbed her thumb and forefinger across her forehead, looking suddenly tired. "Look, I truly believe that everyone connected with Michigan recruiting—the athletic department, the Alumni Association, the M Club, *everyone*—absolutely break their necks to keep this operation clean. The fact is, *it can't be done.*" She chopped air with her hand, sending cigarette smoke swirling around her head.

"What do you mean?"

"Okay, the first problem is, there are more than *four hundred thousand* living alumni from the University of Michigan, and according to the NCAA, the University is absolutely and fully responsible for every single one of them. Never mind that we tell them over and over to leave recruiting to the coaching staff; never mind that we plead with them to make no contact, ever, with any high school athlete. The fact remains, one imbecile alumnus in Backwater, Idaho, can bring down the entire football program at any moment with one, single, stupid act. Even if we don't know anything about it. Hell, especially if we don't know anything about it, because then we don't even know we're at risk.

"Now. The second problem is, NCAA regulations are bullshit—and you can quote me. Their procedures are so convoluted, so bizarre, so totally Byzantine that it's almost impossible *not* to break one of them, no matter how pure your intentions. Did you know, for instance, that the NCAA specifies exactly how far—in miles—a coach may drive a recruit? Or that it has a regulation mandating how many colors a school can use to print its recruiting brochure? Absolute fact," she said to Zoe's look of disbelief. "Did you know that most major universities, including Michigan, have to spend thousands of dollars to operate NCAA Compliance Departments, just to have someone who can keep it all straight? So you tell *me* who's crazy."

SEVENTEEN

"We also have a legal staff, Eleanor, and no one thinks that's inappropriate." Anneke turned to see Frank Novak standing behind her. He looked tired and depressed; his face seemed to sag, and there were deep line down the sides of his mouth.

"We could do without some of them, too," Eleanor retorted. "Pull up a chair, Frank. You look awful."

"I haven't got time. And I don't think we should be making public statements to the press without considering them very carefully." But even as he spoke he sank into the chair Karl had vacated, casting a glance in Zoe's direction. "The NCAA may not be perfect," he continued heavily, "but the student-athlete concept is important enough to fight for." He spoke to Eleanor, but he kept his eyes on Zoe. His earlier hostility seemed to have burned itself out; his expression now was somber but no longer angry.

"Student athletes!" Eleanor snorted. "Give me a break, Frank."

"That's exactly what most of them are," he snapped. "Out of nearly a hundred kids who play football at Michigan every year, how many actually become professional football players? Four or five maybe, and that's in a very good year. The rest of them are exactly what I said—student athletes. Look," he went on more temperately, "I agree that kids who want to be football players shouldn't have to go to college if they don't want to. And believe me, I wish the University could get out of being a minor league for the NFL and the NBA. But just because we're stuck with it doesn't mean we should sell out our educational mission."

"Not to mention giving up all the big bucks those kids bring in," Eleanor said acidly.

"Oh, not that old chestnut again." Novak waved his arms. "What do you people think we do with those 'big bucks'—buy ourselves fur coats and yachts? Sure, football brings in a lot of money at Michigan. And at Notre Dame and Penn State and Miami. But the truth is, half of all NCAA schools *lose* money on their football programs.

"Besides which," he went on, becoming more agitated, "every penny of that 'profit' under Big Ten rules must go directly back into the athletic department rather than to the General Fund, precisely to prevent schools from 'exploiting' athletes. It goes into facilities, and operations, and especially to scholarships in sports that don't bring in the big bucks. Including women's athletics. So every one of those 'exploited' superstars is actually subsidizing the education of dozens of anonymous kids who'd never see the inside of a college classroom any other way."

"Perpetual motion fur farm," a voice interjected.

"What did you say?" Eleanor looked up at Richard Killian, standing next to the table. The black leather jacket he'd worn at the stadium was draped over his shoulders, and his boldly printed brown and black silk shirt was again buttoned to the neck without a tie.

"Oh, hell, I'm sorry." Richard's handsome face managed to look both apologetic and arch. "Sometimes I just *blurt*, if you know what I mean."

"And what was it you blurted this time?" Eleanor inquired curiously.

"*You* know. You feed the rats to the cats, skin the cats, feed the carcasses to the rats. Perpetual motion fur farm." His expression was so self-consciously droll that Anneke laughed in spite of herself. So did Eleanor and Zoe; only Frank Novak remained silent, sunk in gloom.

"Sorry," Richard said again. "I really came by to find out if Ms. Kaplan had any trouble with the police over her source. Because, you know," he said to Zoe, "there's a *Michigan Daily* Alumni Club that would be glad to help out if they're needed."

"It's all taken care of." Zoe gave him the same answer she'd given Eleanor. "But thanks anyway. Look, as long as you're here, do you mind if I ask you a couple of questions?"

"Sure, I suppose." Richard took a sip from the glass in his hand, looking first surprised, then wary.

"I'd better go." Frank Novak stood heavily. "Take my chair, Mr. Killian." He stumped off across the dining room. Anneke noted that he was stopped by Jeffrey Person as he reached the lobby.

"She's already grilled me. Seems only fair for you to take your turn," Eleanor said to Richard. "Have a seat." She pointed to the chair next to her with such an air of authority that Anneke was unsurprised to see him drop into it with only a momentary hesitation.

"You're from San Francisco, aren't you?" Zoe asked Richard.

"That's right. I own a restaurant there, the Maize and Blue."

"Yeah, there're a lot of Michigan alumni out there, aren't there?" Zoe asked brightly. "Do you do football brunches and that sort of thing?"

"Sure, a lot of them." Richard's eyes held a glint of humor, and—something else? Anneke wondered. She noted that Zoe's golden-copper eyes seemed to sparkle in response.

"We're even starting to recruit out there," Zoe went on. "That freshman wide receiver, Tony Rickett, came from northern California. Did you ever see him play in high school?"

"I not only saw him play," Richard said with every evidence of innocent pride, "I'm the one who sent a videotape of one of his games to Ro. It's a shame," he added, grinning pointedly, "that I've never had the chance to meet him."

"So you're pretty seriously involved in football recruiting?" Zoe pursued.

"Actually, I'm more involved in *academic* recruiting. Look," Richard spread his hands, his voice pouring sincerity, "Michigan's reputation is important to me, both professionally *and* personally. When I read your story this morning, I wanted to personally kill the rat bastards who got us into this mess. I wish there were something I could *do.*"

"Too bad you're not on the *Daily* anymore."

"I know. I never had the chance to investigate anything as juicy as a murder—the best I ever came up with was a ticket-scalping scandal. You know," his eyes lit up, "I could help you out on this. I mean, I've got access to some people who might not want to talk to a *Daily* reporter. In fact," he went on animatedly, oblivious to Zoe's dubious expression, "we might be able to come up with some things that even the police won't get."

"I don't think—," Zoe began.

"Look, I don't want a byline or anything," Richard interrupted eagerly. "It would be entirely your story. You give the orders. But I really could contribute, and you can never have enough people doing legwork."

"Depends on the legs." At the voice from behind her, Anneke started. "How're you, Miz Sullivan?" Charlie Cassovoy asked. "And you're Dick Killian, right?"

"Richard Killian, yes." Richard's voice was frosty. Once again, Anneke felt the others draw away slightly at Charlie Cassovoy's approach.

"And you're Zoe Kaplan." He examined her closely. "You're not what I expected." He seemed faintly aggrieved.

"And you're Charlie Cassovoy." Zoe returned his stare. "What did you expect?"

"Someone more . . . I don't know, slick. Sexy." Without waiting for an invitation, he grabbed a chair from an empty table and squeezed in between Zoe and Eleanor, dropping his briefcase on the floor. "More of a bimbo," he said finally.

Zoe burst out laughing. "Sorry to disappoint you."

"So you're not into sports to pick up jocks?"

"Jeez, Cassovoy, not you, too? Is that why you think women become sportswriters?"

"Why else?"

"Well, why did you?"

"That's different."

"No it isn't," Zoe declared. "You think only little boys grow up fascinated by sports? You think only guys can appreciate a great performance or the high you get from a win? We're all coming from the same place—if we can't be jocks ourselves, this is the closest we can come to being part of the team."

"Maybe so." Charlie appeared unconvinced.

"From your viewpoint," Eleanor interjected, "you'd have to figure that I'm involved in Michigan football to pick up guys, too. Right, Charlie?"

"I never said that," he protested.

"Oh? You mean you think an old broad like me isn't interested in a nice tight set of buns anymore?" She laughed aloud at the look of angry discomfort on Charlie's face, and Anneke stifled a giggle.

Charlie made an impolite noise and returned pointedly to Zoe. "How're you doing on the Greenaway thing? Got it solved yet?"

"I suppose you've already lined up an exclusive with the murderer, along with a contract for the TV rights," she retorted.

"Let's just say I got a couple of leads."

"Yeah, right."

"Look, honey, I hate to admit it, but you're not bad. In a few years, you might even be pretty good. But right now you're still a tadpole in a shark tank." He put his elbows on the table and leaned forward. "Lemme ask you this—what's the most important piece of information you've picked up so far?"

"Why should I tell you?"

"Don't let him bait you," Richard warned.

Charlie shot him a look of contempt. "You haven't got anything yet, and you know it. Right?" He leaned back, a smirk on his face.

"Come on, Charlie, you think I'm going to fall for that one? Like you've actually found out something useful?"

"Ah, shit. Sorry, Miz Sullivan. All right," he said to Zoe, "how about you show me yours and I'll show you mine?" He leered. "I'll even go first."

"You're blowing smoke, Cassovoy." Zoe leaned back and folded her arms, grinning.

"Kyle Farmer wasn't at his ten o'clock class this morning." Charlie leaned back and folded his own arms, mimicking Zoe's position.

"Farmer?" Zoe's eyes widened. "He's never cut a class in his life." She shook her head. "That's ridiculous; it couldn't be Farmer."

"I didn't say it was," Charlie shook his head. "Don't get ahead of yourself. When you start out, you're just collectin' information. Now, what've you got?"

"Nothing concrete yet," Zoe admitted a shade defensively. "So far, I've been concentrating on backgrounders and working out an approach."

"Okay." Surprisingly, Charlie nodded approval. "That's where you gotta start, all right. The first thing is always deciding what questions to ask. So how far have you gotten?"

"Hold on, Cassovoy. Why're you so hot to give me advice? You're only screwing your own guys."

"That is why. Because they put McCaffrey on it and I hate his guts," Charlie said frankly.

"You really are a charmer, aren't you, Charlie?" Eleanor said.

"Okay, so it ain't pretty." He responded with a shrug. "What the hell, I don't owe the *News* anything, they owe *me.*"

"Y'know, that's so slimy I almost believe you." Zoe looked at him consideringly. "Okay, let's talk, at least for a while."

"Hang on." Charlie held up a hand. "Lemma get a drink first." He looked around for a waiter, but the restaurant was now nearly full. Their table had long since been cleared, and the few waiters were concentrating on newcomers. "Cheap bastards won't hire enough staff, then they wonder why the take is down," he snorted. "I'm gonna go get something from the bar."

"As long as you're going, get me a Jameson's?" Richard asked.

"And a Coke for me," Zoe put in.

"Do I look like a waiter?"

"Come on, Charlie." Zoe grinned. "We're supposed to be all working press together, right? Would you like something to drink, Ms. Sullivan?"

"Actually, I think it's time for my exit line." Eleanor stubbed out her cigarette and stood up. "I like games as much as the next person, but I don't think I want to play this one. Anneke, good meeting you."

"How about you?" Zoe asked Anneke.

"I should probably leave also," Anneke said, reaching for her purse reluctantly. It didn't seem appropriate, somehow, for her to remain, although she was both interested and curious.

"No, don't. Please stay," Zoe urged. "You can be a kind of police liaison."

"A what?" Charlie asked sharply. "You were at the stadium today, too," he said accusingly to Anneke.

"Anneke's in a relationship with Lieutenant Genesko," Zoe explained easily, "so if we find out anything the police should know, we'll tell her and she can tell the police. Please?" she repeated to Anneke.

"All right. Why not? I'll have a Coke, too," she replied finally. "No, make that a diet Coke." She changed her mind, remembering her snug waistband.

When Charlie had grumbled off, Zoe said, "I want to start making some notes." She reached down to her bookbag, started to retrieve her notebook, then stopped. "Hey, let's use this." She pulled Charlie's laptop out of his briefcase and pushed it across the table to Anneke. "You take notes, okay?"

"All right." She was still uneasy about her presence, but surely there could be no objection to her acting as a kind of recording secretary. Besides, she felt more in control now that she had her fingers on a computer keyboard.

"Okay, why don't we start by making a list of suspects to interview?" Richard asked.

"Just about everyone on campus could be a suspect," Zoe protested.

"I think," Anneke offered, "Charlie had a point. It might make sense to begin by listing the things you want to find out." There was a floppy disk in the laptop's drive; she popped it out, then booted the computer, typed WIN at the C:\> prompt, then opened WinWord and selected Outline from the View menu.

"Well, the first thing we want to find out is who Greenaway's informant was," Richard said.

"I think the actual infraction is more important," Zoe responded.

"Well, yes, those are the big questions," Anneke said. "When we have the answers to those, we'll probably have the solution to the whole thing. But there are other questions—oddities. Things that don't track somehow."

EIGHTEEN

"What do you mean?" Charlie returned with four glasses clustered awkwardly in his bony hands. He dumped the glasses on the table. "That's four fifty for you," he said to Richard, "and a buck and half for each of the Cokes." He picked up a fair-sized glass nearly full of amber liquid and drank off half of it before sitting down. "What d'you mean, oddities?" he repeated, scooping up money.

"Well, for instance," Anneke's fingers typed words as she spoke, "why was Greenaway *at* the stadium?"

"Yeah, that is a good point," Zoe agreed. "He couldn't have just been sightseeing, could he? I mean, he must've been pretty upset after the story came out. I'd guess he was there to meet someone." If she felt any guilt about being the source of Greenaway's distress, Anneke thought, it certainly didn't show.

"But why at the *stadium?*" Anneke stressed the word.

"Because," Zoe said excitedly, "the person he was meeting was planning to be at the stadium for some other reason!"

"Which means," Anneke pointed out, "it's very unlikely that the murderer was someone who just walked into the stadium, stabbed

Greenaway, and walked out again. He was someone who was there for a purpose."

"Like a high-level meeting in the president's box," Charlie said. "So the odds are good that the murderer is one of Big Blue's big shots." He looked unaccountably pleased.

"Jeez, Cassovoy, you really do hate Michigan, don't you?" Zoe snapped.

"Only sometimes, and only a little bit more than most other colleges. So what?" He peered at her, his narrow eyes narrowing even further. "Sorry, I thought you wanted to be a reporter. Do you want to investigate a crime story, or do you just want to protect the old alma mater? Make up your mind, honey. Anyway," he continued when she didn't answer, "I'm not so sure you're right about the killer being there for some other purpose. Seems to me there's one other type who might want to meet at the stadium, and that's a football player. Sort of home field advantage."

"You still on the Kyle Farmer kick?"

"Or any other player who wasn't where he was supposed to be. But yeah, Farmer fits. Wouldn't that be a hoot? Squeaky-clean Kyle Farmer, everybody's favorite stoo-dent ath-a-lete." His voice dripped sarcasm.

"Oh, shit. Cassovoy, take a hike, okay?" Zoe's temper boiled over. "I don't care what kind of contacts you have, I don't want to work with pond scum."

"You really don't get it, do you, kid?" Charlie was unoffended—but then, Anneke thought, recalling some of his columns, that was probably one of the milder epithets he'd been called. "This is a *Michigan* crime, committed by *Michigan* people, and if you're gonna be an investigative reporter, that's what you've got to investigate. If it isn't Farmer, who do you want it to be—Frank Novak? Eleanor Sullivan, a former Regent? How about him?" He jerked a finger at Richard, who shied away in surprise. "Take your pick. *I* don't care; I'll get my jollies either way. But I'll tell you this—" he jabbed the finger at Zoe "—the other media aren't going to use velvet gloves just because it's the great University of Mee-chigan."

"He's right." Richard leaned forward and took Zoe's hand. "Which means our coverage is even more important." The *Daily* story had now become "ours," Anneke noted.

"I suppose," Zoe muttered. "All right." She patted his hand before removing it and turning to Anneke. "What other questions were you thinking of?" she asked Anneke.

"Well, there's something else that's been bothering me." She tapped her fingers on the edge of the computer, filing the contact between Richard and Zoe at the back of her mind. "How did anyone know who Greenaway *was*?" At their blank looks, she explained, "How did the informant know about Greenaway at all—who he was, and especially *what* he was?"

"Wouldn't the informant have just contacted him through NCAA headquarters?" Richard asked.

"Uh-uh." Zoe shook her head positively. "We already checked with them, and they're totally clueless. If the tip had come through channels, they'd know about it."

"Besides," Anneke pointed out, "that would just back up the question a step. It still would mean someone knew him personally."

"Anyway, I don't see it," Zoe said. "I think if he'd gotten the tip that way, he'd have told the NCAA people about it. He was a real straight-ahead kind of guy."

"So we assume the contact was made here in Ann Arbor," Anneke concluded. "Which brings us back to the question—how did the informant know who he was?" For a few moments the only sound at the table was the soft tick of computer keys.

"What else have you got?" Charlie asked.

"All right, try this one: We're assuming that the murderer was the target of Greenaway's investigation—the person who committed some sort of NCAA infraction. Only, how did this person know he *was* Greenaway's target?"

"Well, because . . . " Richard started, then stopped.

"You see what I mean? Was it just guilty conscience? Was it simply that he knew he'd done something wrong and just assumed he was the target?"

"Why not?" Charlie rasped. "Probably every rule breaker at Michigan figures he's the only one breaking the rules. After all, it's so *non-Michigan*, right?"

"You know, there's a point there," Anneke said reluctantly. "It's actually possible that the murderer wasn't even Greenaway's target, but instead just someone who *thought* he was."

"Oh, jeez," Zoe groaned.

"Think about this," Anneke said suddenly. "There's still someone out there who knows what Greenaway was planning to investigate. Who probably knows, in fact, even more than Greenaway did. Which means . . . "

"That there's somebody out there who's auditioning for the role of next victim," Zoe interrupted.

"The informant must know he's in real danger," Anneke agreed. "Surely he'll come forward now, no matter how angry people will be."

"I bet he won't anyway." Zoe shook her head. "Whoever he is, he'll be crucified if people find out."

"Yeah. You bring people bad news, they want to kill the messenger," Charlie said.

"Even so, I think I'd take my chances," Zoe said. "If it were me, I'd be camped out at the police station talking my head off and yelling for protection."

"You and me both," Richard laughed. "Even a brick through your window is better than a flagpole through your stomach."

"Do you know about that story, too?" Zoe asked, diverted.

"Know about it? I was at the *Daily* the night it happened."

"Were you really? It must have been awesome."

"What story?" Charlie asked suspiciously.

"It was back in the late sixties." Richard's voice took on the singsong quality of the born storyteller. "We'd just broken a story about some football players getting free clothing and movie tickets from local merchants, which is of course a violation of NCAA rules, and the campus was in an uproar. The athletic department wanted to shut us down, and the students wanted to crucify us. The night after the story ran, two halves of a brick come flying through the window, one after the other like a pair of banshees, scattering glass all over the office.[2] We all jumped up and ran to the window like fools, of course, but it was too dark to see anything." He paused, with unconsciously perfect timing. "We called campus security, and a guy who came by said, 'Hell, if I catch the boys who did it I'll personally give them a medal!' "

"Hmph. If you're through reliving your youth," Charlie snapped, "could we get back to the business at hand?"

"Sure. Maybe we can reminisce later on," Richard said, grinning once more at Zoe.

"Where were we?" Charlie asked grumpily, directing his question to Anneke.

"Talking about possible danger to the informant," she replied, her eyes on the computer screen but her mind wondering uneasily about Richard and Zoe. Surely the girl has more sense, she told herself.

"You know," Zoe said slowly, "the informant and the target could even be the same people—I mean person."

"How do you figure?" Charlie looked at her curiously.

"Well, suppose it was accidental. I mean, suppose the guy was talking to Greenaway and just let something slip. Or maybe Greenaway saw something he wasn't supposed to or overheard a conversation. Something like that."

"It's possible," Anneke agreed. "And it would answer one other question that bothers me: Why kill *Greenaway*? After all, the murderer had to know there was someone else who knows what he did." They sat in silence for a moment.

"So what do we do next?" Richard asked finally.

"I think it's time to start focusing on the suspects," Zoe replied.

[2]See "Where Opinions are Free, Bricks Fly," *The Michigan Daily*, Feb. 11, 1968, p.6.

"And we're agreed that that means the people in the stadium."

"All right." Anneke stared at the computer screen, tapped keys, then used the pointer to rearrange what she'd typed. "Here are the people in the stadium." She turned the computer around so the others could see the screen:

```
Richard Killian
Daniel Najarian
Jeffrey Person
Eleanor Sullivan
Kyle Farmer?

(Other players who might have been in
  the stadium)
Karl Genesko
Anneke Haagen
Frank Novak
Zoe Kaplan
Charlie Cassovoy
```

"Even without the TV and maintenance crews, that's a lot of people." Zoe looked at the list dubiously. "How are we going to investigate them all?"

"Depends," Charlie said. "For one thing, forget the background checks—what they do back home, how they've been involved in recruiting, their finances, that kind of stuff. The cops have the manpower and connections for that, and you don't. You've got to focus on what happened here."

"I agree." Anneke tapped keys again. "There are three periods of time that look crucial. First, there's the time between Greenaway's arrival in Ann Arbor and his call to Truhorne. We have to assume that that's when he found out about the infraction." The others nodded. "Second, there's all of this morning, beginning with the time the *Daily* hit the streets. At some point, Greenaway either decided to, or arranged to, go to the stadium. If he wasn't simply sightseeing, then someone must either have met with him, or talked to him on the phone, to get him there. And third, of course, there's the period in the stadium, leading up to the murder."

"The police will be zeroed in on that," Charlie commented.

"Which leaves us the other two periods," Zoe said. "I suppose the police will be investigating those also, but that's the sort of thing people are more likely to talk to us about than to the cops. Sounds like a plan."

"Remember," Charlie pointed out, "you have to investigate both the suspects *and* Greenaway himself."

"Right. We need to find out what flight he came in on, whether anyone picked him up at the airport, that sort of thing."

"Exactly. Because the *informant* isn't necessarily someone who was in the stadium this morning."

"Jeez." For the first time, Zoe looked uncertain. "It's more complicated than it looks, isn't it?"

"Just take it a step at a time." Charlie was unexpectedly reassuring. "It's the same old jigsaw puzzle, there're just a few more pieces, that's all."

"That's true," Zoe said more cheerfully. "We just start from the beginning. So we talk to his daughter, we talk to the people in the athletic department, oh, and we check his hotel, too. See if he had any visitors or phone calls."

"Talk to the maids," Richard suggested.

"That's definitely your job." Zoe grinned at him.

"Is that a compliment or a put-down?" he asked, laughing. "Either way, I'll volunteer right now to investigate the hotel. Uh . . . *which* hotel?"

"This one, I assume. He was probably part of the President's Club block. And can you check out the airport, rental car agencies, that sort of thing?"

"Sure." Richard's eyes flashed with excitement.

"Okay. I'll talk to his daughter, and to Frank Novak—I have to work the athletic department anyway. Now about the alumni. I'll take Jeffrey Person, I think. There's something interesting there. And I think we can skip Eleanor Sullivan; we won't get any more out of her than I already got right here."

"Okay, I'll take Najarian," Richard said. "I need to talk to him anyway."

"What about Farmer?" Charlie challenged.

"Yeah, but . . . " Zoe swallowed whatever protest she'd been about to make. "All right, I'll talk to him, too. One other thing." She turned to Richard. "If I'm going to print information from your interviews, I want it on tape. With all respect, it's my name on the story."

"No problem. I can pick up a tape recorder in the morning." Richard drained the last of his drink. "Are we adjourned?"

"I guess so—no, wait," Zoe said. "Can you print out a copy of these notes for me?" she asked Anneke.

"Yes, I suppose so." Anneke looked down at the screen, startled by how deeply she'd let herself be involved. "No problem. Let me dump the file to a floppy and I'll print it out tonight when I get home." The mention of home caused her stomach to lurch. What had seemed like fun an hour ago was suddenly nonsense, even dangerous nonsense. How did I ever get sucked into this? she wondered. Would Karl object to her involvement? How on earth could she possibly explain it to him, she wondered, dismayed over the necessity to do so at all. Do I really have to ask permission?

"How about lunch at Zingerman's tomorrow?" Zoe suggested. "You could bring them along then."

"Yes, all right. I'll just dump it to the disk in the drive." For the moment, caught up in her own thoughts, Anneke simply wanted to get away. She did a final save, closed Windows, and typed COPY A: C:\WINWORD\INVESTIG.DOC. When DOS replied 1 FILE COPIED, she powered down the computer, popped the diskette and shoved it into her purse. "Charlie, here's your computer," she said, shoving it across the table and standing up. "Excuse me, I'm going to try to catch up with Karl." She saw the surprise on their faces at her abrupt departure, but all she wanted right now was to escape.

Once in the lobby, however, she stood irresolute. The Carlton must be nearly full already, she concluded. People decked in every imaginable Michigan accessory swirled around her, laughing and chattering and calling out to each other. Lines snaking from the front desk blocked traffic lanes, and chattering clusters of maize-and-blue-clad figures milled in front of the doors. Next to her, a group suddenly burst into an off-key rendition of "The Victors."

In the maelstrom she could pick out one or two familiar people—Daniel Najarian crossing the lobby, Jeffrey Person deep in conversation with a man she didn't know—but Karl's towering form wasn't among them. Neither was Brad Weinmann; she spotted a policewoman she'd met once or twice, but before she could approach her, the woman disappeared into an elevator.

Well, I don't really want to explain this to him here anyway, she told herself at last. It can wait until we're home. Mentally shaking herself, she thought: maybe they'll actually dig up something that can help. And at least this way Karl won't be mousetrapped by something in the newspaper. Pursuing this and other forms of self-justification, she detoured to the ladies' room, waited her turn in the inevitable line, and then headed out to her car.

The October nip in the air revived her further, and she quickened her steps toward her car, parked at the back of the lot. After all, they're only going to be talking to each other, she reasoned, and people in a situation like this do that anyway.

It was the last thought she had before the world went black.

NINETEEN

"I still don't know why we're driving all the way out to the Carlton just so you can be hassled by the cops." Wendy Coleman, always so in control when she was running Frank Novak's office, didn't want to admit that she was frightened. She squirmed uncomfortably in the passenger seat of the dilapidated Honda, glancing at Kyle Farmer out of the corner of her eye. His dark, serious face was outlined in profile against the passing streetlights. His hair curled tightly against his head in a close, semitraditional style with only a hint of sculpted height. Wendy had to restrain herself from reaching out to touch it. She was glad he hadn't shaved his head, like some of the other guys on the team had.

"I *told* you." Kyle's mouth tightened. "The Man gave me a choice—either come out here to talk to him now or go to the police station tomorrow. And at least here," he added grimly, "I've got a shot at avoiding reporters." Kyle didn't look frightened, he looked angry. He looked like he did sometimes when he'd just been clotheslined by a linebacker—tightly-controlled hostility leaking out, scarier in its way than unbridled fury. It was that combination of anger and control, she thought, that made him a great running back, and wondered if the anger would ever overwhelm the control.

"But why would he want to question you at all?" Wendy asked for the third time. "I mean, why you?"

"I keep telling you, I don't *know.*" Kyle said angrily. "Stop asking and asking, okay? It doesn't have to mean anything. Could be just that I'm team captain."

"Could also be they're looking for a quick scapegoat," Wendy said, feeling fear spiral within her. "I don't see any white players lined up to be hassled."

"Well, it ain't gonna be me." She could see his hands tighten their grip on the steering wheel as he swung the Honda into the Carlton parking lot. Instead of heading toward the main entry he turned left and proceeded around to the side of the hotel, taking the corner too fast so that Wendy had to grab for the edge of the door. "He said we should go in there." Kyle pointed to a doorway marked "Rooms 114–156." "I don't see any cameras or anything," he said. "Let's go."

They jumped out of the Honda and walked quickly into the hotel, finding themselves in a long, carpeted, and blessedly empty corridor. Kyle squared his shoulders and took a deep breath before knocking on a door to their left labeled "Staff Only," which was opened almost immediately by a youngish white man in a nondescript gray suit.

"Please come in, Mr. Farmer." Karl Genesko sat behind a large wooden desk in a room that was apparently one of the hotel offices. No cheap suit for him, Wendy noted; that was custom tailored pure, fine wool. And even sitting down, he looked enormous. She was surprised at how enormous he looked; after all, she spent a fair amount of time among football players. "Ms. Coleman?" he turned his gaze on her. "Did you want to speak to me also?"

"She's here with me." Kyle took two steps into the room and stopped. "I wanted a witness."

"If you like, certainly." Genesko said. "But for the record, Mr. Farmer, are you sure you don't want to have an attorney with you?"

"I don't need no lawyer. I know what I want to say. For the record," Kyle emphasized the words, "I just want someone else to hear me say it."

"By all means." Genesko turned his dark gaze on Wendy. "Actually, I'm glad you're here as well, Ms. Coleman. I'd like to ask you some questions also."

"Sure." Wendy returned his gaze with what she hoped was a calm look. "But I can't tell you any more than I already did at the stadium."

"Possibly not." His eyes seemed to focus on her even more tightly. "But perhaps you can tell me why you were at the stadium in the first place?"

"What do you mean?" Shit, I blew that line big time, Wendy thought, feeling her stomach turn to ice.

"You weren't there at Mr. Novak's request," he said flatly.

"If you already made up your mind I'm lying, why should I say anything?" Wendy poured anger into her voice, pumping herself up. This was the enemy, whitey with a badge. This guy can do whatever he wants, and there isn't shit all we can do about it. She stole a glance at the other cop, the young one, but he was concentrating on the notebook in his lap. Anyway, he was white, too.

"You were looking for Mr. Farmer, weren't you?" Genesko asked.

"No! Why would I . . . Kyle has classes all morning."

"Hey, man, don' you be goin' on at her, you hear?" Kyle interrupted the exchange, his voice harsh with anger. "You wanna buss my ass, you gonna do it, thass okay, but you don' be givin' her no hard time, you hear?" He hitched his chair closer to Wendy and laid a protective arm along the back of her chair, both his hands clenched into fists. Genesko regarded him thoughtfully.

"Mr. Farmer," he said finally, "I was a football player myself, you know."

"Yeah, so? That mean we homies?"

"No." Wendy could almost swear there was a hint of amusement on Genesko's face. "But it does mean I'm less likely to fall for either the 'dumb jock' or the 'gangbanger' routine." He waited for his words to sink in. "Please understand, I'm not trying to trap anyone. I'm simply trying to gather information."

"You're trying to browbeat her into saying something you can use against her," Kyle said, all trace of street patois gone. "Probably trying to protect your buddy Novak. Okay, let's do this up front." He removed his arm from Wendy's chair and sat up stiffly. "For the record, I have never, at any time, accepted money, goods, promises, or any consideration of any kind that is prohibited by NCAA regulations," he recited. "Now, if you want to try to prove different, you go right ahead."

Genesko made a note on his pad. "You're majoring in English, aren't you?"

"So? Actually, I'm majoring in linguistics."

"Really." Genesko looked at him with interest. "An unusual choice."

"For a dumb jock, or a gangbanger?"

"For most people." Genesko seemed not even to notice Kyle's hostility. "What do you plan to do with your degree?"

"Beats me." Kyle shrugged in visible irritation. "What's all this got to do with anything?"

"Mr. Farmer, why *did* you stay in school for your senior year?"

"Shit, if I told you the truth, you wouldn't believe me."

"Try me."

"Because I happen to like college, that's why." Kyle glared at Genesko as if daring him to sneer. "I mean the real college shit, y'know? Classes, and studying, and learning stuff, that whole business. There's just something about it that gets to me, that's all. Now go ahead and laugh."

"I know what you mean." Genesko spoke with no appearance of either surprise or disbelief. "I felt like that too, sometimes, when I was in school."

"Yeah?" Kyle looked at him suspiciously. "You ever just sort of wander through the library? The grad, I mean."

"Yes, a few times."

"Y'know, you almost have to squeeze through the aisles, they're so close together, and the books go all the way to the ceiling, aisle after aisle, floor after floor, and it's like there's so much *stuff*, so much to *know.*" Kyle's voice held a wondering note, displacing the anger. "Everything in the whole world that anyone knows, it's all right there."

"And sometimes you almost feel despair because you realize you'll never be able to read it all." Genesko seemed to be speaking to himself rather than to Kyle.

"Yeah," Kyle said quietly. "Yeah, well anyway, that's why I'm still here," he went on in a louder voice. "Besides, sorry to bust your stereotype, but I don't come from a family of eight barefoot kids and a welfare mother."

"No, I didn't think you did."

"Why? Because I happen to like to learn stuff?" Abruptly, the anger was back. "You think because a kid's poor he doesn't want to learn things?"

"I think," Genesko replied, taking the question seriously, "that intellectual pursuits are fairly far down the list of Abraham Maslow's hierarchy of needs."

Kyle surprised Wendy by bursting into genuine laughter. "Shit, I don't believe this—a couple of jocks sitting around rapping about Maslow."

"Don't tell the media." Genesko smiled broadly. "They wouldn't be able to handle it. It can't be easy for you," he went on more seriously, "living in so many different worlds. Black and white, street and campus, physical and intellectual."

"Nothing I can't handle," Kyle replied shortly. "Can we go now, man?" He started to rise, but Genesko motioned with his hand.

"I do have one more question," he said. "Mr. Farmer, what were you doing at the stadium this morning?"

Wendy started, and knew at once her involuntary motion had

been noted by the man behind the desk. She felt the rising fear once more, and darted a look at Kyle.

"What was I . . . " Kyle, half-standing, threw himself back in his chair. "Shee-it," he said softly. "How'd you know?"

"As a matter of fact, I saw you there."

"Over by the clubhouse, probably." Kyle nodded in thought.

"That's right. And since you cut a class to be there, I assume it was something important?"

"Yeah, it was important."

"Who were you meeting?" Genesko asked in a conversational tone.

"Man, you're pretty good, aren't you?" Kyle shook his head. "Sorry. I can't tell you anything else."

"I assume it wasn't Ms. Coleman," Genesko nodded in her direction, "since there'd be no reason to do so secretly. But I think she went there because she was worried about you, which means she must have known about the meeting." He paused, but Kyle remained silent. "Mr. Farmer," he said at last, "you must know that we'll pursue this. If your meeting, or errand, was perfectly innocent, telling us about it now is less likely to create trouble for you than if we have to dig for it. And right now, the fact that you were at the scene of a murder, with no good reason for being there, has to place you at the top of the suspect list."

"Then arrest me." Kyle jumped to his feet and leaned over the desk, his face inches from Genesko's own. "You're looking for a reason to anyway, aren't you? To get your buddy Novak and all those fatcat alumni off the hook? What the hell, so one more nigger goes bad, who's gonna give a shit, right?"

"Kyle, please." Wendy jumped up in her turn and grabbed at his arm. If he took a swing at Genesko they'd have the perfect excuse to put him away.

Genesko didn't back off—just sat there, linebacker-steady. After a moment he sighed audibly. "I don't think I have any more questions at the moment, Mr. Farmer. Think about what I said, will you?"

TWENTY

The world wasn't entirely black, Anneke concluded. There were those interesting pinwheels of colored light just outside her line of sight, but when she tried to focus on them they danced away. She tried to shake her head clear, which was a serious mistake; brighter lights flashed inside her eyelids, accompanied by a stab of pain that left her breathless. There was pain in her left leg, too, especially the knee. She reached down and felt bare skin where there should have been silk, and when she took her hand away it felt sticky.

She lined up all the facts in her mind, trying to lay out a logical pattern that would account for them all, but she was having trouble concentrating. She wished the voices calling her name would be quiet so she could think clearly.

"Anneke! Anneke? Oh, shit. Richard, go get Genesko. Anneke!"

She blinked two or three times, painfully, until she brought Zoe's frightened face into focus. She realized she was on the ground, crouched on hands and knees as though she had crawled there. She tried to stand, mortified by her position, but her legs didn't seem inclined to propel her upward. I'm really in terrible shape, she thought; I've absolutely got to start exercising more.

And then suddenly there were people all around her. Especially, there was Karl. Only, why did he look so angry?

"Anneke, look at me—no, don't try to stand up, just look directly at me."

"I'm . . . it's all right. I'm fine." Reality snapped in with a lurch, and she scrambled to her feet, holding on to Karl's arm for balance as she brushed at her clothes. "Really, I'm okay." Faces surrounded her, pale ovals just barely visible in the erratic light of the parking lot. A wave of embarrassment washed over her. They must think I'm a clumsy idiot—or drunk. "Please, it's . . . "

"Did you get a look at him?" Karl asked.

"At who?"

"At the person who hit you."

"Hit me? But . . . my purse! Oh, *shit.* You mean I was mugged?"

"I'm afraid so." The concern on his face was relieved by a flicker of a smile. "Can you describe the purse?"

"Yes, of course." Now that she understood what was happening, she found it easier to think. "Gray suede, about ten inches square, with a thin leather shoulder strap. You'll want the contents too, won't you?" She saw the young policewoman from the lobby, scribbling rapidly in a notebook, and addressed herself to her. "Gray ostrich-skin wallet, purse style, with forty-two dollars and change, two twenties and two singles—I stopped at an ATM this afternoon." The effort of recall seemed to be good for her; her head felt clearer as she spoke. "Folding comb, tortoiseshell plastic. Lipstick. Black plastic compact. Keys, on a key ring with a Firebird logo on it. A Mont Blanc fountain pen—damn, I loved that pen—and a small notepad." She paused. "I think that's everything."

"The disk," Zoe said.

"Oh, right. A three-and-a-half inch high-density diskette, PC format. It had a label, but I don't know what it said."

"Do you think . . . " Zoe stared at her, eyes wide.

Anneke stared back. "The disk? That's silly."

"What was on the disk?" Karl asked.

"Nothing, really. At least, nothing that matters." The last thing she wanted was to explain her evening to him under these circumstances.

"It was notes on Greenaway's murder." Zoe came to her rescue. "Richard, Charlie Cassovoy, and I were outlining our investigation for the story. Anneke was taking notes for us on Charlie's laptop. When we were done she put it all on a floppy disk and put the disk in her purse."

"But we were—*they* were just organizing their ideas," Anneke protested. "There wasn't anything that could possibly be a . . . a clue. Was there?" she appealed to Zoe.

"It doesn't seem like there was," the girl spread her hands in a gesture of indecision. "But maybe we came up with something without realizing it. Richard?"

"If we did," Richard said with a shrug, "it sure went right by me."

"There needn't have actually been anything useful on the disk," Karl pointed out, "so long as someone thought there might be. I assume everyone in the Carlton knew what you were all up to?" His voice was perfectly matter-of-fact, but Anneke winced.

"I suppose so," Zoe muttered. "Well, hell, they all know I'm a reporter anyway," she said defensively, looking down at the ground. "Besides," she said suddenly, "the disk was in Charlie's computer to start with, remember? And he's been sniffing around all day. Maybe someone wanted to see what *he'd* come up with."

"In which case," Anneke interjected anxiously, "Charlie could be in danger right now."

"Yes." Karl nodded. "Is he still inside?"

"No," Zoe answered. "He left right after Anneke. We did, too—Richard said he'd drive me back to the *Daily*. Only, I had to stop at the john, and of course there was a humongous line . . . " Her voice trailed away.

"We'll send someone after him. And we'll get a copy of your file as well."

"It's in the WinWord directory," Anneke told him. "Filename investig.doc." She spelled it out for him.

"Good." Karl turned away and spoke to the policewoman. Most of the other onlookers had moved on, Anneke was relieved to note; the only person she didn't recognize was a well-dressed middle-aged man who was looking at her with a worried expression on his face. When she caught his eye he came forward, clearing his throat.

"I'm Lawrence Cutler, the Carlton night manager," he introduced himself. "I'm delighted to see you looking better."

"I'm fine, really." Anneke shook his outstretched hand.

"As far as you can tell at the moment, you mean." Richard's voice held a note of warning. "I doubt that she's ready to sign a release yet."

"Believe me, I had no such intention in mind." The poisonous look Cutler gave Richard belied his words. "If the hotel can help in any way," he said to Anneke, "please don't hesitate to ask." He turned and stalked away.

Richard chuckled. "I've done the same thing at the Maize and Blue, when some idiot stabs himself with a steak knife, or walks into a wall because he's too drunk to see the doorknob. You get them to say they're okay; that way, you have it on the record. On the other hand," he scanned the parking lot thoughtfully, "there really isn't enough lighting out here. You might actually have a good case."

"I really am fine," Anneke insisted.

"Sure, but wouldn't you be even finer with, say, a quarter mil in your pocket?"

"I think I'll pass on insurance fraud, if you don't mind." She must have spoken more sharply than she intended, because Richard held up a hand in protest.

"Hey, I was only joking, you know," he said with a disarming grin.

Only you weren't, Anneke thought even as she returned a tired smile. *Just for a moment, you were thinking about making a money-for-nothing killing.*

Killing. She could have been killed out here. She shivered from more than the chill in the air. Where had Richard been when she was mugged—with Zoe? No, Zoe had been standing in line in the ladies' room. So it could have been Richard. Or Zoe, for that matter.

"We've done all we can here," Karl interrupted her thoughts. "I want to get you to the hospital to be checked out."

"The hospital? Don't be silly, I'm fine."

"Probably so, but I want you examined for concussion anyway."

"Look, you know what will happen if we go to the hospital," she said, struggling for a reasonable tone of voice to cover her unreasonable loathing of hospitals. "We'll sit there for three hours while I keep getting bumped to the bottom of the triage queue, and when I do finally see a doctor he'll shine a light in my eyes, then tell me to take two aspirin and call my family doctor tomorrow if I still have a headache. Besides, even if I did have a mild concussion, it's not that big a deal. After all," she smiled at him, "you must have had at least a couple of them in your playing days, and it doesn't seem to have scrambled your brains any."

"Linebackers don't get concussions," he growled, "they give them. And we always had a doctor right there."

"Who held up three fingers, asked you what city you were in, and sent you back out on the field," she retorted, then asked curiously: "Did you really never have a concussion?"

"Yes, I had one once," he admitted. "And no, you don't seem to be acting the same way."

"What happened?"

"It was against the Oilers. I remember Earl Campbell plowing through a hole in the line and coming straight at me. And I remember being on the plane back to Pittsburgh. I don't remember a single thing in between. They do tell me," he grinned slightly, "that I played a hell of a fourth quarter."

"Lieutenant?" Zoe broke in.

"Yes?"

"Did you make the stop on Campbell?"

"So I've been told." He threw up his hands. "All right. Let's all go home."

TWENTY-ONE

"Did you call and cancel your credit cards?" Karl asked.

"As soon as we got home." They were sipping hot chocolate, of all things—Anneke hadn't even known there was any hot chocolate in the house, let alone that Karl knew how to make it. She was curled in a corner of the big brown velvet sofa that dominated the living room, wearing the long-sleeved nightgown and heavy blue flannel bathrobe she always thought of as her cold-and-flu clothing. She wasn't supposed to sleep immediately after a head injury—that much she'd dredged out of her maternal-period memory—and anyway, despite the long and event-filled day, she wasn't particularly sleepy. Another good sign, she had pointed out to Karl as they waited for the eleven o'clock news to come on.

"Just in case, how much of what was on that disk can you remember?" he asked.

"I guess I could recall most of it if I had to. But honestly, there just wasn't anything on it worth getting excited about. It was mostly a list of questions to ask." She shook her head. "I still think it was just a random mugging."

"Maybe. But I have an abiding distrust of coincidence."

"Do you? I don't. I guess working with computers forces you to have a high tolerance for ambiguity. Anyway, we can get everything off Charlie's computer, and you can see for yourself."

"I suppose so." He looked at her. "How did you get yourself involved with this crew, anyway?"

"Honestly, I'm not sure. It just sort of happened." He remained silent, and after a moment she said, "I suppose I should have left, but, well, it was interesting. And besides . . . "

"Besides what?"

"I didn't want to be the *adult*," she blurted, embarrassed. Was it really necessary to be sober and mature and responsible every single moment?

To her relief, Karl didn't laugh. Instead he asked, "How are you feeling?"

"Better. In fact, the headache's almost gone." She checked the antique marble clock on the mantel. "It's time for the news."

The Greenaway murder fit the rubric "If it bleeds, it leads." Besides, this one had star appeal. Under an aerial view of Michigan Stadium, the portentous voice-over described the murder as the camera zoomed in on the concession stand under the seats, then cut to an exterior shot of Weidenbach Hall before moving to the athletic department's press conference and finally a brief interview with Karl, politely saying as little as possible. There was a sidebar explaining the NCAA and its investigative procedures, during which Karl counted four factual errors—"about par for the course," he said.

"The one thing they didn't mention was Greenaway's secrecy," Anneke noted. "I take it you didn't find any kind of paper trail?"

"Not a damn thing. And we practically dismantled his hotel room. We're assuming the killer got anything there was to get when he rifled Greenaway's briefcase. Aside from the notebook next to his briefcase, there wasn't a thing."

"And nothing turned up in the search of the stadium."

"No. Although we're not finished yet. We've got it sealed off, and we'll continue the search tomorrow, but I don't expect to turn up anything. I think if Greenaway had wanted to leave a paper trail he'd have worked through his own people at the NCAA."

"Well, what *about* his office? Or his home?"

"The Overland Park police did a full search at their end—nothing there either. They even checked his home computer, but they didn't find any files dealing with Michigan."

"Was he usually so secretive?" Anneke asked.

"I don't know." Karl sipped his chocolate thoughtfully. "The NCAA said he was a first-rate investigator, and that to their knowledge he was always absolutely by the book." He reached for the television remote. "Let's see what ESPN is doing with it."

To the surprise of neither of them, the cable sports network provided far better, more expert and even-handed coverage than the local channel had managed. Leading off SportsCenter, the late-night anchormen gave a brief account of events, covering known facts but avoiding conjecture. They had brief interviews with Russell Truhorne and an NCAA spokesman, and a somewhat longer one with a former NCAA investigator who explained the organization's normal procedure. Only when they moved on to the police investigation itself did they get cute.

"One unique element of this investigation," the announcer stated, "is the detective in charge of the case. Football fans are unlikely to forget Ann Arbor police lieutenant Karl Genesko, the former Pittsburgh Steeler Pro Bowl linebacker whose greatest moment will forever be remembered as . . . The Pass."

And as his voice dropped dramatically, there was the film. Anneke, who had seen it when it occurred and two or three times since, nevertheless watched in fascination the play that had made Karl Genesko forever famous.

Last game of the regular season, last minute of the game, Steelers down by three, fourth and six on the Cincinnati 23-yard line. Roy Gerela back to kick the game-tying field goal on the frozen tundra that was Three Rivers Stadium in January.

Even knowing what to look for, it was difficult to follow exactly what happened. Somehow the snap went wrong; players hurled themselves forward; and then the ball squibbed out of the pile and, in the manner of footballs, bounced erratically toward the sideline.

Number 94 broke into the scene from the left of the screen, scooped up the ball in midstride and broke toward the end zone. Two Bengal defenders appeared midscreen; number 94 cut sideways, then scrambled backward as two more Bengals approached from the side.

And then—and this was the part that always left Anneke breathless—he held the ball aloft in his right hand and *pointed* downfield with his left, scrambling to avoid an onrushing Bengal, screaming inaudible directions to an invisible receiver, before finally releasing the ball in a tight, wobbly, but effective spiral that the tight end caught standing up, all alone in the end zone, while the Bengals stood there with their jaws dropping open and the sellout Three Rivers crowd went happily and utterly bonkers.

"There." Anneke pointed to the screen. "That's the part that always blows me away—when you're back there pointing—*directing traffic.* It's such a . . . a *quarterback* thing. I don't understand how it even occurred to you to pass the ball."

He shrugged. "There was nowhere to run."

"That's not really an answer." She shook her head. "You were a *linebacker*, for heaven's sake. When a linebacker has nowhere to run, he gets tackled. Period. He *doesn't* pass."

"No. I know. People have been asking me that for years, and the truth is I really don't have an answer to it. It was just one of those moments when your unconscious mind takes over—when you don't think, you feel. You act on instinct. If I'd actually had time to think about it, I probably would never have done it."

"What a great moment." She stared into space. "So few people can pinpoint the one ultimate moment of their lives."

"I wouldn't call that the best moment of my life. Oh, it was certainly the most lucrative," he explained to her surprised look. "It got me a lot of endorsements and a big contract the next year. But winning that first Super Bowl was a much bigger moment. For one thing, that was a team moment."

"Yes, I suppose the greatest moments are ones that are shared, aren't they?"

"I've known a few players who were more interested in their own individual performances than in whether their team won. In my experience, they never lasted long—and not just in football." SportsCenter moved on to news of two baseball managers being fired. "Well, at least they didn't have film of me crashing across the field this afternoon," he said, sounding relieved.

"Why? You looked like you could still take out Ken Stabler," she teased.

"Sure. Remember, Kenny's the same age I am."

She suddenly remembered Zoe's comment. "Where were you coming from, anyway?" she asked.

"After I found Frank at the TV trailer, I accompanied a third assistant director around to the clubhouse." He made a face. "He wanted to set up for a 'really cool camera angle' for a post-game show. I was with him right up until the moment Greenaway appeared."

"Thank goodness." She breathed out a gust of relief. "It's going to be a mess, isn't it?" she asked after a moment. "I mean, it's an awfully . . . *illustrious* group of suspects."

"More illustrious than you know. As I was heading toward the clubhouse, I spotted Kyle Farmer leaving the stadium."

"Kyle Farmer! He was in the stadium this morning?" She stared at him. "Still, he's a football player—is his presence there so unusual?"

"At that particular time, yes. He was supposed to be in class, and he won't tell me why he was there."

"You said he was just leaving the stadium when you were heading toward the clubhouse." Anneke thought for a moment. "That would have been fairly early, I assume—probably not much after eleven o'clock. Could Greenaway really have been stabbed that long before we saw him?"

"I'm afraid so. The preliminary forensics report said Greenaway was stabbed just below the rib cage. The post went through a lot of soft abdominal tissue, but it didn't hit any vital organs. He actually died from loss of blood, and that could have taken anywhere up to forty minutes or so."

"God, how bizarre." She shuddered and turned back to the television set, where SportsCenter had given way to beach volleyball. She reached for the remote and clicked off the set. "You know, that was really good coverage," she said. "Very professional, clean, not sensationalized at all."

"Of the Greenaway murder? Yes, it wasn't bad. Better than we're likely to see from the rest of them, anyway."

"The police never do think much of the media, do they?" she asked.

"Neither do most athletes," he replied tartly. "And both groups for good and sufficient reason, believe me."

"Still, it is a necessary function," she argued. "And there are some decent journalists, after all."

"Oh, decent." He waved away the word. "That's not the real issue, at least not across the board. The issue is that, to a reporter, we're not people, we're *subjects*."

"Well, but to a policeman we're *suspects* rather than people. And to a football player, the other team is the *opponent*, not people."

"Exactly." He seemed to pounce on her words. "Each of those examples represents an adversary system, and that's just what journalism is. The people who get into trouble with the media are the ones who forget that."

"I see your point, of course," she said reluctantly, "but I do think you're overstating the case."

"Why don't we wait and see what the *Daily* prints tomorrow," he zeroed in on her real concern. "I know you think Zoe is a friend," he spoke over her protest, "but *she* thinks of herself first and last as a reporter."

"That's not fair," Anneke objected. "She was perfectly straight with you."

"Maybe. We'll see if she continues to be."

He could be right to be suspicious, Anneke admitted to herself;

after all, she'd only just met Zoe. But she liked the girl a lot. And she discovered that it was important to her, somehow, that Karl like her as well. Another facet of building a relationship, she realized; how do you manage if the person you love dislikes your friend? Drop the friend, and lose something important? Or compartmentalize your life, and lose a kind of closeness that was perhaps more important still?

The shrilling of the telephone from Karl's office cut through her musing. He left to answer it and returned almost immediately.

"We got your file off Charlie Cassovoy's computer," he told her.

"That was quick."

"Jon Zelisco met him at his apartment and copied it onto a disk. I'll look it over tomorrow."

"Did he say what else was on the floppy that was taken?"

"According to Charlie, it was a blank disk." His voice was carefully neutral.

"You sound like you don't believe him."

"He's a reporter." Karl smiled slightly.

"Well, at least you're consistent," she said, laughing. "And tomorrow you'll see there's nothing on it worth getting excited about."

"I hope you're right." Karl looked at her soberly. "At least it would mean that whoever has it will know you're not a threat to him."

"You'll see." Anneke sighed. "I feel too wired to sleep. I think I may crawl into bed and watch television for a while. Is there anything on that's good and soporific?"

"All of it, as far as I'm concerned. Here, take a look." He tossed her the TV magazine. She opened it to late night Thursday and moved her head until the listings came into focus.

"Oh, damn it to hell," she said.

"What is it?"

"They took my bloody glasses."

TWENTY-TWO

"Here we are." Richard Killian swooped around to the back of the *Daily* with a flourish, a gesture marred principally because the rental car he drove was a small, underpowered Chevy painted that unpleasant shade of green usually reserved for government office buildings. Zoe was sure that, back home in San Francisco, Richard drove something far more status-conscious. Probably a Porsche.

To confirm her hunch, she asked, "What kind of car do you drive at home?"

"Not one of these, I promise you." He made a disgusted face. "I've got a burgundy red Mercedes convertible, such a little beauty. Ah, wait'll you come to San Francisco. I'll take you up to Twin Peaks with the wind in your hair and the whole gorgeous city spread out before you." He reached over and ruffled her hair. "Did no one ever tell you that you have the *most* beautiful hair?"

"Actually," Zoe replied, "when they're handing me a line they usually tell me what beautiful eyes I have."

Richard burst out laughing. "What a cynic you are. Promise me when you come to San Francisco you'll let me show you the most romantic city in the world."

"What makes you think I'm coming to San Francisco?"

"Because all beautiful women come to San Francisco eventually," he said grandly.

This time it was Zoe who burst out laughing. "Shit, you really know how to ladle it on, don't you?" She was having fun, enjoying the verbal riposte, letting the cautions rest at the back of her mind.

"But if you weren't worth it, would I waste my best lines on you?" Richard grinned and curled a strand of her hair around his finger.

"Sure you would," she retorted. "You need the occasional practice run."

"Ah, now you've truly wounded me." He placed a hand over his heart.

"Sell it to someone who's buying," she said, but she grinned back at him before opening the car door. "See you tomorrow."

Jeez, what a pseudo, she thought as she unlocked the door to the *Daily* and trotted up the slate staircase. But she had to admit the flirtatious exchange left her with a warm, faintly sensual glow. Guys like Richard were at least fun. The trouble was, that was usually all they were.

"Zoe, where the hell have you been?" Gabriel Marcus demanded. "It's almost eleven o'clock."

"Chill, Gabriel. I've been out getting you more for your money. Can you give me about fifteen inches for a sidebar comment story?"

"Who've you got?" His voice quickened with interest.

"Eleanor Sullivan and Frank Novak in a head-to-head argument about the NCAA. With some *very* nice quotes."

"Good stuff?"

"Grade A."

"Okay, you can have . . ." Gabriel peered at his layout sheet dubiously, "ten inches, I guess. Sorry," he held up his hand to stem her outraged protest, "it's the best I can do."

"Okay, okay." She grumbled over to the row of computers and dumped her bookbag on an empty chair, nodding hello to Jeff Bryson in the next chair. "Anyone want to call out for a pizza? I'm starved."

She'd finished the main story on the murder itself—page one lead again, of course—earlier in the evening, before going out to the Carlton. Now she dug out her notes and started typing, shutting out the noise and controlled chaos that was the city room's customary ambience. There wasn't space enough to be clever, but the quotes themselves were good enough to carry the piece. Still, there was an awful lot of stuff to cram in. She typed furiously for a while, just getting it all down. Then she checked for length and stared at the numbers in dismay. Swearing, she highlighted a particularly colorful graf and hit the delete key.

She looked up at the clock. Past midnight, less than an hour till deadline. Swearing again, she paged through the on-screen text, dragging grafs and reorganizing ideas, occasionally typing a few words. The conversation between Sullivan and Novak became clearer. Good; point counterpoint, the basics of the argument set out as dialectic.

"Done the bugger." She stretched out her arms to ease tight shoulder muscles and swiveled to face Gabriel. "How were the press conference photos?"

"Mostly feeble, but there's one good one of Ro pointing at that airhead from Channel Three."

"Full color page one?"

"No. For that we got a shot of the concession stand where he was killed." Gabriel was reading her story as he spoke; now he dragged on his mouse and clicked keys.

"What are you changing?" she asked suspiciously.

"I think you can guess."

"*Not* the Eleanor Sullivan quote. Gabriel, you *have* to leave that in."

"Darlin', this is a newspaper. We don't print words like *bullshit.*"

"Oh, puh-leeze. This is the *Daily*, not some sanctimonious suburban rag. If a former University Regent can say it, we ought to be able to print it."

"She's right." Katie Sparrow, reading over Gabriel's shoulder, sounded both serious and gleeful. "Come on, Gabriel, one *bullshit* is pretty tame stuff. Except for a couple of little old ladies, who's it going to piss off?"

"Shit, even the LOL's are pretty hip around here," Zoe insisted. "After all, that describes Eleanor Sullivan herself, doesn't it? And besides," she brought out her big guns, "the *Daily* has printed stronger stuff than that."

"I doubt that," Gabriel shook his head.

"Oh, yeah? Hang on and I'll show you." She raced the length of the city room and across the hall to the library. For a wonder, the bound volume she wanted—Fall, 1971—was actually in the right place. She dropped it onto a table and riffled through it. It would be a Sunday paper—they published on Sundays back then—after the Iowa game . . . there. She wrapped her arms around the big book and carried it back to the sports desk. "There." She dropped it in front of Gabriel and pointed to the story.

"Hey, watch it." Laid open, the volume covered most of the desk.

"See?" Zoe reached for the pizza box on the corner of the desk and extracted a last uneaten wedge, cold and congealed. Munching pepperoni, she read the story again over his shoulder:

> "We got the fucking shit kicked out of us today." Thus did a none-too-happy Frank Lauterbur begin his post-game press conference yesterday.[3]

"Yeah, okay." Gabriel was grinning as he closed the bound volume. "But that was the sixties."

"Oh? I know the country's gone into the toilet since then, but did they repeal the First Amendment and forget to tell me? And I wrote it exactly the way she said it," Zoe continued persuasively.

[3]See: "Lauterbur Laments," *The Michigan Daily*, Nov. 7, 1971, p. 6.

"She specifically said 'and you can quote me.' Gabriel, she was challenging us to print it."

"She was, wasn't she? And I suppose a single *bullshit* isn't going to bring the building down around our ears. Oh, all right." He turned to his terminal and tapped keys, a broad smile on his face.

"What did Jimmy get from the NCAA?" Zoe changed the subject, just in case Gabriel might be prone to second thoughts.

"I didn't get diddly." Jimmy Tarbell, a small, chubby junior, came up behind her and peered mournfully into the now-empty pizza box. "Either they don't know squat or they're just not talking."

"Bummer," Zoe said sympathetically. "Didn't they even tell you whether they're planning a full-scale investigation of Michigan?"

"They didn't say," Jimmy said after a pause that Zoe translated to mean: I didn't think to ask. Oh well, some people just weren't meant to be investigative reporters. She smiled amiably at him and wandered over to the assignment sheet, a mass of frantic scribbles overlaying the original neat typing. She located her name beside two ongoing stories, the murder follow-up and the President's Club Weekend. Well, she'd do some of the suspect interviews tomorrow morning, and then talk to the cops in the afternoon, when they'd probably have more information. The President's Club stuff didn't start until Friday, thank God; this murder investigation was going to chew a lot of time. She could blow off her morning lecture tomorrow—like everyone on the *Daily*, she had a list of people she could cadge lecture notes from—but she kind of hated to miss her afternoon poli sci discussion section. . . .

"Want a ride home, Kaplan?" Jeff Bryson interrupted her mental planning.

"Yeah, I guess, thanks." She was still so wired that she felt more like going out somewhere, but underneath, she knew, she was tired. And she had another big day tomorrow. Mostly, she hoped her roommate would be asleep when she pulled in.

She kept the hope alive through the oak-paneled lobby of East Quad and up the windowed stairwell to the second floor of Cooley House. But when she turned down the corridor, she was annoyed but unsurprised to see light spilling from the doorway of her room.

"Kaplan, you're back! Finally!" Zoe heard the note of complaint in Paula's voice, felt a guilty pang and then stiffened with resentment. The mixture as usual.

"*Every*body was talking about your story all day," Paula Schiffer bubbled. "And then the murder! Are you going to be covering that, too?" She bounced up and down on the upper bunk, peering at Zoe excitedly. She was a tall, fair girl with indeterminate-colored hair and washed-out light brown eyes. She wore a long cotton nightgown, flowered and ruffled, and a pair of owlish pink-framed glasses that accentuated her waiflike appearance.

"Yeah, I'm covering the murder." Zoe dropped her bookbag on top of her desk, dislodging a stack of books and narrowly missing the keyboard of her Mac. She dropped her coat over the back of the chair and yanked her nightshirt from under the pillow of the lower bunk.

"There's hot chocolate." Paula pointed to the illegal hot plate on the dresser. "And I've got some cookies—I bet you're starved."

"I'm too tired to eat." Zoe peeled off her sweater, dropped it on the floor and stepped out of her jeans.

"That cop was on the TV news. The one who used to be a football player?" Paula, who was from Flint, had the annoying Southern-belle habit of turning statements into questions. "He looked really hunky. Did you get to interview him?"

"Yeah, I talked to him." Zoe shrugged into a terrycloth bathrobe and rummaged on the floor of her closet.

"What was he like? Is he as good looking in person?"

"Paula, he's just a cop." Zoe unearthed the rubberized shower bag and reached up to the top shelf for a towel.

"It must have been really exciting today," Paula pressed, sounding both eager and plaintive.

"Mostly just frantic."

"All right, if you don't want to talk about it, why don't you just say so?" Paula, abruptly offended, flounced on her bunk. "And of course you don't want to be bothered talking about *my* day." She squirmed under her blanket and ostentatiously turned her face toward the wall. "And please try not to wake me up when you get back," she flung over her shoulder.

The trouble is, Zoe thought gloomily as she located a (mostly) clean towel and escaped down the hall to the women's shower, by tomorrow morning she'll have forgotten all about being dissed and go into that eager-puppy routine all over again, like we should be joined at the hip.

What is it about the Paulas of the world, she wondered, that brings out the worst in everybody else? Well, in me anyway. She disliked herself for the curt, even nasty way she treated Paula, and then she blamed Paula for making her act that way. The original vicious circle.

Standing under the hot spray, she wished for the twentieth time that she'd scored one of East Quad's rare single rooms. An only child just isn't going to be real good at this group living crap, she excused herself; maybe she'd be better off pulling out of the dorm at the end of the semester and getting herself an apartment. Except, dorm living was so much easier; she didn't really want to be bothered with shopping and cooking and all that crap.

The problem is, I really would like to talk about today, she admitted as she toweled herself dry. If only Paula wouldn't glom on to her like a fucking leech or something. If only Paula would get herself a life.

Her freshman roommate had been a small, driven girl in the throes of Inteflex, the University's accelerated pre-med program. Between Zoe's hours at the *Daily* and Ginny's hours at the library, they'd barely gotten to know each other before the end of the year, when Ginny decided to move to an apartment to get away from dorm noise.

After Ginny, Zoe had been unprepared for Paula's demanding togetherness. Paula expected them to have breakfast together; she expected them to study together, to have long, intimate talks, to share ideas and secrets and clothes. Some hope, Zoe snorted, looking down at her short legs and round hips.

For a while, Zoe had even wondered if Paula were gay—that, at least, she could have understood and dealt with honestly. But that wasn't it; Paula had occasional dates (which Zoe was expected to help dissect endlessly), and she never made a pass. I expected a roommate, Zoe thought, but Paula expected a soulmate.

When she got back to her room, the door was locked, and when she dug out her key and unlocked it, the room was pitch black. Great, she thought, stubbing her toe on something unidentifiable but painful. Sighing, she tossed her robe and towel and shower bag in the general direction of the closet and crawled into bed.

TWENTY-THREE

They had left the window open during the night, one life choice, at least, on which they agreed. Anneke came awake muzzily, with a feeling of such vast depression she almost cried aloud. For a moment she couldn't remember where she was. Images of bedrooms past flickered through her mind—the ugly suburban room filled with fake French Provincial that she'd slept in when she was married; the spare, light-filled room in her burned-out house; the tiny, cozy bedroom of the rented cottage. All of them were empty, abandoned.

She pulled the down-filled duvet more tightly around her, shivering. Nightmare? The fire nightmares, those beautiful, terrifying visions of crystal and flame, had ended long ago. She tried to recall dream images, but there was nothing she could recapture.

She forced her eyes open. Dark, polished walnut furniture. Dark green carpet. Drapes in a handsome, subtle stripe of dark green and burnt orange. Karl's bedroom, not abandoned but filled with the sense of him. She felt rather than heard his slow, even breathing next to her, felt warmth from his body flow toward her. Amazing, she thought, how much warmer two people are than one.

She rolled over toward him, fitting her body to his, running a hand down the line of him, feeling the hard muscles of his chest and the slight softening of waist and stomach. Even Karl, who worked out religiously, couldn't hold back time forever, she thought, and to her surprise the notion was more comforting than disturbing.

"There's nothing sadder than an athlete gone to seed, is there?" he growled sleepily, turning toward her. "We'll just have to crumble away together." He moved his hands down her body, touching and stroking. "Will you still love me when I'm old and flabby?"

"That depends." She ran a hand down his leg and up along the inside of his thigh, shivering with pleasure as his palms moved lightly over her breasts.

"Oh? On what?" His arms circled her and he lifted her on top of him, hands stroking the backs of her thighs.

"On which parts . . . are going to get flabby," she said breathlessly.

"Well," he gave her a sleepy grin, "there's the old athlete's motto—use it or lose it."

Afterward, he turned on his elbow to look at her. "What's the matter?"

"Nothing," she lied quickly. "I was just thinking about the work I have today."

"Not very complimentary," he grumbled. "All right, I suppose we'd both better get moving."

"In a minute." She pressed up against him, trying to recapture the glow. The thought that had popped into her head was silly enough, certainly; lying about it was preposterous. Now why, she wondered, did I refuse to admit that I absolutely hate those drapes? She sat up and mentally shook herself.

"I take it your headache is gone?" Karl asked.

"Completely. I feel fine." She swung her legs over the side of the bed, shaking her head experimentally. "No headache at—what was that?" She jerked her head toward the door, startled.

"Just Marianne."

"Oh, hell, I forgot. Today is Thursday, isn't it?" At the mention of the maid, all her determined cheerfulness seemed to drain away in an instant.

"Is it a problem?" Karl asked.

"No, not at all," Anneke lied again. "I just forgot she was coming, that's all." She stood up quickly and reached for her robe before heading toward the bathroom.

She'd never had a maid before, or even a cleaning woman. As Tim Mortenson's wife, of course, caring for the house was her job, and in truth it had never occurred to her to want help. And after the divorce, living in small quarters with only herself to care for, there had never been the need. Besides, household help is vaguely suspect in Ann Arbor, just this side of politically incorrect, snarled in issues of exploitation, overemphasis on appearance, and other such social issues. At the very least, a maid requires constant justification.

Now, of course, the justification was self-evident. Even the most hypersensitive of Burns Park residents couldn't expect two people with two demanding jobs to manage a house this size on their own. And God knows, she thought, standing under the shower and letting hot water stream over her, I have no possessive instinct toward housework. But Marianne's cloaked hostility was becoming more than she could bear.

She finished dressing, in black jeans and a black velvet shirt, without finding an answer. She added a pair of silver hoop earrings and a silver ring with a large stone of clear quartz crystal. By the time she was done, Karl was already downstairs, drinking coffee at the dining table they'd placed in a bay window at the side of the living room. Anneke detoured to the kitchen to get herself a cup, only to find Marianne busily washing out the coffeemaker, although she knew Anneke had not yet had any.

"Good morning, Miss Haagen." Marianne, chunky and gray-haired, dipped her head in a nod. Her broad face, innocent of makeup, wore its usual grimly impersonal expression.

"Good morning." Anneke had given up trying to get the woman to address her as "Ms." Or, for that matter, to provide her with coffee. Without commenting on the coffeepot, she took a mug from the cabinet, filled it with water from the tap, and set it in the microwave. When it boiled, she spooned instant coffee into it and took the resultant mess into the living room, sighing in frustration.

Marianne had been working for Karl, Mondays and Thursdays, ever since he arrived in Ann Arbor, she reminded herself. It was only reasonable that she might feel possessive toward him, and resentful of Anneke's intrusion. Anneke had to admit the house was spotless, and the home-cooked meals twice a week more than welcome. And finally, there was absolutely nothing concrete she could object to in Marianne's manner or expression—the hostility was so carefully measured that once or twice Anneke herself wondered if she was imagining it.

"Do you want to see what your friend wrote?" Karl offered her the newspaper.

"Is that the *Daily*?" Anneke took the paper eagerly. "Where did you get it?"

"Marianne brought it with her."

"Oh. Good." Anneke shoved the Marianne problem aside for the twentieth time and turned her attention to Zoe's story, her eyes widening as she read the lead.

NCAA INVESTIGATOR
SLAIN IN 'M' STADIUM

> Special to the *Daily*—Alvin Greenaway went over the brick barricade like a playing card folded in half. The dark blue banner with the big yellow Block M was clutched in his hands like a sideline judge's down marker. Only, the other end was sunk deep into his stomach.
>
> For Alvin Greenaway, it was fourth down.

Anneke looked up from the paper. "Wow."

"Yes. It's quite a lead, isn't it." Karl's tone was so neutral she couldn't tell if he was complimenting or condemning. She returned to the story, reading it rapidly to the end before looking up again.

"It seems to me," she said carefully, "to be perfectly straightforward. There's nothing inaccurate in it, is there?"

"No, nothing at all," he said grudgingly. "Barring the sensationalism of the lead, it's as you say, perfectly straightforward. It would have been better, perhaps, if she hadn't named names." He pointed to the paragraph near the bottom, that began "Among those present in the stadium when Greenaway died . . . " followed by a list of names that included Anneke's own.

"Well, she had to, after all. It's not as though they can be kept out of the media."

"Probably not," he said, and then: "Read her other story." This time Anneke thought she heard a hint of amusement in his voice. She returned to the *Daily*, located Zoe's second byline under the headline "Can Even Michigan Keep It Clean?" and saw the quote about halfway down:

> "NCAA regulations are bullshit, and you can quote me," Sullivan said.

"Eleanor did that on purpose, you know," Anneke said, recalling the scene. "I was there."

"Oh, I'm sure she did." Karl was smiling.

Anneke read the remainder of the article, interested to see how Zoe had organized the random conversation around the restaurant table. "It's excellent," she said when she finished.

"You sound surprised."

"Relieved, I guess," Anneke admitted. "She really is good."

"Yes, she is," Karl conceded. "She's captured the student-athlete argument very cogently."

"Well, then." There was a moment of silence. "Are you going

to print out that file from Charlie Cassovoy's computer this morning?" she asked finally.

"Jon should have it on my desk this morning. Would you like a copy?"

"Yes, please." She carefully avoided mentioning that she'd promised a copy to Zoe. Or that she was planning to meet her at Zingerman's for lunch. "Why don't I stop by your office for it later this morning?"

"Fine. I'll see you then."

TWENTY-FOUR

Charlie Cassovoy had the Super Bowl of all hangovers. It started at his lower back and worked its way up to the top of his head, with detours for fun and games in his stomach and behind his eyeballs. He opened all the windows of his car and gulped fresh air, but it didn't do any good. He was well and truly fried.

He vaguely remembered an Ann Arbor cop showing up at the door of his Redford Township apartment, just minutes after he'd pulled in himself. The guy'd copied that file off the laptop, Charlie remembered that much, but other than that it was a blur. His last coherent memory, in fact, was of a bar out on Schoolcraft Road. He remembered regaling a dozen or so local boys with a highly colored description of Alvin Greenaway's death, and he remembered the gratifying way they bought him drinks and hung on his words. Then it all went fuzzy.

He tightened his grip on the steering wheel and swung off Beech Daly onto Plymouth Road, heading toward Ann Arbor. Sweat beaded his forehead, but try as he might, he couldn't remember another thing about last night. Well, shit, it didn't really matter.

What did matter was that he could still pull this off—still come up with a story that would have everyone pissing green with envy.

So okay. First he'd go corner Frank Novak and play a little squirming music. There was dirt somewhere, and if Frankie knew about it, he oughta be an easy one to break. He'd scrounge around for something on Genesko, too—no way could he have helped with recruiting all these years without breaking *some* sort of NCAA reg. The notion made his headache feel better. The lead for his Sunday column took shape in his mind:

> Michigan looks after its own. When Alvin Greenaway, a supposedly impartial NCAA investigator, got information implicating a Michigan alumnus in a football recruiting violation, he went first to the Michigan athletic director before going to his bosses at the NCAA. When Greenaway bought the farm, it was through the agency of a Michigan banner, in Michigan Stadium, surrounded by a group of Michigan alums. And when it came time to investigate that death, the cop in charge of the case turns out to be—surprise—Ann Arbor police lieutenant Karl Genesko, one of that very same group of Michigan alums, a former Go Blue football player and himself a sometime recruiter for Michigan football.
>
> At Michigan, they apparently don't see anything wrong with putting the fox in charge of the chicken coop.

Not bad, Charlie thought. He might even be able to work that broad into it—Anneke, it was. Yeah, she's bonking Genesko, which gives her a motive, too.

He'd have to pin the guy to the wall, find out his excuse for being on the wrong side of the field when he was supposed to be talking to the TV people. He and Novak couldn't claim to be together the whole time, because they'd showed up from different directions. He recognized in himself a reluctance to confront Genesko directly, and decided he was merely being sensible. Novak would be a lot easier to break. First he'd tackle Novak

No. First he'd stop at that roadhouse for a little drink.

TWENTY-FIVE

Richard Killian was having the time of his life. The little hotel maid, a charmer from Nicaragua, fixed gorgeous dark eyes on his face and said breathlessly in Spanish:

"No, no tuvo visita que yo vi." (No, he had no visitors that I saw.) "Aunque no vigilo quien viene o va, me entiende." (Although I don't keep watch on his door, you understand.) "¿Piensa que eran drogas?" (Was it drugs, do you think?)

"Aun no se sabe." (There is no telling yet.) "Pero revelarémos el culpable, se lo aseguro." (But we will expose the culprit, I assure you.) "Es lo que hacen los periodicos en este país." (That is what newspapers do in this country.) He took both her hands and held them between his own, looking at her with keen sincerity.

"No pienso que le creo su historia." (I do not think I believe this story of yours.) She laughed up at him. "Pero le mostraré el cuarto de cualquier modo." (But I will show you the room anyway.) She kept hold of his hand and led him down the corridor.

Richard let himself be led, grateful he'd made the effort to learn Spanish. In San Francisco he'd found it useful for both business and pleasure—he had a smattering of Chinese for the same reason—but he hadn't expected to use it in Ann Arbor. The world was getting more multicultural all the time, he smiled to himself. Beautiful women came in all colors and flavors.

But then, Richard had never met a woman he didn't like. Richard loved women. All women. Women were marvelous creatures, soft or strong, timid or fiery, shy or sophisticated or aloof. He could always find something in a woman to please him, whatever her appearance or age or social condition. Some of his best friends—and best customers—were elderly San Francisco dowagers whose reminiscences of Baghdad-by-the-Bay never failed to delight him. These he never hit on, of course, although he flirted a little to let them know he appreciated them. He always seemed to know when a woman simply wanted a little male attention or when she wanted something more, and he tried never to disappoint them.

He squeezed the little maid's hand gently, but she turned and frowned at him, putting her other hand to her ripe red lips in the universal gesture of silence.

"Where are we going?" he whispered in Spanish.

"Upstairs," she replied in the same language. "He had one of the new Business Special rooms." She continued toward the back of the hotel and up a flight of stairs Richard hadn't known existed. On the second floor she turned once more before stopping. "Here," she said, taking a ring of keys from her pocket and turning the lock.

Inside, it looked like every hotel room Richard had ever seen. A king-size bed took up most of the floor space, a low dresser with a color TV was opposite, and a minuscule desk sat under the window. Richard crossed to the desk and opened the one small drawer, which contained a folder of stationery and the usual miscellany of room service menu, hotel directory, and other flotsam. He withdrew the Gideon Bible, held it open and shook it, but to his disappointment nothing fell out.

"You see, it is as I told you," the maid said. "I had to clean it twice. First, the normal time this morning, then after the police were done I cleaned again, and a fine mess they left, I can tell you—the bed all pulled apart, all the drawers turned out, even the pictures unscrewed from the walls. And dust and powder covering everything."

"Fingerprint powder," Richard said, more to himself than to her. "It doesn't sound like they'd have missed anything." He surveyed the room in frustration, until his eye lit on the empty wastebasket under the desk. "What about the trash?" he asked.

"I emptied that before the police came."

"Damn." He paced back and forth, trying to think of something else to ask. There wasn't much room in which to pace, though. "I thought this was some kind of special room," he said, sitting down on the bed.

"It is. It has two telephones, see?" She pointed to the instruments, one on the desk and one on the night table.

"That doesn't seem all that special," he said grumpily.

"I think there is something to send faxes and other things like that, but I don't know anything about that." She shrugged.

"Well, what about his phone calls?" Richard asked. "Did he get many of them?"

"We-ell, I don't know for myself, but Linda on the switchboard says he was on the phone most of the evening. She is angry with herself now that she didn't listen in, so she could feel important instead of just someone who pushes buttons all night." The girl laughed. "She is jealous because I was actually inside his room."

"Were his phone calls incoming or outgoing?"

"According to Linda," the maid's voice left no doubt she considered this a suspect source, "there were three or four incoming calls, but outgoing it was mostly one long call. To someplace in Kansas."

"Kansas." Richard pondered. To the NCAA, or to his home? But he lived alone. Still, he could have had a woman friend back home. The police probably already knew, but of course they wouldn't reveal it. Or if they did, it would be for all the media, not for a *Daily* exclusive. Damn.

Still, it was something, he decided, his cheerful disposition reasserting itself. Maybe he could squeeze it out of Genesko right at deadline—too late for TV or the other papers.

He sighed and sat down on the bed, wearing his best sorrowful look, but when he patted the bedspread next to him the girl laughed and shook her head.

"Oh, well." He favored her with a regretful look. "You can't shoot a guy for trying."

"In my country, you can," she retorted with a brilliant smile.

TWENTY-SIX

She had managed to escape Paula's importunings by the simple process of getting up early and skipping breakfast, which Zoe now realized was a mistake. The sweetish smell of pot that filled the filthy basement room in the old rooming house on Oakland was making her stomach do unpleasant calisthenics.

Melissa Greenaway sprawled on the unmade bed in a nest of graying sheets and stained blankets. She was thin in an unhealthy way—gaunt, really, with narrow, pinched features and snarled and matted brownish hair. She wore only a pair of formerly white bikini underpants and a cropped sweater that had once been blue.

She was also totally zoned out. Wrecked. Hopeless.

Zoe curled her feet under her to avoid the half-eaten pizza on the floor in front of the only chair in the room. She mentally ran down the list of questions she'd prepared, and discarded all of them. The girl on the bed was too stoned to give coherent answers.

Zoe sat still, momentarily baffled, and then a sudden flash memory popped into her head from a book about interviewing she'd just read: "A good question elicits a specific answer. A great question open floodgates. The very best question starts with the words 'Tell me about . . .' "

"Tell me about your father," Zoe said quietly.

"Dear old dad? There's nothing to tell." Melissa rolled over onto her back and stared at the ceiling. "He was a nothing, a social cypher." She blew smoke and watched it drift upward with every evidence of interest. "He never did anything *valid* in his life," she said. "Just went to work and came home, went to work and came home, workhomeworkhomeworkhome." The words seemed to fascinate her. "Just went to work, came home, paid his taxes, obeyed the law." The last word was said scathingly, like profanity. Her voice sharpened. "If there was a law, my daddy obeyed it. Obeyed. Love, honor, obey."

"He sounds like a good guy," Zoe probed.

"Have you ever read Baudrillard?" Melissa pulled herself to a sitting position and crossed her legs under her, giving Zoe a clear and unwanted view of her crotch. "Dear old dad was a perfect specimen of late-twentieth-century European American. If the media told him something, he believed it. If the media told him to buy something, he bought it." Her high-pitched voice was scathing. "He had to have all the latest toys, y'know? He bought into the techno-conspiracy big-time." She took another puff from the rapidly diminishing joint, coughed, and laughed raucously. "Computerize all the jocks," she declared. "And the microchip shall make you free. The preceding has been a live re-creation of actual events that never happened until we re-created them." Her voice dropped to a mumble and she stared into space, and Zoe saw that her face was wet with tears.

After a long silence, Zoe concluded that Melissa had forgotten she was there. With a sigh she shoved her pen and notebook into her bookbag, stood up, and picked her way across the littered floor. The postmodernists had a lot to answer for, she concluded in disgust.

Outside in the bright October morning, she took several deep gulps of blessedly clean air, decided she was hungry, and wondered if it were lack of breakfast or a bad case of the munchies from a contact high. Either way, she'd better eat something before trying to interview Jeffrey Person.

She unlocked her bike and headed toward Packard. There was a clutch of coffeehouses at Packard and State, and she was so busy concentrating on the question of cinnamon roll versus blueberry scone that she almost missed them. Only when the white Ford Escort zoomed past and cut her off at the intersection did she note the two people in it. The driver was Jeffrey Person. The passenger was Kyle Farmer.

She told her rumbling stomach to bag it and turned in behind them. Heading north through the usual State Street traffic scrum, she had more trouble staying behind than keeping up with them, and plenty of time to consider implications. Farmer was keeping his head down, face turned away. She tried to recall the little she knew so far about Jeffrey Person, and came up with former cornerback, Miami, lawyer. Sports law . . . The dirty word popped into her head suddenly. Agent.

It all fit, she thought gloomily, still unwilling to believe the worst about Kyle Farmer. Jeffrey Person was ideally positioned to jump to the big-money world of athlete representation. And ten percent of Kyle Farmer's future NFL contract, projected to be in the neighborhood of seven million dollars, would give Person one hell of a jump start. Not to mention ten percent of potential endorsement dollars.

The only trouble was, signing a contract with an agent while still in school—or even orally agreeing to sign—was one of the NCAA's biggest no-no's.

Suppose it were true. And suppose it got found out. First thing, Jeffrey Person gets barred from every campus in the country. No; first thing, Kyle Farmer gets declared immediately ineligible. So no Heisman, no football season. Out of the public eye, out of school, out of shape. Out of the money, both of them.

The Escort plowed through campus traffic, turned left on Huron and then right on Division, where it accelerated rapidly up the broad one-way street. Zoe pedaled madly behind them for two blocks and finally gave up, gasping, as the white car swung into the Beakes Street turn and disappeared. She was fairly sure where they were going, anyway; she'd just have to hope they'd be there long enough for her to catch up with them.

Besides, she was only a block from Zingerman's. First, she was damn well going to stop for a cheese danish.

By the time she pedaled the two miles out Plymouth Road to the Carlton, Zoe was hungry again. A brief reconnoitre revealed, to her relief, that the white Escort was safely in the parking lot. She pushed the thought of food firmly aside and approached the hotel desk casually, holding the folded sheet of paper she'd prepared outside.

"I'd like to leave a message for Jeffrey Person, please."

"Yes, ma'am." The desk clerk was clearly not a fan of second-rate TV detective shows. He took the paper from her hand, consulted his computer screen, and shoved the paper into a slot above the number 143. Zoe nodded politely and turned away, hiding her grin until she was back outside. Jeez, just like on television, she giggled to herself.

She walked around the outside perimeter of the hotel until she reached the end of the west wing. There she peered carefully through the glass door before pushing it open and padding down the carpeted corridor to room 143.

Only when she stood in front of the door did she pause as sensible caution kicked in. She'd always hated those books in which the heroine (it was always the heroine, never the hero) charged into the abandoned warehouse after the bad guys. She stood still for a moment, wondering if she should call Genesko. Except what did she really have to tell him? Merely that she'd seen Jeffrey Person and Kyle Farmer together, which was hardly a criminal offense and would probably lower Genesko's opinion of her even further. Well, she could at least call Gabriel. . . .

As she stood irresolute she heard the low rumble of voices from behind the door. At least she knew they were still inside. She leaned forward and pressed her ear to the door, but she couldn't make out any actual words. Shit. She squeezed her ear closer to the crack between door and jamb.

And fell forward, her bookbag catching her painfully between the shoulderblades, as the door swung inward and a dark brown hand grasped her wrist.

"What the hell do you think you're playing at?" Jeffrey Person yanked her into the room and slammed the door behind her. The sound of it was not reassuring. He spun her around and glared at her, fury in every line of his face. He kept his hand wrapped tightly around her wrist.

"I'm not playing." Zoe heard her voice shake with fear and fought to steady it. "It's all over, you know. We know all about it—not just me, but my editor, too."

"She's lying." The raspy voice spoke from the other side of the room. Zoe whirled toward it. At the desk under the window, looking sick to his stomach, was Kyle Farmer. Stretched out on the bed, smiling grimly, was Eleanor Sullivan.

"Shit!" Jeffrey Person released Zoe's wrist but kept his position in front of the door. "What the hell are we going to do with her?"

TWENTY-SEVEN

Anneke went first to the Secretary of State's office for a replacement driver's license, then to her office, where conversation ceased and wide-eyed faces turned to look at her as she walked in. She saw a copy of the *Daily* on Ken Scheede's desk and grimaced.

"Yes, I was there," she said to forestall questions. "But I don't know a single thing more than what's printed in the paper."

"Is Kyle Farmer really the target of the investigation?" Calvin Streeter asked, looking angrier than usual.

"Kyle Farmer? Not that I know of," Anneke replied. "Why Farmer?"

"Because it's all over Confer," Max Loeffler said excitedly. "They're saying that Farmer was paid half a million dollars to stay in school for his senior year instead of turning pro."

"What?" Anneke stared at him.

"It's true." Ken nodded. "Log on and see. It's all anyone's talking about."

Anneke went swiftly to her desk and logged her Compaq on to Confer, the university's computer conferencing system. She downloaded her e-mail to read later and went directly to the Sports Conference, where she read the most recent postings with growing dismay.

```
>So what if Farmer took the money? Why shouldn't
>he get a piece of the action--after all¬ he's the one
>who's responsible for putting butts in the seats¬ isn't he?
```

The next one read:

```
>But why would he take a payoff to stay in school
>when he could just have come out for the NFL
>this year? I still think it's nuts.
```

followed by:

```
>Yeah¬ but this way he gets to keep his status as
>Saint Kyle¬ the Perfect Student Athlete <gag>.
```

and:

```
>Can the U sue him? That's what they're saying
>in the Law Conference.
```

Anneke moved to the Law Conference, where there was indeed an erudite discussion of possible liability proceedings against Kyle Farmer for potential lost revenue should the University be placed on NCAA probation, as well as "punitive damages for causing irreparable harm to the University's reputation." In the Social Issues Conference several dozen postings flamed angrily about exploitation of young African American males, ethical absolutism, and postmodern morality, all as it applied to Kyle Farmer's transgression. And in the Campus Issues Conference there were dark hints of athletic department complicity, an administration cover-up, and more.

But was it true about Farmer? Surely if it was, Karl would have known. If not, where had it all started? She backtracked through several different conferences, but couldn't seem to find the thread that started it all. The rumor, if it was a rumor, seemed to have begun in half a dozen places almost simultaneously. She toggled her printer and printed out a representative sample of the postings. Then she picked up the phone and called Karl.

"Have you found any evidence that Kyle Farmer was the player being investigated?" she asked without preamble.

"So you've heard it, too." His voice over the phone sounded disgusted. "No, we don't have any more now than we had yesterday. I don't know how these things get started."

"I think I may have an idea about that," she said slowly. "No, wait. When I come to your office to pick up that printout, I'll show you."

"All right. I'll see you later."

She hung up, picked yesterday's mail off her desk, and carried it to the small office that housed the Sun workstation, quelling her young staff's curiosity with a glare. The mail was as bad as usual. Software catalog, office supply catalog, bank statement. Invitation to an investment seminar, and another to a workshop entitled "How to Be the Perfect Secretary," presumably sent to every female name on some sort of business list. Forms to be filled out from the IRS, the state treasurer, and the Michigan Secretary of State. Three requests from small local businesses to install server networks that they didn't understand, didn't need, and wouldn't be able to keep operational. Still, it was business. She put the requests aside for consideration.

At the bottom of the stack, just as she was preparing to pitch the rest, was a Request For Proposal that stopped her. A consortium of Great Lakes shipping companies wanted to develop an Internet service, to be called LakeNet, which would provide instant access to a range of information from weather to cargo pricing. Now that's more like it, she thought, putting it aside with the others. She returned to the stack of mail feeling mildly cheered. She put the business forms in a different stack, tossed the rest of the mail, and reached for the LakeNet RFP again.

It was eleven o'clock when she finally came up for air. All right, she didn't have time. But this one was too interesting to pass up. It was also, she conceded to herself, a big—a very big—project. Maybe Ken had a point about expanding. She put aside the Lake-Net notes reluctantly and checked in again to Confer. The Kyle Farmer debate continued to rage. Sighing, she logged off, picked up her briefcase, and headed out of the office to the police department.

City Hall was a zoo. Instead of proceeding directly to Karl's office, she had to fight her way through a pandemonium of media people, explain her purpose to a harried security guard, and then wait several minutes for confirmation before being allowed through the door.

"It's incredible out there," she said to Karl in amazement when she finally reached his office. "I thought it would be calmed down by now."

"Some hope." He looked grim. "It's been a madhouse all morning—we practically have to scrape the reporters off the walls to get any work done."

"But why? Is there something new?"

"Primarily the Kyle Farmer rumor."

"Oh, God. It didn't occur to me that the media would be on to it. But it is just a rumor, isn't it?"

"As far as we know." He threw up his hands in disgust. "We can't begin to figure out how or where it started."

"I think I can help there, anyway. Take a look at this." She handed him the Confer printout, and while he read through it she sat down in front of his terminal and logged on again. The flames were continuing, pro and con—blaming Kyle Farmer, blaming the NCAA, blaming society.

"Hardly anyone seems to question Farmer's guilt," Karl noted, reading over her shoulder.

"No." She shook her head. "I've seen this sort of thing before, but I've never seen it become so . . . all-encompassing."

"Has anyone from the Athletic Department posted a denial yet?" he asked.

"Not that I know of. Anyway, it wouldn't do any good." She riffled through the printout until she came to a section from the University Conference. "If they did, you'd only get more of this." She pointed to an entry that read:

```
>Of course, the U just wants it all
 to go away.
>You can bet they've got their cover
 story all ready.
>Can you spell deniability?
```

"Once something like this gets started, any official denials are just taken as evidence that the administration has something to hide. Until things start to cool down, it's a no-win situation."

"So you think the rumor could have started on-line?"

Instead of answering him directly, she asked: "Have you ever read Larry Niven? The science fiction writer?"

"No."

"Niven created a universe that had invented matter transmission—universal, instantaneous travel from any point on earth to any other point. And one of the things he extrapolated from that was the concept of the Flash Crowd."

"I see. You mean that any time something interesting was going on, anywhere in the world, millions of people might zap in."

"Right." She was relieved, as always, by his quick understanding. "Now, what we have here isn't universal instantaneous travel, but universal instantaneous communication—or at least, universal within the University. So what *we* have is—"

"Flash Rumors." He completed her sentence, shaking his head in disgust. "Wonderful. So now a single idiot can panic a whole city instead of just his little corner of it."

"There's more."

"Somehow I had a feeling there would be." He grimaced.

"Niven also postulated criminals who *created* Flash Crowds for various illegal purposes." They digested the implication in silence for a few moments.

"So the rumor could have been purposely planted," he ruminated. "Tell me this: Is there any way to trace it back to its first instance?"

"Not really. And even if you did, on-line anonymity is so easy I doubt that it would tell you anything. Not to mention how porous Confer is."

"Porous?"

"Easy to break into. With all the amateurs floating through it, I could probably find a back door in about thirty seconds."

"So we have just what we need—another dead end." He twisted the big Super Bowl ring on his finger in an unconscious, and uncommon, gesture of tension. Anneke felt her own tension level, high to begin with, rise several more notches in response.

"Look," she said rather desperately, "if you can't solve the 'who,' what about the 'why?' "

"True." He paced the length of the small office and back. "All right, what is the *result* of this rumor?"

"Well, first and most obvious, Kyle Farmer's reputation is trashed."

"Second," Karl pointed out, "the media—" he made the word a loathesome sound "—go haring off after Farmer, to the exclusion of other possible targets. And third," he sat down finally and glared at the computer screen, "the police are now going to have to turn a great deal of their attention, time, and resources to investigating Farmer. Also to the exclusion of other suspects, at least for the moment."

"I never thought of that." She stared at him.

"For that matter, I suppose I should be grateful that the rumor focused on Farmer. It could just as easily have been me."

"You! Don't be silly."

"Realistically, I probably *shouldn't* be handling this investigation," he said. "I have far too many personal connections among the suspects."

"It's a small city," she protested. "Contacts like that are inevitable."

"Which doesn't make them any less compromising," he pointed out. "If it's not wrapped up within forty-eight hours, I have a feeling the prosecutor's going to call in the state police."

"Would that necessarily be a bad thing? Yes, of course it would," she answered her own question. "It would be like a vote of no-confidence, wouldn't it?"

"That's exactly what it would be." He swiveled his chair to face the computer, where flames continued to scroll down the screen. "As you noted, Ann Arbor is a small city, and I know a lot of people here. If I'm to be taken off every case in which I know someone involved, I can't do my job."

"It's all ridiculous." There was a tightness in her chest that she recognized, after a moment, as fear. Fear of what? she wondered, and had no answer, or too many. It occurred to her that she'd asked herself that same question more than once recently.

"Probably so." He smiled briefly and picked up a small sheaf of papers from one of the neat stacks on his desk. "This is a printout of your notes from last night."

"Have you read through them? Sorry; of course you have. So you can see why they couldn't be important."

"There certainly isn't anything there to cause a murderer to lose sleep," he agreed.

"That's what I've been saying."

"On the other hand, the murderer wouldn't know that until he'd read it, would he?"

"But it was just a group of people sitting around brainstorming," Anneke protested. "Why would the murderer even think we had anything to threaten him?"

"Because he's scared," Karl said forcefully. "By the very nature of their situation, murderers become increasingly paranoid."

"Well, now that he's seen what's on the disk," Anneke said, as much to reassure herself as to answer Karl, "he'll know we don't have anything to threaten him with."

"But he knows you're hunting him."

"*I'm* not hunting him," she pointed out. "All I did was type some notes into a computer. It's . . . never mind." She took the printout from him, blinking down at the text. Her eyes felt hot and tired.

"Did your headache come back?" he asked.

"No. I've just been poring over forms for too long."

"Did you arrange for a new pair of glasses?"

"Not yet," she replied defensively. "Look, I'd better get out of your way. Will you be home late tonight?"

"Probably. I'll call and let you know, all right?"

"All right." She didn't tell him that she was on her way to Zingerman's to meet Zoe and the others. Well, the subject simply hadn't arisen, that was all. And of course she'd give him a complete accounting of the conversation this evening.

TWENTY-EIGHT

She arrived at Zingerman's a few minutes after noon, to find Richard already there, holding down a picnic table on the patio.

"Is Zoe here yet?" she asked.

"Not yet." Richard stood up. "Why don't I go in and order for us while you guard the table? It's a madhouse in there."

"It always is at noon," she agreed. She asked him to order her a Tom's New Job—turkey, Swiss cheese, and cole slaw on rye bread—and coffee, and when he left she pulled her own laptop out of her briefcase and set it on the table in front of her. As she hit the switch, Charlie Cassovoy materialized suddenly and dropped onto the bench across from her, a large paper cup of Coke in his hand.

"I figured I'd come by and see how the chick was doing, see if I could give her a boost." He peered at Anneke. "Hear you had some trouble last night."

"Nothing serious." She returned his gaze. He looked pretty awful, she thought, even more red-eyed and rumpled than last night, but he seemed as alert and acerbic as ever. "I take it you didn't have any problems?"

“Not until you sicced the cops on me,” he replied acidly.

“I’m glad to hear it.” She was, in fact, very glad indeed; if no one had tried to get hold of Charlie’s computer, it could only mean that the attack on her had been exactly what she’d thought it was—nothing but a random mugging.

“Here you go.” Richard slid in next to her, setting two steaming cups on the table. “It’s a real circus in there,” he jerked his head toward the building. “Hi, Charlie, what’re you doing here?”

“Just thought I’d drop by and see how you amateurs were doing.” His smile did nothing to soften the insult. “Where the hell is that chick from the *Daily*?”

“I can’t imagine,” Anneke replied. There wasn’t much point in taking offense at Charlie, she concluded, looking around the patio. It was now completely full, but there was still no sign of Zoe.

“Shit,” Charlie said angrily, “I thought she might just have something. I don’t suppose,” he said to Richard, “that you got anything.”

“Even if I did, why should I share it with you?” Richard asked reasonably.

“Because, shit-for-brains, I’m gonna have some stuff *you* people’ll want.”

To Anneke’s surprise, instead of taking offense Richard burst out laughing. “Charlie, one of these days someone’s going to stuff a football into that mouth of yours and use you for a kicking tee. All right, why not? Another round of ‘you show me yours and I’ll show you mine?’ Would you take notes again?” he asked Anneke.

“All right.” She opened a file on her laptop and looked at Charlie expectantly.

“I didn’t get much yet,” Charlie grumbled. “But I did manage to corner Novak, at least. He says,” Charlie invested the words with deep suspicion, “that he was with one or another of the TV people the whole time. Hard to figure what ‘the whole time’ means, though. But he could’ve done it going to or from the TV trailers. The main thing is,” he added pointedly, “that Genesko wasn’t with him. Novak either didn’t know or wouldn’t say where he went.” He looked directly at Anneke.

"Have you asked Karl where he was at the time?" She kept her voice neutral, unwilling to give away information. If Karl wanted the press to know his whereabouts, he should be the one to tell them.

"Have you?" he challenged her.

"This isn't my party," she pointed out. "I'm just the recording secretary. Is that it?" she asked firmly, typing his comments into the computer.

"Just for the moment," Charlie grunted. "I'll be getting some hot information this afternoon. What about you?" he asked Richard.

"Not a lot," Richard admitted. "Oh, good, here's our food." When the young server had deposited baskets of sandwiches in front of them, he continued, "I did get into Greenaway's hotel room."

"Did you? Not bad," Charlie said grudgingly around a mouthful of pastrami. "What'd you get?"

As Richard outlined what he'd found out from the maid at the Carlton, Anneke typed, took bites of her sandwich, and scanned the patio for Zoe, wondering if she should be worried. There was no way the girl would have simply forgotten the lunch meeting; on the other hand, any number of things could have come up to prevent her from getting there. She reminded herself firmly that maternal responsibilities were well behind her and returned her attention to the matter at hand.

"Did you get to Najarian?" Charlie asked Richard.

"Yes, he 'got to' me." Daniel Najarian stood next to the table, his strong, almost-ugly face impassive. "Ask him anything about the role of recombinant DNA as a potential source of food for the next century." Najarian favored them with a grim smile that made him look more than ever like a Mafia don. "I thought I'd better find out what you people are playing at."

"How did you know where we were?" Richard demanded. "Did you follow me?"

"Good lord, no." Najarian shook his head in disgust. "You mentioned getting to lunch before the line got too long." At Richard's blank look he continued, "You're a restaurant owner, which means you're hardly the Burger King type, nor are you the type to eat alone. Where in Ann Arbor does one meet others for first-class food where one nevertheless must stand in line?" He spread his hands, and Anneke could practically see the word "elementary" hovering over his head.

"You're a real doctor, aren't you?" Charlie alone seemed unimpressed by Najarian's deductive tour de force.

"If you mean a medical doctor as opposed to a Ph.D., it happens that I'm both."

"So tell me, how long could a guy live with a flagpole in his gut?"

"I'm afraid you'll have to ask the coroner that question." Najarian's face darkened. "I came here to make sure all of you understand something. I have no intention of becoming the target of a group of post-adolescent Hardy Boys. If you follow me, call me, or harass me in any way, I will *make you sorry.*" He spit out the last words with such venom that Anneke flinched. Then, without another word, he turned and left.

"Now I do wonder," Charlie commented, "exactly what the wild hair is that he's got up his ass." He looked first thoughtful and then annoyed. "So bottom line, we got nothing," he grunted, shoving the last of his sandwich into his mouth. "Bubkas on the alumni, the Kaplan chick doesn't bother to show, and on top of it, I have to pay Ann Arbor prices for lunch." He stood up. "Never mind. This wasn't much of an idea in the first place."

Anneke watched him stomp off, glad to see him go. It was nearing one o'clock, she noted, and her worry over Zoe intensified. She'd worked with students long enough, she reminded herself, to know which ones were erratic and which were steady and responsible. For all her hyperactive energy, Zoe was in the latter category.

"I can't understand why Zoe isn't here," she said to Richard.

"Oh, I'm sure she just got held up by something." He looked as worried as Anneke felt, but he was gazing into the distance, in the direction that Najarian had taken.

TWENTY-NINE

What *had* Daniel Najarian been so upset about? Anneke wondered as she drove back to her office. She shook her head and tramped on the accelerator as she turned onto Huron, belatedly checking the rearview mirror for police cars.

The first thing she did back in her office was check her calendar for messages. When she saw only noncrisis business messages on screen, she picked up the phone and pressed Ken's extension.

"Ken, were there any messages for me besides the ones you posted?"

"No, that was all of it. Were you expecting something?"

"Not really." She hung up, reached for the University directory and looked up the number of the *Daily*. "Sports desk, please," she said when she was connected.

"Sports desk." A male voice came on the line.

"May I speak to Zoe Kaplan, please?"

"Sorry, she's not here. Can I take a message?"

"Is the sports editor there? Gabriel Marcus?"

"He's around somewhere," the voice said. "Hey, Marcus!" it shouted. "For you."

"This is Gabriel Marcus."

"This is Anneke Haagen," she said quickly. "We met yesterday." When he made a sound of recognition, she asked: "Have you seen Zoe today?"

"No, I haven't. Sorry."

"Is she expected in any time soon?"

"Not really, although she usually checks in around lunchtime."

"And you haven't heard from her?" Anneke's worry spiked sharply.

"No. Is something going down?" His voice quickened with interest.

"No, nothing like that," she said quickly. "Will you ask her to call me as soon as she gets there?"

"Sure. Look, if something's about to break, I can handle it. Zoe and I are on the same team, you know."

"Yes, I know. Just ask her to call me please?" She hung up the phone, swearing at the one-track mind of the reporter. On the other hand, there was no reason for him to suspect trouble. She wasn't sure herself why she felt such foreboding, but the feeling was becoming stronger by the minute.

She called Student Locator for Zoe's dorm number and when a girl answered she once again asked for Zoe.

"She's not here." This time the voice sounded sullen.

"Have you seen her this morning?"

"Me? She couldn't be bothered."

"Well, will you take a message for her please?" Taking the grunt at the other end of the telephone for assent, she asked the girl to have Zoe call her as soon as she got in.

"I'll leave the message on her desk," the girl said, "but don't hang by your thumbs waiting. Zoe's just too, too busy to bother with other people." The phone banged down and Anneke stared at the receiver. What on earth was that all about?

Zoe was probably in class, she told herself. She was a student, after all. She fought with herself for a moment and then called the *Daily* again. When Gabriel Marcus was back on the line, she asked, "Do you know if Zoe has a class now?"

"She has a three o'clock, but nothing right now," he said. "Look, is something wrong? You sound worried."

"No, nothing's wrong, I guess. It's just . . . Never mind, Gabriel. I'm sorry to bother you." She hung up and stared at the telephone, chewing on her lower lip in worried frustration. She could think of nowhere else to call. Finally she stood, picked up her briefcase and returned to the outer office.

"I'm going over to Karl's office," she told Ken. "If a Zoe Kaplan calls, would you please call me there and let me know?"

"Sure," Ken replied.

"Zoe Kaplan?" Marcia Rosenthal looked at her with wide-eyed curiosity. "Isn't that the *Daily* reporter who broke the NCAA story?" Anneke noted that Max, too, was staring at her. She gave them all a curt nod and hurried out of the office to avoid further questions.

She found herself looking over her shoulder uneasily as she walked through the Arcade and up the stairs of the Maynard parking structure to her car. She locked herself in and drove to City Hall even faster than usual, pulling into the parking lot with an absurd feeling of relief. After once again fighting her way past crowds of media people to Karl's office, she didn't waste words coming to the point.

"It's about Zoe."

"What about her?" Karl's voice was sharp.

"She's missing."

"What do you mean, missing?"

"She was supposed to meet us for lunch, and she never arrived." Now that she'd said it aloud, Anneke realized how foolish it sounded. "We'd arranged to meet at noon today at Zingerman's—Zoe, Richard Killian, and myself," she confessed, feeling her face redden under his tight-lipped gaze. "I'd promised to bring her a copy of the notes from last night," she said defensively. "Only, Zoe never showed up. Karl, she wouldn't have just skipped the meeting, not without calling. If nothing else, she wanted those notes."

"I imagine she just got busy with something else," Karl said with an irritated shrug. "She's probably at the *Daily.*"

"No. I called there. She missed an appointment with Gabriel Marcus, the sports editor, too. They haven't seen her all day, which is apparently unusual. Her roommate hasn't seen her, either. I left messages at both places, and I asked Ken to call me here if she returned my calls."

"Damn," he said grimly. "I knew that girl was going to be trouble."

"That's not fair," Anneke protested. "For one thing, we don't know yet that there *is* trouble. For another, you have to admit she gave you everything you asked for."

"Agreed, and irrelevant. Look, I like the girl, but she's a student, and she's a reporter, two categories that produce more pains in the ass per capita than any other group alive." He still, to Anneke's relief, looked more annoyed than worried. "And now I have to waste time searching for her."

"That's very probably entirely my fault, not hers."

"Also agreed." He smiled slightly to take the edge off his words, but Anneke felt her face redden. "Look, let's first check out the places she was expected to go." He had kept a copy of her notes, she realized; now he picked up the printout and read through it rapidly. "All right, she was supposed to interview Melissa Greenaway, Jeffrey Person, and Kyle Farmer." He riffled through a different sheaf of papers, picked up the phone, and dialed.

"Ms. Greenaway? This is Lieutenant Genesko, of the Ann Arbor police. I apologize for bothering you again. Have you spoken to a *Michigan Daily* reporter named Zoe Kaplan today?" He listened, then asked, "What time did she leave?" After a moment he hung up, dialed again, and waited for nearly a full minute before hanging up. He dialed a third time and said, "Jeffrey Person, please." When he was connected he once again identified himself and repeated the question, "Have you spoken to Zoe Kaplan today?" Finally he hung up and turned to Anneke.

"She left Melissa Greenaway around ten o'clock, at a guess. Take it with a grain of salt—the girl sounded completely stoned. Kyle Farmer's phone doesn't answer; he may be at practice, or at the training center, or almost anywhere. I can try him later, if necessary. Jeffrey Person says he hasn't heard from her at all."

"It's after two o'clock." Anneke checked her watch. "That means no one has seen her for almost five hours. Unless," she said suddenly, her throat catching, "one of them is lying."

"It's possible, of course. But honestly, I don't think there's any need to worry. Reporters and students are both notoriously unreliable, and in combination . . . " He threw up his hands. "Anyway, we'll follow up. Why don't you go back to your office? You'll probably hear from her before we do."

THIRTY

Unhappily, Anneke walked back to her car, wondering if Karl was letting his prejudices get in the way of his judgment. Of course some students were irresponsible, but she didn't think Zoe was one of them. On the other hand, suppose I've simply analyzed the situation wrongly? she asked herself. If Zoe did skip the lunch, what could the reason have been? The answer was immediately obvious—to chase down a story.

She slid into the Firebird but sat there without moving, following the chain of logic. Presumably Zoe was still working on the NCAA/murder story. All right, there were two places where the main players in that story could be found—the athletic department, and the Carlton Hotel. The athletic department could be checked by phone, but she couldn't very well call the hotel and ask them to search the whole place for one unregistered visitor. She backed the car out of its slot and headed it toward Plymouth Road and the Carlton.

But at the hotel there was no sign of Zoe. The restaurant was nearly empty; the lobby and its attached bar were filled with maize-

and-blue revelers, but Anneke searched in vain for Zoe's head of curly black hair. A few people sat on the outdoor patio, but Zoe wasn't among them either.

Anneke walked the length of the hotel, and then all the way around the outside perimeter, before giving up. Finally, she returned to the lobby and approached the desk.

"I'm trying to find a young woman who I think was here earlier," she told the man behind the high counter. "She's not a guest here, she's a student. Eighteen years old, about five foot three, with a lot of black, curly hair and unusual eyes, almost copper colored."

"Hey, yeah, I did see her." The clerk was barely beyond student age himself, short and skinny with a dark crew cut and an amiable, pock-marked face. "Awesome eyes."

"You did!" Anneke felt such a gust of relief that her legs felt weak. "When was she here?"

"Dunno the time, but it was this morning, because I'd just gotten back from my break. That'd make it around ten thirty, I guess. Maybe a little later, because I hadda wait for the doughnuts to get here—the bakery's always screwing up our order, 'cause they figure we're only staff, they can screw with us and nobody'll complain."

"Did you see where she went?" Anneke short-circuited his complaint, uninterested in the Carlton staff's doughnut problems.

"Sure. She just left her message and split."

"Message! What message?"

"Sorry, it wasn't for you." The clerk shook his head. "It was for one of the guests."

"Oh, of course." Anneke, belatedly crafty, nodded her head. "It must have been for Daniel Najarian."

"Nuh-uh. I think the name was Peoples, Peepers, something like that?"

"Peoples?" It took Anneke a second to get it. "Oh, of course." She forced a hearty laugh. "I'll bet you mean Jeffrey Person."

"Person! Yeah, that was it." The clerk joined in her laughter.

"You know," Anneke was now in full character, "I bet Jeffrey left a message for me. We were all supposed to meet this afternoon," she improvised on the fly, "only they forgot to let me know where they were going to be. Could you check for me? The name is Anneke Haagen, H-A-A-G-E-N," She spelled out automatically.

"Lemme take a look." The clerk tapped keys on his computer, then shook his head. "Nothing for you, sorry."

"Damn." Anneke tapped her fingers on the counter, arranging her face in an expression of anxiety without difficulty. "Where the hell could they be? I wonder," she said, miming a sudden idea, "do you think there's anything in the message the girl left for Jeffrey?"

The clerk glanced automatically toward the rack of numbered pigeonholes and then shook his head. "Sorry, the message is gone. Your guy must've picked it up."

"Damn," Anneke repeated more forcefully. "Well, thank you anyway. Where are your phones?" She headed in the direction he pointed, feeling slightly ill as she fitted data together. One: Zoe had left a message for Jeffrey Person. Two: The message had been picked up. Inescapable deduction: Jeffrey Person had lied when he said he hadn't heard from Zoe.

She started for the pay phone, stopped, and picked up the house phone instead. "Jeffrey Person, please," she said to the operator.

"Hello?" She recognized Person's Southern-tinged voice and heard a mutter of other voices in the background.

"May I speak to Zoe Kaplan, please?" she asked as coolly as she could manage, using her best businesswoman's voice.

"Sorry, there's no one here named Kaplan."

"Hey!" Zoe's voice called out, perfectly clear in the distance, as Jeffrey Person gently replaced the receiver.

Anneke had to dial the police number twice because her hands were shaking. "I've found her," she said without preamble when Karl came on the line.

"Tell me."

She told him where she was, and described her discussion with the desk clerk and her call to Person's room. When she was finished, there were several long moments of silence.

"Is your car outside?" he asked finally.

"Yes, of course. Why?"

"I want you to hang up the phone, go out to your car, and drive away. All right?"

"Yes, all right," she said reluctantly.

"Good. We're on our way." He hung up, and she obediently turned from the phone, headed outside and drove out of the parking lot. But when she reached the street, instead of turning left back toward town, she crossed Plymouth Road into the parking lot of a restaurant directly across the street. There she pulled into a slot facing the Carlton, and settled down to wait.

It didn't take long. She heard the siren in the distance, but the sound cut off before Karl's Land Rover came into view, carrying two people. She peeled the Firebird out of its parking spot and, when the Land Rover swung into the Carlton parking lot, she drove back across the street and pulled in behind it.

"Isn't there something about the spirit as well as the letter?" Karl asked when she caught up with him, but to her relief he looked more amused than angry.

"How do you want to handle it?" Brad Weinmann climbed out of the passenger seat and offered Anneke a sketchy wave, his youthful face intent and serious.

"Let's find out what the situation is first," Karl replied. He led the way into the hotel lobby and up to the desk, where the same clerk looked startled and then wide-eyed when Karl withdrew his badge and asked for the number of Jeffrey Person's room.

"It's room one-forty-three," the clerk said without having to consulting his computer this time. "Is there gonna be a bust?"

"Which way is the room?" Karl didn't bother to answer the question.

"That way." The clerk pointed, licking his lips.

"Inside or outside room?"

"Inside. That is, it faces an interior courtyard. You can get to the courtyard through those doors there," the clerk volunteered, pointing again. "One forty-three'll be the fifth door to the left."

Karl nodded at Brad, who trotted away through the indicated doors.

"Look, I better call the manager," the clerk said, as though suddenly realizing the seriousness of what was going on.

"By all means," Karl agreed. "But I don't really expect any trouble."

Brad reappeared through the doors, shaking his head. "Drapes are drawn," he said. "Can't see anything, and I couldn't get close enough to hear. There's a patio door, and a little concrete patio with a low fence around it. I was afraid if I went too close they'd hear me."

"Okay, we wait for backup then." Even as Karl spoke, Anneke saw two uniformed patrolmen enter the lobby. Brad motioned them over. One of them had curly red hair spilling out from under the back of his uniform cap; the other was the color of milky coffee with no hair visible at all. Neither of them looked more than sixteen years old, and both of them looked nervous.

"You made good time," Karl said to them, then to Anneke, "Please stay here in the lobby." He spoke quickly and quietly, in what she always thought of as his policeman's voice, the one that seemed to engender automatic obedience. "You two cover each end of the corridor," he told the two patrolmen. "Brad, you take the outside. I'll go to the door." He drew his gun, holding it close to his body with the barrel pointing toward the ceiling. Then all four of them nodded tensely at each other and trotted to their assignments, leaving Anneke standing in the lobby feeling both frightened and extraneous.

"Awesome." The desk clerk still had his hand on the house phone, but he seemed to have forgotten his original purpose of calling the manager. He licked his lips again with suppressed excitement, craning to see down the corridor. *He's acting like he's watching a television show,* Anneke realized. *To him, it isn't real. It doesn't occur to him that there's real danger.*

Even though he was a policeman, she'd never really worried about Karl before. In the nature of things a plainclothes detective in Ann Arbor, especially one whose work is primarily administrative, is rarely if ever in any danger. She'd become so accustomed to the gun under his jacket that she, too, had forgotten its reality. Now she felt her stomach twist in fear. Dry-mouthed, she eased around the corner until she could see down the hallway.

He stood to one side of the door, gun still in position. Reaching sideways, he knocked sharply and waited. There must have been a response from inside, because he said, "Lieutenant Genesko. Ann Arbor police." For a frozen second, Anneke saw the tension on his face, saw the knob turn, saw the door begin to open. Then Karl slammed through the door and disappeared inside; the two uniformed patrolmen ran toward the room; and finally there was a voice from inside.

"Jesus, Karl." Eleanor Sullivan's raspy voice carried down the hallway. "You really know how to make an entrance."

THIRTY-ONE

"We're four people in a private hotel room having a private conversation. When did they make that illegal?" Jeffrey Person was stonewalling. Zoe thought he was wrong, but she was waiting for the right moment.

"You are four suspects in a murder investigation," Genesko pointed out. "A former University Regent, a sports lawyer, a Michigan football player and a reporter—an unlikely group to be getting together for a casual pregame celebration. Your coach," he said to Kyle Farmer, "would be particularly interested in your presence here."

"Leave the boy alone, Karl." Eleanor Sullivan was stubbornly uncompromising, the light of battle in her eyes. "He won't crack either." He wouldn't, either, Zoe concluded. Farmer had that second-effort look on his face, like when he was fighting his way through half a dozen defenders for those couple of extra yards.

"All right, apparently we're going to have to do it the hard way." Genesko stood up, looming over them. "I'll have to ask all of you to come with me, please."

"Oh, phooey." Eleanor settled back in her chair defiantly.

"Mr. Person," Genesko said, "would you please confirm for Ms. Sullivan that I have the right to hold all of you as material witnesses to a murder?"

"A former Regent, an attorney, a football star and a reporter?" Person repeated his list back to him. "You'd be crazy to try it."

"Nevertheless. Will you all come with me, please."

If it's a bluff, it's a good one, Zoe decided. He's perfectly capable of taking us all in, all by himself. She had better things to do with the rest of the day than spend it in an interrogation room at City Hall.

There had been other cops behind Genesko, but they were gone now. After Genesko had catapulted into the room, scaring the shit out of everyone but Eleanor, they'd sorted it out a little—they'd been afraid she'd been kidnapped, for pete's sake—but when Genesko had asked what they were doing here, everyone had dummied up. Anneke had shown up too, with a sick look on her face that had changed to embarrassment and finally a kind of weird expression, like she wanted to laugh but didn't dare.

Zoe would have laughed too if she hadn't been so exasperated. She looked at her watch, then spoke finally for the first time since the argument began.

"Look, we've got to tell him what's going on. I think you all know it, too."

"Not until tomorrow." Jeffrey Person was being even more stubborn than Eleanor. "You agreed you'd hold it until then, to give us time to get everything in place before it goes public."

"I'm not talking about going public, I'm talking about getting clear with the cops," Zoe insisted. "If we don't get them off our backs," she pointed out shrewdly, "we'll spend the rest of the day like this and then you won't have *time* to get things in place."

"She's right." Kyle Farmer stared at Genesko. "I'd rather Coach heard the truth from me than sit around wondering if those lousy rumors are true."

"Good." Zoe didn't wait for objections from the other two conspirators. "I'll take care of it, then. You guys still have a lot of work to do. If you'll drive me back to the *Daily*," she told Genesko, "I'll give you all of it, on one condition. That you say nothing to anyone—and I mean *anyone*, cop or civilian—until five-thirty A.M. tomorrow morning."

"Why five thirty?" he asked curiously.

"Because that's when the *Daily* hits the streets."

"I see. So that's what you get out of it." He made a face, then nodded. "All right. If, as you've been insisting, it has nothing to do with the murder, certainly."

"Uh-uh." Zoe shook her head, stung by his obvious disgust but determined to follow through. "No loopholes. We know this has nothing to do with the murder, but it'd be easy for you to find something to open an escape hatch with. Look," she persisted as he shook his head, "if you go ahead and blow it anyway, we can't stop you. But if this gets out before tomorrow morning because of something you do, the people in this room will know you broke your word. That's all."

"No they won't, because I haven't given my word." He stood up. "All right, let's go."

This time she really didn't trust him, Zoe thought dispiritedly as they drove back to town, with her bike in the back of the Land Rover. Still, she didn't see where she'd had much choice. At her insistence, Anneke was following behind in her own car, but Zoe doubted that even her presence was going to help much.

To Zoe's relief, Gabriel was at the *Daily* when they arrived. They settled in at the big table in the library, with Cokes from the machine in front of them.

"We've got to stop meeting like this," Zoe said, eliciting smiles from Gabriel and Anneke but no reaction at all from Genesko. "Look, I know you think I'm being obstructive," she said to him, "but honestly, it wasn't that way at all. I got on to this by pure accident. I'm sorry I didn't call," she turned to Anneke, "but it just didn't occur to me that anyone would be worried."

"Please tell us what you know, Ms. Kaplan," Genesko said without expression.

"All right," she snapped, finally angry. "Apology not accepted. I guess I can live with that. Here's what you want to know in three words—college athletes' union." She leaned back and folded her arms. Gabriel looked absolutely stunned, and even Genesko looked gratifyingly surprised.

"Jesus, are you sure?" Gabriel asked.

"Give me some credit," Zoe snapped back. "Am I sure."

"How much have you got?" He licked his lips.

"The whole package."

"Holy shit." Gabriel sounded awestruck. "This week, darlin', is going to go down in *Daily* history." He leaped to his feet and dashed out of the library.

"So that's why he was there," Genesko said, to himself rather than to them.

"That's why who was where?" Zoe asked quickly. "When?"

"And how did you get involved in it?" he asked. Well, she hadn't expected an answer, so she wasn't really disappointed.

"I saw Kyle Farmer and Jeffrey Person driving through town together, and I followed them," she replied simply. "I thought it was evidence for the hot rumor going around. When I confronted them with that, they told me about the union organizing."

"So you know about the rumor, too," Genesko said.

"The Kyle Farmer rumor?" Gabriel bounded back into the library. "Is it true?"

"Of course it's not true, Gabriel," Zoe said scornfully. "It must have gotten started somehow as a spillover from the union thing." She stopped, thinking. "Could it be someone who found out about the union forming and was trying to get Farmer out of the picture? No, what would be the point of that?" She shook her head. "Anyway, I'm glad it isn't true."

"Because you've got a better story this way," Genesko pointed out.

"No! Because I think Kyle Farmer is a good guy. Jeez, you're an unforgiving bastard."

"Tell me about the union." This time Zoe thought she saw a hint of amusement on the big man's face. "And why they told you of all people about it."

"Well, it was sort of an accident, I guess."

It sounded so simple. Zoe didn't want to admit, even to herself, how scared shitless she'd been when Jeffrey Person yanked her into his hotel room. For a minute there, being an investigative reporter hadn't seemed like so much fun anymore. Then she saw the list on the bed. From where she stood, with Person's large hand still clutched around her upper arm, she could make out two columns, one headed "Locals Established," the other headed "Local Presidents." The first column contained the names of more than a dozen major universities, including Notre Dame, Berkeley, and Nebraska. And Michigan.

The word *locals*, plural, could mean only one thing. Zoe wasn't a union brat for nothing. She turned in Person's grasp and stared at him, seeing the whole scenario in one breathless moment.

"How many schools have you signed up so far?" she asked. "Are you going to be ready to go during the regular season, or are you holding off until bowl season? What percent participation are you expecting? Are any coaches in on it?"

"Oh, shit," Kyle Farmer groaned. "It's her. What are we going to do now?"

"Chill, Kyle." Person released Zoe's arm but remained standing with his back to the door.

"What we're going to do," Eleanor Sullivan spoke for the first time, "is give her the whole package, in exchange for her word that she won't publish until we say so." The look she gave Zoe was a challenge. "I think her word can be trusted."

"When I give it, yes," Zoe agreed. "But I don't think I can do that here."

"And why not?" Eleanor asked with interest.

"Because you're all kidding yourselves." She took two steps forward and plucked the list from the bed. "You've got—what—seventeen major colleges already involved." She counted down the column. "Each of them has nearly a hundred football players and God knows how many other athletes. You've probably got people recruiting at a couple of dozen other schools. And all those people have parents, and girlfriends, and roommates, and high school coaches, and—well, you get the idea. I don't know when you were planning to go public, but it better be soon—you've been mondo lucky already. The thing is," she overrode Person's incipient interruption, "I'd promise to hold it back if you could guarantee that it wouldn't break somewhere else. Only you can't. This is a balloon that's going to go up any day now, and you can't just expect me to sit on it."

"She's right." Eleanor nodded with every evidence of approval.

"Dammit, all right." Behind Jeffrey Person's clever, mobile face, Zoe could almost see the thought processes racing. "Look," he said to her, "we'll give you the lot. Just give us one more day."

"I can't." This time Zoe was embarrassed. "Tomorrow's Friday, and the *Daily* doesn't publish on weekends. If I don't go tomorrow, I don't go until Monday. And I can't—*you* can't hold it that long."

"Ah, hell, we're just about ready to announce anyway," Eleanor said. "There was always the risk that it would break prematurely, and the risk's been getting higher every day. And it could be worse, you know—we could've been blown by that antijock fascist on Channel Three, the one who thinks that all athletes should be grateful to the massa for giving them a chance to play."

"I suppose there are some advantages to having it break in the college press, too," Person said thoughtfully. "They're more likely to be sympathetic to the movement." He turned to Zoe. "We need to get in touch with our people, to let them know it's going down. That means you don't say word one to anyone until it hits the paper."

"Except for my editor, you have my word," she agreed this time. "What's more, if you want me to, I can hang around for a while and help you write up the press material."

"All right." Eleanor rubbed her hands gleefully. "It's showtime. Jeffrey, you get on the phone while I fill Zoe in on the background."

"The thing is, I gave them *my* word that it wouldn't break until tomorrow morning," she said to Genesko. "They need to contact all their people, prepare press materials, generally get ready for the explosion. So if you don't keep it locked down until then, you'll be breaking my word, even if you aren't breaking your own."

"A college athletes' union." Genesko sat and thought. "What are their basic demands?"

"Number one, an equitable spending allowance." Zoe held up fingers, counting off the demands. "Second, student-athlete representation on all NCAA committees. Third, player input on issues like scheduling and training limits. And one biggie." She made a fist. "The right to profit from their own person."

"You mean," Gabriel asked, "they want the right to get money for endorsements, posters, personal appearances, things like that?" When Zoe nodded, he gave a low whistle. "That's going to make waves."

"All it does," she pointed out, "is put them on an equal footing with every other college student. If I can sell a story to a magazine, why can't they sell a poster? Anyway, they may as well go for the whole package, because they're in for a bloody fight no matter what kind of demands they make. After all, nobody gives up power and money without a fight. That's what unions are all about." She looked at Genesko. "Well? What about it?"

"I plan to interrogate Jeffrey Person, Kyle Farmer, and Eleanor Sullivan," he said carefully, "but at the moment I have no plans to discuss this matter with anyone else."

"Y'know," Zoe said, pushing back her chair and standing up, "you're not nearly as grim as you try to look." She grinned at the expression on his face. "Anneke, could I ask you some questions about this Farmer rumor?"

"Me?" Anneke looked alarmed.

"Just the computer stuff—how it could have been planted, and like that."

"I suppose so, although I can't tell you very much."

"I'm going back to the department," Genesko told Anneke. "Enjoy yourself."

He seemed to mean it, Zoe thought as she led Anneke out of the library and through the city room. Gabriel was scrambling through sheets of page dummies, scrawling viciously with his pencil. Katie Sparrow was standing behind him demanding to know what the big story was. When she saw Zoe she aimed a half-amused, half-envious glare in her direction.

"What now, Kaplan? You breaking the start of World War III?"

"Nope." Zoe flashed her a grin. "Just the end of civilization as we know it. C'mon over here," she said to Anneke, "where we can get what passes for peace and quiet around here." She looked around the city room, seeing the mess of papers and books, the discarded food and clothing, the scarred counters and battered terminals, the couple of dozen people sitting at or on top of desks, or pounding up and down corridors, or shouting back and forth to each other across the huge room. "What a zoo this place is," she said with absolute pleasure.

THIRTY-TWO

The tensions of the afternoon had left Anneke feeling exhausted and drained, yet paradoxically wanting to go back to the office. Partly, it was the *Daily*, she realized. The level of excitement, the sheer energy, the sense of shared purpose left her oddly envious. When was the last time, she wondered, that I felt that excited about anything?

She wouldn't be able to get any real work done, she admitted to herself, turning the Firebird south toward home. What she needed was a hot bath and a cold drink. But as she pulled the Firebird to the curb in front of the house on Olivia she saw a figure standing on the porch.

Oh, hell, what now? she thought crossly as she stepped out of the car, and then, with a sudden smile: "Michael! What are you doing here? I haven't seen you in ages." It was true, she realized. Michael Rappoport was an antique dealer who specialized in Victoriana, an old and treasured friend whom she hadn't seen in a long time. Too long.

"Well, since you wouldn't return my phone calls, I decided I'd simply have to commit the social solecism of dropping in uninvited." Michael's impossibly handsome face wore a smile that almost contradicted the sternness of his words.

"What phone calls?" Anneke asked.

"I called you twice last week. Didn't you get my messages?"

"No." She shook her head, confused. "As far as I know, my machine's in working order."

"I didn't leave them on your answering machine. I talked to your maid."

"Oh." That made three messages in the last month that Marianne hadn't given her—three that she knew of, that is. Too many to be accidental. "I'm sorry, Michael. It's been . . ." She sighed. "Please, come on in and let me give you the grand tour."

"I thought you'd never ask." But once inside, he stood perfectly still in the wide front hall for several moments before speaking. "Not bad at all. Nineteen twenty?"

"Twenty-two."

"Hmm. Not Victorian, of course, but a lot of elegance. Style." He ran his hand over the elaborately carved woodwork surrounding the open doorway to the living room, then lifted a latch and pulled. An oak-framed door of beveled glass panes slid out from its concealment in the wall. "Pocket doors. Nice. You'll have all this woodwork refinished, of course," he stated.

"Some year."

"Call Les Castagna when you're ready," Michael told her, and Anneke filed the name away in the back of her head; if Michael recommended a refinisher, she'd take his word for it. "Now," he went on, "show me the rest of it."

Anneke led him into the living room, feeling idiotically nervous as he moved from room to room almost silently, pausing now and then to examine a mantelpiece or run his delicate fingers over Karl's Queen Anne dining table.

"My office is through here." She took him through the kitchen and across the back hall, opened the door to the former dining room, and stopped dead in the doorway. Marianne, dust rag and spray cleaner in hand, was scrubbing industriously at the monitor screen of her computer.

"Marianne," Anneke struggled to keep her voice level, "I've asked you several times not to clean any of my computer equipment. That cloth will leave scratches on the screen."

"Sorry, Miss Haagen." Marianne picked up her cleaning caddy and turned away, but not before Anneke saw the flash of malice on her face. Michael raised one eyebrow at her retreating back but said nothing.

"Breaking-in period." Anneke made what she hoped was an amused grimace.

"Oh? Well. Why don't you show me the upstairs." He said nothing more as he examined the second floor, beyond an acid comment about the pumpkin-colored tile in one of the bathrooms. Back downstairs, he returned to the living room and ran his practiced eye over the furniture once again.

"Queen Anne table and chairs," he cataloged aloud. "Georgian breakfront. That chest next to the sofa, if I'm not mistaken, is pre–Civil War American. Superb pieces. And the house," he waved an arm to encompass the whole, "is wonderful."

"I'm delighted you like it." Anneke felt an absurd gust of relief. Michael's opinion was important to her.

"I have only one question." He faced her squarely. "When are *you* moving in?"

"When . . . What on earth are you talking about?"

"Don't pretend to misunderstand me." He glared at her. "This is a wonderful house filled with marvelous things. But aside from your office, there isn't a single, solitary iota of *you* anywhere in it."

"But I didn't have anything," she protested angrily. "Everything I owned went up in flames, remember?"

"And what have you bought with the insurance money? T-bills?"

The barb was so close to the truth that Anneke reddened. "That's not fair. You said yourself, it's a beautiful house. Besides, I don't spend that much time here."

As soon as the words were out she wanted them back. Michael

stared at her without expression for what felt like a very long time. "If you don't put something of yourself into your home," he said finally, "it can never *be* a home. Now," he said, changing the subject firmly, "have you heard the latest about Carolyn Herbert?"

They chatted for a while about various scandalous doings in the Ann Arbor antiques world—Michael attracted gossip like a magnet—and made arrangements to meet for lunch the following week. Then, after walking him to the door, Anneke started toward her office, stopped, and forced herself to return to the living room, where she sank down on the sofa and examined her surroundings closely. Brown velvet sofa, the only contemporary piece in the room; two wing chairs upholstered in crewel-patterned linen; polished dark wood tables and cabinets; one good-sized oriental rug on the refinished oak floors. On the brass-trimmed coffee table, one large modern pottery vase in tones of gold and brown, a handsome square leather box, and an antique brass bowl.

It was a beautiful room. She couldn't wait to get out of it, back to her own spare, white office. Only when Karl was here did she feel at home in this room.

How on earth did I let this happen? she asked herself in dismay. And more to the point, what do I do about it? It was a question that clearly called for large amounts of caffeine. She stood up and started for the kitchen, then halted at the slight clatter of sound from within. Damn. She'd forgotten about Marianne. With a sigh, she turned and headed toward her office.

And stopped.

Back in the seventies, when working women were first beginning to move out of clerical ghettos into management positions, several how-to books recommended that the first thing a woman should do when she took over in a new job was to fire somebody. First, to prove to everyone else that she had the balls to do it. Second, to prove to *herself* that she was in control of her own world.

The books also offered advice on how and when to perform the execution. Anneke checked her watch and was relieved to see that it was nearly four thirty. Squaring her shoulders, she crossed the hall and pushed open the kitchen door, where Marianne, to her relief, was just putting on her coat.

"Are you leaving, Marianne?" she asked.

"Yes, Miss Haagen." Marianne picked up her purse and started for the door, brushing past Anneke with a finely judged mixture of avoidance and contempt.

"Just a minute before you go, please," Anneke halted her.

"Yes, Miss Haagen?" Marianne turned in the doorway, her purse clutched in front of her. Without changing her usual impassive expression, she nevertheless managed to convey impatience.

"I'm afraid," Anneke declared firmly, "that we won't be using your services any further after today." She held out her hand, relieved to see that it was rock-steady. "If I could have your house keys, please?"

"You mean you're firing me?" Marianne's eyes widened, then narrowed. "You can't fire me. I don't work for *you*, I work for the lieutenant."

"Ah, but you see," Anneke said pleasantly, "your job was to work for both of us. And since you don't seem able to do that, I have to let you go. I'll send you a check for one month in lieu of notice." She kept her hand extended. "May I have the key, please?"

"Just you wait till he finds out." Marianne dragged a set of keys out of her purse, her face dark with anger. "He's gonna be real mad, and you're gonna be real sorry." She hurled the keys at the kitchen counter, where they bounced against the toaster and clattered to the floor. Anneke ignored them. "The lieutenant isn't gonna want to eat *your* cooking," Marianne declared spitefully.

"God forbid." Anneke laughed aloud. "Thank you for your work here, Marianne. I'll see you out."

Only after she'd escorted Marianne to the door and shut it firmly after her did Anneke consider the woman's barbs. Shouldn't she have discussed it with Karl before firing Marianne out of hand? After all, say what she might, Marianne had worked for Karl rather than for her. And for that matter, who *would* do the cooking and cleaning now? Obviously, neither she nor Karl could manage a house this size with their workloads. She returned to the kitchen and was relieved to see the oven set on low and a beef stew quietly simmering within. Well, they could get through the weekend, anyway. She'd simply start calling agencies on Monday.

THIRTY-THREE

As it turned out, in fact, the stew went into the freezer. Karl called at six to say he'd be working late, and Anneke microwaved a baked potato, topped it with slices of chive-spiced cheddar cheese, and ate at her desk with guilty pleasure, surfing the Internet between bites. She discovered a Web home page set up by a young San Francisco 49ers fan, which led her to a Pittsburgh Steelers site, which led to a rec.sports.philosophy newsgroup. Then, munching one of Marianne's admittedly superb brownies, she tracked down a gopher site in California that listed seismic retrofit projects to be let out for bids in the next six months, exactly the sort of data a small Ann Arbor electrical supply company was looking for.

Only when she finally logged off, at nearly midnight, did she realize how tired she was. She tried to wait up for Karl, sitting up in bed watching a breathless actress explain to David Letterman how exhausting it was to work six whole hours a day for four whole weeks at a stretch. But somewhere between a description of an artistically necessary nude scene and a particularly obnoxious commercial for a long-distance telephone service, she must have fallen asleep. When she woke, sun was leaking through the edges of the drapes and the bed next to her was still empty.

No, not still, again, she realized after a moment of disorienting panic. Karl's side of the bed had been slept in, at least. The bedside clock said seven o'clock; she stood up, feeling sleep-heavy and still obscurely uneasy. Throwing on a robe, she padded barefoot downstairs. Karl was there, she saw with an unaccountable sense of relief, sitting at the dining table drinking coffee and reading the newspaper.

"Good morning," he greeted her with a smile. "Coffee?"

"God, yes. Thank you." She sank into the chair opposite and filled a cup from the coffeepot, burying her face in the steam and inhaling gratefully before she drank. "What time did you get in last night?"

"Around one." He waited while she drank more coffee. "Here." He handed her the newspaper. "I went out to pick up a *Daily*. And there are chocolate croissants."

"I may have to keep you." She smiled at him, took the paper in one hand and reached for a croissant with the other. "What does the story say?"

"More or less what we've already heard."

For the second straight day, Zoe's byline appeared under a screaming banner headline. This one read

COLLEGE ATHLETES TO FORM COLLECTIVE BARGAINING UNIT

By Zoe Kaplan

© Copyright 1996 *The Michigan Daily*

Athletes at seventeen major universities will announce today the formation of a collective bargaining organization, to be called the United College Athletes of America, with the intent of establishing negotiations with the National Collegiate Athletic Association.

Kyle Farmer, Michigan's superstar running back, will lead the Michigan group until elections can be held.

The list of included schools read like a Top 25 football poll, the list of player representatives like a Who's Who of college sports. "Wow." Anneke looked up from the paper.

"They certainly did their homework," Karl commented.

"Yes, but I wonder about them creating a formal labor union," she said. "I mean, I'm more or less on their side, I think, but are they really 'workers' in the union sense?"

"Absolutely." He nodded firmly. "These aren't kids who are just playing at some extracurricular activity; they're working their way through school. It's equivalent to graduate students who work as teaching and research assistants, and they're represented by a union."

"You're right; I never thought of it that way." She was about to ask him if he thought they were prepared to strike, when Kyle Farmer's name popped out at her again. This time the headline type was much smaller, over a one-column story that began just above the fold.

KYLE FARMER TARGET
OF ON-LINE RUMOR

Michigan running back Kyle Farmer was the apparent victim yesterday of what a local computer consultant referred to as a "Flash Rumor" disseminated on Confer.

The rumor accused Farmer of accepting money to remain in school for his senior year. According to both police and NCAA sources, there is absolutely no evidence to suggest that the rumor is anything but a practical joke or prank.

Computer expert Anneke Haagen explained that anyone with a working knowledge of Confer would be able to plant such a rumor, and that the original source

> would be virtually impossible to trace. She compared the spread of such on-line rumors to author Larry Niven's conception of "Flash Crowds."
>
> Kyle Farmer himself was not available for comment. Coach Ro Roczynski has sequestered the entire football team and closed all practices until after Saturday's game against Wisconsin.

The story said little more except to reiterate the absence of evidence against Farmer. "She asked me if she could quote me, of course," Anneke said uncomfortably, "but it's different when you actually see it in print."

"It is, isn't it." Karl let a short pause make his point. "You might want to compare her story to this one," he suggested, handing her the sports section of the *Detroit Free Press.* He pointed to a large, two-column story that was headed

RUMORS LINK FARMER
TO UM FOOTBALL SCANDAL

By Cliff Dobie

> The University of Michigan's computer conferencing system, known as Confer, was awash yesterday with rumors that Kyle Farmer, star running back, had accepted money from an unnamed alumnus to play out his senior year on the Wolverine football team. University spokesmen say they have no idea how the rumor began and maintain they know nothing about the accusation.

"Amazing." Anneke placed the two stories physically side by side and stared down at them. "How can two stories be so much alike and mean such different things?"

"Nuance is everything. Your Zoe was trying to protect Farmer. The *Free Press* reporter was trying to be 'objective.' "

"She isn't 'my' Zoe. And the *Free Press* reporter *isn't* being objective, he's being neutral, which is entirely different. His absolute neutrality is actually suggesting that the rumor may or may not be true." She made a face. "You know, if he'd gotten an anonymous letter about this, he wouldn't have printed a word without some sort of corroboration. But when the anonymous letter is dumped on-line, it becomes news."

"On the other hand," Karl pointed out, "the *Daily* story couldn't be called value-neutral, either."

"Yes, but in the end it's more accurate," she insisted. "Oh, hell." She shoved both newspapers aside and finished the last of her croissant. "Have you made any progress on the investigation?"

"Not so you'd notice it."

"It's still hard to believe that someone in that group at the stadium could be a murderer." Anneke sipped coffee moodily. "I mean, can you imagine Eleanor Sullivan killing someone?"

"Actually, I think I could." He laughed at the look of surprise on her face. "Don't let that little-old-lady appearance fool you—Eleanor is one tough broad. She also has a handgun permit, and I have no doubt she'd use it without blinking if she were threatened."

"That's different, surely," Anneke protested.

"Yes, it probably is. Still, if there's one thing you learn as a cop, it's that you can't ever assume that someone 'isn't the type' to commit murder."

"No, I suppose not. But not everyone is equally likely to commit a *particular* murder. Would Eleanor kill merely to protect her reputation?"

"I doubt it, but I can't eliminate her purely on my gut instinct."

"And the others, too. The great Daniel Najarian, killing someone this way?"

"Ego," Karl said promptly. "The fixed belief that he is vastly better—and therefore more important, more *valuable*—than other people."

"All right, but what about Frank Novak?" She wasn't sure why she was protesting so strongly. "He's such a . . . a teddy bear of a man."

"Who thinks of Michigan as his family," Karl pointed out. "How far will a man go to protect his family?"

"Damn. I suppose you're right. And Wendy Coleman might kill to protect Kyle Farmer."

"And Jeffrey Person or Richard Killian—or Kyle himself, for that matter—might kill to protect themselves." He looked at her over his coffee cup. "Remember, this was an opportunistic crime, not a planned one. The murderer didn't wait, or didn't have time, for second thoughts. Sometimes people commit spontaneous acts that they'd never do if they gave themselves time to think it through."

"I suppose," she said again. "What about all the other people in the stadium?" she went on. "Have you really cleared all of them?"

"Not cleared, exactly, but set aside to some extent. The TV people seem to be out of it. There were only four of them there Wednesday morning, and they were all either together or with Frank or me all morning. We identified five Plant Department employees in the stadium at the time, and three security guards, and none of them seems to have even the remotest connection to football, or recruiting, or the athletic department. We're still investigating, of course, but I really don't think anything will come of it."

"Well, what about that little cluster of people you had on the other side of the stadium?"

"There were seven of them all together," he said. "One group of five was a husband and wife and three children. The oldest boy is a high school junior looking over colleges he might want to apply to. They were basically just sightseeing."

"And the other two?"

He grinned. "Husband and wife, in their late sixties. He was showing her the site of the greatest moment in his life, when he scored the game-winning touchdown in Michigan Stadium."

"Well?" she demanded. "Isn't that a connection to Michigan football?"

His grin widened. "He scored the touchdown for Ohio State."

"Oh, hell." Anneke managed a laugh. "All right, I give up. So if you continue to assume Greenaway was at the stadium to meet someone who had to be there for some other reason, you're back to square one."

"Afraid so." He drained his coffee and stood up. "I'd better get going. It's going to be a long and probably ugly day."

"With the banquet at the end of it," she reminded him. "Which you are damn well going to enjoy," she added severely. She thought for the fourth time about telling him she'd fired Marianne, and for the fourth time decided to wait for a better moment, jeering at her own cowardice.

"Yes, ma'am." He grinned at her. "Are you going to those seminars?"

"I don't know. I suppose." She had wanted to go, but somehow her office sounded infinitely preferable. "I'll go to the Virtual Reality session, at least."

"Good. I'll meet you back here at six o'clock."

After he left, she pulled open the drapes behind the dining table, usually left closed because the window they covered was barely ten feet from the neighboring house. Outside, on the small mulberry tree growing between the houses, a squirrel perched on a low branch peering in at her. He had something clutched between his front paws, Anneke saw; an acorn, probably. Fall was the busy season for squirrels, after all. But no, it was the wrong color. In fact, it was blue, a small blue plastic spiny object that she recalled was known as a Nerf ball. As Anneke watched, the squirrel rolled over on his back, held the blue Nerf ball aloft, and proceeded to pummel it with his back feet. After a few moments of this, the little creature rolled himself right side up, scampered across to another branch, and repeated the game. Finally he stood up on his hind legs, dangled the Nerf ball from one paw, and very deliberately dropped it to the ground, raced headfirst down the trunk of the tree, grabbed the ball in his teeth and went straight back up the tree until he disappeared from Anneke's line of sight.

Well, even squirrels are entitled to take time off from work, she thought, laughing aloud all by herself and wishing Karl had been there to see the squirrel antics with her. Hell, even computer consultants need some downtime. When *had* she last taken time off from work? But I haven't wanted to, she thought defensively, and then asked herself suddenly, Why not?

She poured herself another cup of coffee and tried to analyze the question. H/A, Inc., was busier than it had ever been, thanks largely to the explosive growth of Internet activity. She wasn't just burying herself in work; she was legitimately busy.

Yes, but why am I accepting so many contracts? She'd always maintained a careful workflow, aware that the kind of operation she ran could easily be swamped by overextending itself. Yet right now, she realized, they were in danger of doing exactly that. What's more, instead of hiring more staff, or making a conscious decision to expand, she was simply taking on more and more of the workload herself. But I'm enjoying the work, she argued with herself, and asked, Why aren't you enjoying other things as well? and had no answer. With a sigh, she put down the coffee cup and headed upstairs to get dressed. She would go to the seminars, and she would bloody well force herself to enjoy them.

THIRTY-FOUR

"Zoe! It's him! Zoe, wake *up*!"

Zoe forced one eye open and tried to focus on the fuzzy outline of her roommate's face. "Whu? What time is it?"

"Eight thirty. Never mind that," Paula said impatiently to Zoe's squawk of outrage. "*Parker Bolling* is on the phone for you."

"Parker? You mean the stud muffin from American Political History?" Zoe snapped awake, ignoring the fact that she hadn't gotten in until nearly two A.M. the night before. "You're joking." She jerked herself to a sitting position and instinctively reached up to fluff out her hair. With her other hand she grabbed the phone receiver from Paula's grasp.

"Hi, Parker," she said, keeping her voice casual.

"Hi, Zoe." He had a voice like silk, as befitted a politician-in-training. He was also semibrilliant, semirich, and altogether gorgeous. "Sorry to call so early, but a frat brother just dropped two Crash Worship tickets on me, and I wondered if you'd like to go."

"Sounds great," Zoe said coolly, pumping her arm in the air and grinning maniacally. Across the room, Paula mouthed a silent war whoop.

"Terrific," Parker said. "I'll pick you up at seven thirty, okay?"

"Seven thirty? You mean tonight?" Zoe's heart sank with a thud. "Oh, *shit.* Parker, I can't go tonight. I have to cover a testimonial dinner for Karl Genesko."

"You have to do what?" She could hear the disbelief in his voice; women didn't say no to Parker Bolling.

"I have to cover this dinner. For the *Daily.*"

"Let them get someone else."

"I can't. It's not a 'them,' it's me. It's my story. Honestly, I would if I could. Let's make it some other time, okay?"

"Okay, sure. Some other time."

Yeah, right. In my dreams, Zoe thought, hanging up the phone glumly.

"Zoe, you just blew off *Parker Bolling.*" Paula's voice held a mixture of shock and accusation.

"I didn't blow him off. I have to work. In fact, I've got about a week's worth of stuff to do today."

"You'll be here for the TGIF, won't you?"

"Not a chance." Zoe shook her head. Hell, if she'd passed up a date with Parker Bolling, she sure wasn't going to find the time for a monthly dorm mixer.

"Zoe, you promised," Paula said, her face stormy.

"Paula, you don't need me there." Shit, she had promised, Zoe recalled, feeling the all-too-familiar spiral of guilt and resentment. "You'll make out better on your own. Guys don't like to come over if they see two women together."

"If you don't want to go with me, just say so," Paula snapped. "I should have known you wouldn't keep your promise." She flounced out of the room, leaving Zoe sitting on her bed in angry frustration.

At least there's no weekend paper, she thought as she climbed the slate staircase to the city room shortly after eleven, having miraculously made it to her ten o'clock class.

"Oh, good." Gabriel caught up with her as she reached the upper landing. "There's a call for you on line two. Actually, the phone's been ringing off the hook for you all day," he added as they trotted down the aisle to the sports desk, "but I think you probably want to take this one. It's Wendy Coleman."

"Farmer's girlfriend. Right." She picked up the phone. "Zoe Kaplan here."

"This is Wendy Coleman." There was a pause so long that Zoe wondered if they'd been disconnected. "I . . . wanted to thank you for the way you wrote about that rumor. About Kyle."

"I just wrote it the way it was."

"No, you did more than that." Wendy's voice was stronger now. "You bothered to go out and *find out* how it was."

"How're the union preparations going?" Zoe changed the subject, more uncomfortable with praise from a subject than she would have been with anger. It made her wonder if she'd subconsciously slanted the story to protect Kyle Farmer.

"Well, the official press conference is at one o'clock."

"I know." She wouldn't bother to go. ESPN was televising it live, and she'd arranged to tape it. By Monday, the next time the *Daily* came out, it would be old news. "I assume Kyle's in hiding until then."

"More or less. Ro's closed practice to the media, so he's okay there. But it's going to be rough on him."

"Yeah. Look," Zoe said impulsively, "if you need a place to hide out for a while, the *Daily*'s pretty empty today. You or Kyle, or both of you."

"I don't know. Maybe. Thanks."

"No problem." She hung up and turned to Gabriel. "Anything going on so far that I should know?"

"Nothing to know. Ro's got the team sequestered until after the game tomorrow. The official word is that nobody has anything to say until after the official announcement, and then they'll 'have to study the matter' first. How about you? Anything new at your end?"

"You mean besides having to pass on the hottest date of the year?" she said bitterly. "You'll never know what I just gave up for the greater glory of the *Michigan Daily.*"

"Join the club." His grin was wholly unsympathetic. "Why do you think most *Daily* people only date other *Daily* people? We're the only ones who can put up with each other, that's why. Besides," he added pointedly, holding up the day's paper, "you wouldn't trade *this* for a date with Tom Cruise."

"You're probably right," she admitted. "Is that healthy, do you think?"

"Who knows? Ask me again in twenty years." He paused, but made no move to leave. Finally, he said, "There is something else."

"What is it?" Zoe was instantly suspicious.

"We've decided to go to team coverage on the Greenaway story. Russ Blake from the news staff will handle the murder investigation, you'll handle the NCAA part of it." He stepped back a pace, as if waiting for an explosion.

It didn't come. "I suppose that makes sense," Zoe admitted, grinning at Gabriel's visible relief. "I am getting kind of overextended. Is Blake here?"

"Not right now."

Gabriel shook his head. "He's got classes all day." Zoe almost snorted, then thought better of it. Friday, with no paper to get out, was the one day *Daily* staffers tried to get to class. And Russ Blake had done some good stuff. "He said he'd get together with you tomorrow," Gabriel said. "We'll want to run a full update for Monday's paper."

"Okay. I'll pull my notes together for him this afternoon. Oh, hell."

"What's the matter?"

"I forgot to get that printout from Wednesday night."

"What printout?"

She described the events in the Carlton restaurant, including the apparent mugging of Anneke. "That's totally off the record, by the way. Anyway, I was supposed to get a copy of the notes she took, but I got sidetracked by the union story. Oh, and Richard Killian," she recalled suddenly. "He was going to do some research for me, and I never got back to him either." She shook her head, embarrassed. "I guess I do have a little more on my plate than I can handle."

"Richard Killian?" Gabriel cocked his head. "He was here about an hour ago."

"Oh, shit. Did he leave a message for me?"

"Just to tell you he'd come by. He wandered around for ten minutes or so talking about some story he did back in the sixties or seventies—ticket scalping or something. I figured he was just doing the alumni thing."

"Probably was. He was getting pretty soggy with nostalgia the other night."

"It's a big alumni weekend, too," Gabriel pointed out. "We'll probably have a few of them come through today and tomorrow." They would, of course, be unfailingly polite to these wandering *Daily* alumni, but they did sometimes get in the way.

"Right. I better give Killian a call." Zoe dumped her bookbag on an empty desk. "And I'll get hold of that printout. Then I need to do some heavy-duty background research for the players' union story." She sighed theatrically, pulled a notebook from her bookbag and attacked the phone, but with little success. Richard, not surprisingly, wasn't in his hotel room, and Anneke was neither at her office nor her home. The NCAA had no comment "until such time as we have received formal notice"; neither did any of the presidents, athletic directors, or head coaches of any of the schools on Jeffrey's current union list. Everyone in the college sports world was running for cover.

She made a dozen futile calls, spent what seemed like three days on hold, and then raced across to Angell Hall for her one o'clock psych lecture. From there she went to the basement of Nat Sci for an Urban Ecology quiz, and finally back to the *Daily*, with a quick stop at a sandwich shop on the way.

"You know, this would be a great school if it weren't for the classes," she said to Katie Sparrow as she dumped her bookbag on a vacant desk.

"Isn't that the straight," Katie agreed.

"Where's my list?" Zoe dragged papers out of her bookbag with one hand and unwrapped the sandwich with the other. "God, I'm starved." She took a bit of tuna salad and glared at the notebook in front of her. "I better see the tape of the press conference before I call the rest of them." She tilted her chair back on its hind legs and propped her feet on the desk, thinking as she ate.

Right. Her chair dropped to the floor with a thud. What was the point of being a union brat if she couldn't use it? She grabbed the phone, called Detroit information, dialed, and was shortly talking to Joe Sawicki, an old family friend who just happened to be the number three or four man (she could never remember which) in the UAW.

"It's going to raise some very interesting questions," he said when she explained her interest. "Even defining the bargaining unit is going to be a problem."

"What do you mean?"

"Look, the first step in forming a new collective bargaining unit is to file a statement of intent. That statement has to declare *exactly* what group of workers will be represented by the new unit. That defines everything else. But in this case, how would you define your group?"

"All college athletes? No, wait, that's too broad, isn't it? Okay, all scholarship athletes in Division One-A schools."

"Not impossible," he said grudgingly. "But what about walk-ons—athletes who play for a team but aren't receiving scholarships? What about redshirt freshmen—who *are* receiving scholarships but aren't officially on the team because they're sitting out their freshman year? And are you going to include every intercollegiate sport, including golf and fencing and polo? Yes, there are college polo teams. Or are you just going to include the major sports? Because the interests of, say, basketball players and swimmers are very different."

"That's true," Zoe admitted.

"Good. Now," Sawicki continued, "there's also the problem of defining the employ*er* unit. Consider the players on the Michigan football team. Their 'employer' is functionally the University of Michigan Athletic Department, just as a Penn State player is 'employed' by Penn State. But this particular collective bargaining unit is going to have to negotiate with the NCAA, because that's where the rules are made. And in terms of labor law," he said thoughtfully, "I'm not sure the NCAA can be said to exist. Fascinating. I think I'll have to give Jeffrey Person a call."

"If you do, and anything comes of it, you call me first, okay?" She thanked him profusely, then hung up and stared at her notebook for a while. She now had a whole new list of questions for Jeffrey Person, but she'd better view the tape of the press conference first. She stood up and looked around. The city room was nearly empty. Katie Sparrow was gone; a couple of people sat bent over textbooks in the far corner of the Business Staff area; and Charlie Cassovoy was walking down the center aisle toward her.

Well, weaving, really. He dropped his briefcase on the floor at the end of the aisle and leaned against the oak cabinet, both hands flat on the wide countertop, peering at her from red-rimmed eyes.

"You got another big one for tomorrow?" Despite his condition, his voice was as steady and irascible as ever. "Or you gonna take a day off?"

"You're drunk, Cassovoy."

"Drunk?" He considered the accusation seriously. "Not really. I will be later, of course, but not now. You must be feeling pretty special."

"Damn straight I am."

"Good. You should enjoy it while you've got it." He seemed entirely serious. "You're not a bad kid. I feel kind of sorry for you."

"You're just jealous, Cassovoy," she retorted, made uneasy by the oddity of his manner.

"Jealous?" This too he seemed to consider. "No, I don't think so. I was, but I'm not anymore. Y'know," he said conversationally, "the biggest story of my life came when I was twenty-seven years old. You're . . . what? Nineteen?"

"Eighteen."

"Even worse. How does it feel to know your whole life is gonna be downhill from here?" It wasn't a cynical jab; he was really waiting for an answer, and for a moment Zoe felt a chill of belief. "You know what my biggest story was last year?" he went on. "Whether a couple of Eastern Michigan basketball players were holding illegal practice sessions before the season began. And you wanna know the worst part of it? They weren't." This time he didn't seem to wait for a response, for which Zoe was more than glad since she didn't have one. "See ya around, kid." Charlie picked up his briefcase and stumped away down the aisle.

Jeez, Zoe thought, if I ever get to that point I hope someone shoots me. Twitching her shoulders in disgust, she scrambled her papers together, shoved them back into her bookbag, and headed back to the dorm to change for the Genesko dinner.

THIRTY-FIVE

It wasn't easy to make virtual reality boring, but Henry Baker had managed it, spending most of his time warning his audience about what it wouldn't do instead of telling (or showing) them what it would. When it was finally over, Anneke almost decided to go to the office; it took an annoyingly strong effort of will to force her footsteps away from the comforting confines of the Nickels Arcade. After lunch she was scheduled for the Old English Dictionary seminar, a project in complex semantics that usually fascinated her, but today she couldn't face it. On a whim, she headed instead toward Margaret Rohr's session in the Museum of Art.

Rohr had draped the entire room in flaming red satin. The *entire* room—walls, floor, ceiling, chairs, even, as it turned out, the audience. At the door, each participant was required to don a hooded red satin cloak. At that point, Anneke very nearly fled; only, having come this far, she decided she might as well go through with it, as an exercise in self-discipline if nothing else.

She stepped through the door, allowing herself to be engulfed in shimmering red. She had no idea how she was expected to feel;

what she did feel was uncomfortable and faintly ridiculous. Around her, she could hear nervous giggles from other—what? Participants? Subjects? Victims? Once again she nearly fled, but one of the hooded figures strode to what was probably the front of the room—it was difficult to maintain one's bearings amid the coruscations of red satin—and began to speak, in a powerful voice filled with so much energy that Anneke found herself caught up in the woman's own excitement.

"It was halfway between seminar and performance art—all about perception and reality, the way the brain filters sensory data to create an image the mind accepts as 'real.' " She was still talking about it as she climbed into Karl's Land Rover at six o'clock to drive to the President's Club dinner. She looked down at the dark navy blue silk pants and tunic she'd bought especially for this dinner, draped with a silvery-blue shawl scarf. "Thank God I didn't plan to wear red tonight—I don't think I could have taken it. Although the paisley was even more disorienting—did I tell you? Toward the end, she had us all move to the edges of the room, and she dropped a huge covering from the ceiling, pulled down the red drapes and had us all turn our cloaks inside out—and suddenly everything was covered in a bright paisley print. It was a kind of visual chaos. Everything seemed to be moving; you couldn't make out even elementary shapes. Sorry," she interrupted herself. "I'm babbling, aren't I?"

"Only a little." He grinned at her as he turned the car onto Washtenaw. "It sounds . . . interesting."

"You mean it sounds ridiculous, don't you?" She laughed. "Well, it does, of course. It's easy to make fun of this sort of thing—I can only imagine what some right-wing congressman would do if he got hold of it. But it *works*. And what she's doing—the work, the research—is the real thing."

"Are you thinking about the application of Rohr's work to artificial intelligence?"

"No, not really, although it might apply. AI isn't my thing. No, it was just pure intellectual pleasure. It was such a delight to listen to someone so excited about their work."

"And you think perhaps you aren't anymore?" he asked.

"I don't know." Abruptly, the euphoria engendered by Margaret Rohr's performance disappeared. She suddenly recalled the afternoon before, at the *Daily*. There too she'd sensed the same kind of excitement, the electricity of total involvement. When was the last time she'd felt like that? "I'm working more than I ever did," she admitted, "but sometimes it feels more like . . . escape . . . than intellectual enjoyment."

"There have been an awful lot of changes in your life in the past year," he pointed out. "It's not surprising that you'd feel most comfortable with the one part of it that's remained stable."

"I suppose. But how do I break out of it?"

"You'll know it when the time comes," he smiled, turning into the circular drive in front of the Michigan League. He nosed the Land Rover to a stop in front of a sign that said "Reserved" and cut the ignition. "Now let's go to the party."

The Michigan League is a unique treasure of a building, arguably the most beautiful building on campus. Built in the 1920s for, and by, women students, at a time when the Michigan Union was for men only, it has miraculously survived building booms, remodeling frenzies, and political upheavals to remain an elegant architectural gem. Climbing the wide slate staircase, between paneled walls of burnished golden oak, past warmly lit stained glass windows, Anneke felt some of her euphoria return. They stepped out onto the sweeping second-floor landing already filled with people, brightly colored swirls of movement under the huge, glittering chandeliers high overhead.

"I'm probably going to be taken over by administration VIPs," Karl warned her as they stood in line to check their coats. "Don't feel you have to hang around if there are more interesting people to talk to."

"Trying to ditch me, Lieutenant?" But Anneke found her eyes

sweeping the lobby for faces she recognized. Although she'd never have admitted publicly to such an unfashionable taste, she always rather enjoyed the kind of mob-scene cocktail party most people professed to loathe. The predinner reception, with its opportunities for mingling, was more to her preference than a sit-down dinner. Especially trapped at the head table.

"Just remember," Karl grinned slightly at her, "I'm a cop. I know where you live."

He was, as predicted, immediately engulfed in administrators. Anneke made polite noises for a few minutes, then left them. The wide reception area directly in front of the stairs was filled with people, as were the two large rooms opening off either side. She plunged into the festivities, snagged a glass of mediocre champagne, and nibbled shrimp and chunks of cheese. She chatted for a while with a famous faculty mathematician who also happened to be a ferocious Minnesota Vikings fan; discussed the recent Jupiter fly-by with a cardiac surgeon/amateur astronomer; and quickly broke off a diatribe by an insurance executive about illegal aliens. She was in the middle of an argument about the relative merits of Nintendo versus 3DO game systems when she saw a woman waving to her from the other side of the room. It took her a minute to recognize the figure, and when she did, her mouth dropped open in amazement.

"Zoe!" She crossed the room quickly and stared at the girl. No, not girl, woman. "You look . . . well, fantastic is the only word for it."

"Yeah, I clean up real good, don't I?" Beneath the mocking words, Anneke discerned real pleasure in the compliment. Zoe was utterly transformed, in smoky topaz silk pants and low-cut jacket, the neckline filled with a tangle of amber beads. Her normally wild mane of hair was piled on top of her head, and she wore artfully applied makeup that made her copper eyes look even more astonishing. "Sometimes I feel sorry for men," she said. "I'd hate to only be able to look the way I look, if you know what I mean."

"Wouldn't that be depressing?" Anneke agreed, laughing. "I see you've not only changed your look, you've also changed your name." She pointed to the name tag pinned to Zoe's lapel, which read "Berniece Kaplan" in computer-printed block capitals.

"When I do a makeover, I go all out. You think I can get away with it?"

"That depends on what you're trying to get away with." Anneke decided that, this being Zoe Kaplan, she'd better take the question seriously. "I don't think anyone is likely to recognize you, if that's what you mean."

"Even Genesko?" Zoe's eyes sparkled with mischief.

"Don't even think about it," Anneke warned her, laughing again. "Remember, that's his job."

"Well, it would be fun to give it a try," Zoe grinned. "Don't rat me out, okay?"

"Not me. I think he's in the next room." But as they started toward the doorway they were stopped by a voice behind them.

"Champagne, ladies?" Richard Killian held out three long-stemmed glasses, gathered in his hands like a bouquet. "You're looking particularly fine this evening, Ms. Haagen. And the beauteous Berniece, perfectly grand."

"Well, so much for disguises." Zoe wrinkled her nose in disgust.

"Ah, I'd know you anywhere, in any guise," Richard declared.

"Phooey." Zoe took one of the glasses and held it aloft. "What shall we drink to?"

"Why, to beauty and truth, of course." Richard handed Anneke the second glass, raised his, and downed it at a gulp.

"Speaking of truth," Zoe said after taking a sip of champagne, "I tried to get hold of both of you today. Anneke, you don't happen to have a copy of that printout with you by any chance, do you?"

"Oddly enough, I think I do." Anneke reached into her purse, large by evening standards, and pulled out a small leather calendar book. "Here." She withdrew a folded sheet of paper. "I tucked it into my calendar and forgot about it."

"Thanks." Zoe stuffed the paper into her own handbag.

"Richard, did you get anything on Greenaway's movements?"

"You're a hard taskmaster, darlin'," Richard complained. And indeed, Anneke thought, Zoe managed to look thoroughly businesslike when she talked about her work. "I can tell you," Richard said sorrowfully, "that airlines and rental car companies hire the *most* suspicious people. However," his voice brightened, "hotel personnel are far more accommodating." He filled her in quickly on what he'd learned from the hotel maid.

"Good stuff." Zoe nodded approval. "Did you get it on tape?"

"Alas, no." Richard looked abashed. "But it's the pure gospel, I swear."

"Never mind." Anneke was mildly surprised at Zoe's casual response. It occurred to her that perhaps the girl hadn't expected to get anything from Richard in any case. "We can use what you got to get confirmation from the cops. I wouldn't have wanted to quote the maid anyway—it could be worth her job."

"What about your own investigation?" Richard asked. "Did you get anything more on the murder before you got onto the players' union story?" The Irish lilt was gone from his voice, which now sounded faintly . . . aggrieved? Worried? Anneke wasn't sure.

"The only one I had a chance to interview was Melissa Greenaway," Zoe confessed. "It was real strange, too." She recounted the drug-sodden conversation in the filthy apartment, making a face as she described the scene. "I mean, I'm no neat freak, but at least I own a garbage can."

"Nothing much there," Richard commented when she finished. "What do you want me to do next?"

"Nothing *to* do," Zoe said. "I'm going to be working on the union story for the next few days."

"All the more reason you need me to help," Richard insisted. "I'll even be available tomorrow. This is a lot more fun than a football game." His voice sounded almost wistful. "I'd forgotten how exciting it is to chase down a big story."

"Sorry." Zoe shook her head again, more firmly this time.

"You sound like you miss the *Daily*," Anneke commented.

"I guess *Daily* alumni always do, a bit," Richard replied. "It's such an intense time of your life; nothing afterward quite measures up." The wistful note was still in his voice. "Well, that was then," he went on more briskly. "I think they'll be calling the dinner any moment. Madame Berniece, will you walk?" He bowed to Zoe, who grinned but shook her head.

"I'll be along in a bit."

"Ah, well, it was too much to hope." He put his hand over his heart, then sketched a salute and walked away, leaving Anneke and Zoe rolling their eyes at each other.

THIRTY-SIX

"As a performance, it's a bit over the top, isn't it?" Anneke suggested.

"Oh, I don't know. It makes a change from grungy frat rats, anyway." Zoe looked after him. "All that *Daily* nostalgia kind of creeps me out, though. Besides, I don't think it'd be a good idea to walk in with him. People would be more likely to recognize me. Anyway," she turned back to Anneke, "I wanted to ask you what you thought of my Flash Rumor story."

"I thought it was very good," Anneke replied promptly. "I'm glad you made it so clear that anyone at all could have started the rumor."

"I just wrote it the way you gave it to me." Zoe shrugged, but Anneke thought she sounded pleased. "It's too bad, though. I'd give a lot to know if it had anything to do with the murder."

"There's no reason to assume it does," Anneke said, but even as she spoke her mind was clicking over possibilities.

"Yeah, but it's just too freaking convenient, you know?"

"It could just as easily be connected to the players' union business," Anneke pointed out. "In fact, that seems even more likely."

"But either way," Zoe persisted, "I don't believe it was one of those random on-line flames that pops up out of nowhere. I'd bet my last dollar it was planted on purpose."

"But why?" Anneke protested. "What would anyone get out of it?"

"I don't have a clue, but I bet there's something," Zoe said stubbornly. "Look, I know you said it couldn't be traced, but are you really absolutely positive? Suppose you had a finite list of suspects to search for?"

"I still doubt it. Besides, where would you get your finite list?"

"The same place we got the one Wednesday night. Look," Zoe overrode Anneke's objection, "you've got to admit, there's just too much all going on at once—the NCAA investigation, the murder, the players' union, the Flash Rumor. And the same people keep cropping up."

"I suppose that's true," Anneke agreed reluctantly.

"Well then, couldn't you search for each of *them?* I mean, don't all computer messages have some sort of identifying code or something?"

"Not exactly." Well, yes and no, Anneke thought. All right, more yes than no. Suppose she did track the rumor back . . . each message would be time-stamped, of course . . . and there just might be a trail to follow. . . .

"You're on to something, aren't you?" Zoe broke into her musings sharply.

"No, not really. Okay, maybe. Zoe, I don't know."

"But you'll give it a try?"

"Yes, I suppose." She threw up her hands. "All right. But right now," she said severely, "I have a very important dinner to attend, and I think it's time to go inside."

The crowd around them was thinning rapidly, flowing across the hall toward the ballroom. Anneke let herself be swept forward, and shortly found herself being seated at the head table, between Karl and a gnomish University vice president who introduced himself as Gerald Arlen.

"Isn't this fun?" Arlen gestured with his salad fork. "We get to sit up here on display while three hundred people watch us eat. I can't decide whether I feel like British royalty or a zoo animal." He forked salad into his mouth cheerfully.

"Worse than either." Anneke smiled, liking Arlen at once. "Royalty are accustomed to it, and zoo animals aren't aware of it." She looked out at the sea of round tables under pristine white tablecloths, and the chattering people seated around them. Suddenly and acutely self-conscious, she conveyed a small piece of lettuce to her mouth and chewed carefully. Next to her, Karl was deep in conversation with the president, seated to his left. Occasionally he took a bite of his salad with what appeared to be perfect equanimity. Well, if Karl could handle being the center of attention, she should be able to put up with a small overflow of it, she scolded herself.

"It's a bit like mountain climbing," Arlen encouraged her. "You'll be fine as long as you don't look down."

"And at least I don't have to be afraid of falling off my salad." Anneke stifled a laugh, and Arlen beamed at her. He had a rather large head on a rather small body, and the total effect was almost Disneyesque until you noted the sharpness of his gaze. Anneke reminded herself that he was, after all, a University vice president. "You were in anthropology, weren't you?" she recalled suddenly.

"Indeed I was." His oversized head bobbed up and down. "The Function of Ritual." Anneke heard the verbalized capital letters and understood him to be referring to a course title. He paused as a waiter snatched up both their salad plates with one hand. "Unfortunately," he added sadly, "year by year we see ritual disappearing from our lives. That's why I rather enjoy these admittedly boring functions."

Not very complimentary to Karl, Anneke thought with amusement. But she was spared the necessity of response by the arrival of a plate on which half a chicken and some anonymous vegetables huddled under a layer of thick yellowish sauce. This was followed by another, smaller plate containing a large baked potato nearly invisible under a mound of sour cream. There was a flurry of wine-pouring, salt-passing and silverware-sorting, after which Anneke spent several minutes scraping toppings off her food as unobtrusively as possible. By the time her attention returned to the people around her, Gerald Arlen was concentrating happily on his chicken, and Karl was looking at her with a half-smile on his face.

"Well, tomorrow you can eat nothing but rice cakes," he told her.

"And miss out on those marvelous stadium hot dogs?" she retorted.

"No hot dogs for us." He shook his head. "We'll be in the President's Box, remember? Bagels and lox and cream cheese, roast beef sandwiches and potato salad."

"Oh, Lord. And I suppose cheesecake for dessert." She sighed theatrically. "Have you ever *tasted* rice cakes?"

"Nobody has," he replied, making a face. "They have no taste." He turned to reply to a question from the president, and Anneke looked out cautiously across the ballroom. Eleanor Sullivan was holding court at a table near the dais, waving her fork as she talked. Daniel Najarian, on the other side of the room, was eating quickly and silently, his head bent over his plate. And in the far corner, she saw Zoe sitting next to Richard Killian. That can't be pure luck, she concluded; Richard must have nipped in and switched place cards. Resourceful of him.

Well, they were a resourceful group; they wouldn't be major University donors if they weren't. Any one of them, for instance, could be resourceful enough to insert an anonymous rumor onto a computer conferencing system. Still, there ought to be *some* way to track it down. . . .

She came out of her analytic trance with a start as a general scraping of chairs signaled the next stage of the dinner. The president made introductions as waiters served dessert—not cheesecake, but a slab of chocolate cake topped with cherry sauce and whipped cream—and various people were introduced from the floor. Gerald Arlen made a speech, as did a woman poet whose work Anneke loathed. By the time Karl stepped to the podium, Anneke's foot was asleep, and she desperately needed to go to the bathroom.

He spoke graciously and humorously and, thank God, briefly. Only toward the end did he turn serious.

"Being a fan," he said, "of a sports team or of a university, allows us to be part of something wider than our own circumscribed world. It allows us, in a way, to be participants in a broader variety of experience than any one of us could possibly achieve on our own.

"I'm not speaking only of athletics. Through our attachment to the University of Michigan, we have been connected to every sort of endeavor, from an archaeological discovery in Peru to a walk on the moon. Through our attachment, we can share part of the high that comes from a brilliant intellectual breakthrough or a groundbreaking scientific achievement. Or an athletic victory.

"Is this just vicarious enjoyment? Perhaps. But it is no different from books, or movies, or theater. In each case, we enter a world outside our own, and share feelings we would otherwise never know."

When he had finished, after presenting the two Super Bowl rings to Russell Truhorne, there was prolonged applause that Anneke thought went beyond mere politeness and had perhaps a touch of defensiveness to it. The audience seemed to appreciate his defense of their Michigan partisanship, as though the events of the last few days had left them feeling tarnished.

THIRTY-SEVEN

The dinner broke up then. People stood and stretched and wandered out of the ballroom. After a quick whisper to Karl, Anneke rose and headed for the ladies' room as quickly as she could without disgracing herself by actually running. On the way back, Zoe caught up with her.

"Hang back," she said, grinning. "I'm going to find out if Genesko's as good as you say."

"Lunch at Zingerman's says he'll recognize you even dressed like that," Anneke retorted on impulse.

"You're on. Just let me take this off." Zoe removed the name tag from her lapel and walked away—glided away, moving smoothly on high heels back toward the ballroom. Anneke followed at a little distance, struggling to maintain an impassive expression.

Karl was standing by a table near the door, part of a small knot of people which included Russell Truhorne and Eleanor Sullivan, and Charlie Cassovoy as well. If Zoe can pull this off, Anneke thought, she deserves an Oscar. Zoe glided toward the group, and Anneke thought she saw Eleanor's eyes widen slightly, but the former Regent, resplendent in gold-embroidered blue silk, made no comment.

"Lieutenant Genesko." Zoe held out one French-manicured hand, her voice lower than its usual tones. "I wanted to tell you how much I enjoyed your speech."

"Thank you. I'm glad you liked it." Karl shook her hand gravely. "Although," he added, "I doubt that there's much of a story in it."

"Damn." Zoe pushed out her lips in an exaggerated pout as Anneke burst out laughing. "You just cost me a lunch."

"I'm sorry to hear it." His eyes flicked from Zoe to Anneke, and there was the trace of a smile on his face. "Or perhaps not."

"It's not that I mind buying the lunch," Zoe said, "it's just that I hate *losing*." Her voice was still cheerful, but Anneke detected a hint of steel underneath. Karl, she thought, heard it too; he looked at the girl carefully for a moment.

"I'll leave you now, Karl," Russell Truhorne said. "Thank you for everything." He spared one penetrating look at Zoe before he left, but gave no indication that he knew who she was.

"He'll recognize you the next time he sees you," Eleanor warned her. "Anneke, you look gorgeous. I don't think you've met my husband." She indicated the tall, elegant white-haired man next to her. "John McKinley Sullivan. John, this is Anneke Haagen, Karl's friend. And this is Zoe Kaplan, the *Daily* reporter who's caused all this trouble."

"Reporters don't cause trouble," Zoe said, smiling. "We just tell people about it."

"I'm very glad to meet you both." He had finely chiseled, patrician features softened by a good-natured expression. "That was a very fine speech, by the way," he said to Karl.

"Yah." The rude noise came from Charlie Cassovoy. The drink in his hand was a dark amber, and his face was flushed. "I gotta admit, it put a good gloss over all this rah-rah stuff." Charlie waved his drink at the room, which still contained a good number of chattering alumni, many of them dressed in various shades of yellow and blue. "You use the alumni obsession to squeeze money out of people, and then you use the money to feed the obsession."

"Perpetual motion fur farm." Richard Killian appeared suddenly, looking at them owlishly. "Oh, right, I already used that one, didn't I? Amazing how often it works into a conversation."

Even as she smiled, Anneke found herself examining the alumni remaining in the ballroom and contemplating the notion of obsession. The word was excessive, surely?

Alumni fever is generally a direct function of distance from the University, Anneke knew. To most Ann Arborites, there is always something faintly ludicrous about the teeming throngs of alumni racketing around town on football weekends. But ludicrous was a long way from obsessive. Could something as essentially harmless as school spirit turn that ugly? Well, any attachment could turn obsessive, as Anneke had cause to know. Even so . . . She looked at Eleanor Sullivan. To what lengths would Eleanor go for the greater good of the institution to which she'd dedicated a large portion of her life? How far would Frank Novak, for instance, go to protect his beloved athletic program? Was Novak a harmless if overenthusiastic booster, or a man dangerously obsessed?

"It's been real," Charlie said. "See ya." He stomped off angrily.

"I'd better get going, too," Zoe said.

"Do you want a ride back to the dorm?" Anneke asked her, and then wondered if Karl would object.

"I'd love one. Thanks." Zoe looked down at her feet. "These shoes are killing me."

"What about you, Eleanor?" Karl asked. "Are you and John driving back to Bloomfield Hills?"

"No. We took a room at the Carlton for the weekend. We're using the shuttle bus to and from the hotel."

"Why don't we drive you out there when we take Zoe?"

"I'll take Zoe home," Richard interjected, grasping the girl's elbow with a proprietary air.

"Sorry, Richard, I'd better not." Zoe shook her head. "I need to ask the lieutenant a couple of questions." She patted his hand as she casually withdrew her elbow from his grasp. "Tell you what—

why don't you drive Mr. and Mrs. Sullivan to the Carlton? If that's all right?" she asked Eleanor, her eyes wide and guileless.

"Best offer I've had all day." Eleanor Sullivan winked at Zoe and slipped one hand through Richard's arm and the other through her husband's. "Good night, all." She marched both men away. Richard turned and gave Zoe a last look of melancholy reproach as they disappeared toward the stairs, leaving Zoe looking thoroughly self-satisfied and Anneke snorting with suppressed laughter.

THIRTY-EIGHT

"That was . . . impressive, Ms. Kaplan," Karl said with a hint of amusement in his voice.

"Impressive enough to get you to call me Zoe?" she challenged.

"Very possibly."

They retrieved their coats and climbed into the Land Rover, still parked in the driveway space reserved for the guest of honor. Zoe clambered into the backseat and leaned forward as Karl turned on the lights and started the engine.

"How do you like it?" she asked.

"The Land Rover? Very much," Karl replied. "It handles better than any other four-wheel drive I tested."

"You still shouldn't be driving a foreign car," she scolded.

"Did you have some questions to ask me?" He refused to be drawn.

"Not really. That was just, you know, a kind of management technique." Zoe leaned forward and propped her elbows on the back of the passenger seat. "Actually, I'm more or less off the murder investigation. I'm concentrating on the players' union story for the next while. I haven't got time to do a thorough job on both. It's been a hell of a week, though." She leaned back against the leather seat and sighed happily.

"I can imagine," Anneke commented, feeling a sudden, surprising gust of envy. "This must be the greatest week of your life."

"So far, you mean." Zoe seemed abruptly serious. "Cassovoy said something about that this afternoon—that it'd all be downhill for me from here." She shuddered. "You know, that's no joke. Wouldn't it really creep you out to think that your future will never be as good as your past?" They rode in silence for a few minutes. "What about you?" Zoe asked. "What was the greatest moment in your life? So far, I mean," she added.

Anneke considered the question. "I think," she said finally, "it was the day I moved into my office in the Arcade. I'd been working by myself, out of my home," she explained, "and I kept turning down contracts because I couldn't handle any more work. I finally gritted my teeth and decided that if I were going to be in business, it ought to *be* a business. I was scared witless the day I signed that lease, but it was also the most exhilarating feeling I can remember."

"I don't even have to ask what your greatest moment was, Lieutenant," Zoe said to Karl.

"Oh?"

"You mean The Pass?" Anneke smiled to herself.

"Oh, no." Zoe shook her head. "I didn't even think of that. I was assuming it was that first Super Bowl." She leaned forward, seemingly anxious for some reason to be correct, and appeared gratified at Karl's brief nod. "The Pass was just, like, a kind of freak thing. The Super Bowl was the real accomplishment."

"It was also a team accomplishment," Karl pointed out.

"Right. That makes any special moment more special," Zoe agreed. "This has been a great week for the *Daily*, too."

"You mean that, don't you?" he said.

"You don't have to sound so surprised," she said, laughing. "Everything's better when people do it together."

But is that true for everyone? Anneke wondered. Were some people simply born loners? She shivered. She didn't want to be a loner.

"Thank heaven that's over." Karl poured sherry into two glasses and set them on the coffee table, sinking onto the long sofa with a sigh. "It feels good to be home."

He really did look at home here, Anneke thought, sitting down next to him and reaching for her glass. The room suited him perfectly. Abruptly she asked, "Why Ann Arbor?"

"What do you mean?"

"Well, you lived and worked in Pittsburgh all those years, all your friends were there. Why did you decide to move back to Ann Arbor?"

"I don't know that I did 'decide,' " he said, considering. "I think something in the back of my head decided for me. There was a period when I'd find myself thinking that it was time for me to go home, only I didn't know exactly what I meant by that. When I finally figured it out, it turned out 'home' didn't mean western Pennsylvania, it meant Ann Arbor. I guess this place felt like home to me from the first day I got here—even with Bump Elliott chewing out my freshman butt three times a day at practice. Anyway, when this job opened up it just seemed destined."

"Ann Arbor does have that effect on some people, doesn't it?" "Home" was another of those concepts that was too often fraught with emotion, she thought, not amenable to logic. People either felt at home in a place, or not. For Karl, this city—and this house, this room—were home.

"I think I'll see what SportsCenter has on the players' union." He opened the leather box on the coffee table and withdrew the TV remote.

"That reminds me. Zoe gave me an idea this evening I want to follow up. No, not really about the murder," she said to his inquiring look. "About the Kyle Farmer rumor."

"Oh? Have you thought of a way to track down the start of it?"

"It's very unlikely," she warned him. "But I want to try a couple of things."

"Are you sure you don't want to wait until morning? No, of course you don't." He smiled at her. "Don't stay up all night."

"I won't. I just want to see if I'm on the right track." She finished her sherry and went into her office, where she powered up the Compaq and logged on to Confer. She scanned the latest posts briefly, glad to note that the flames had died down. In fact, several discussion threads indicated that many people now realized they'd been had.

All right, backtrack. Each entry had both a UserID and a time stamp, of course. Any UID could easily be a phony, but let's assume the time stamps are accurate. There were so many different discussion areas, though . . . The same people? No, here was something . . . At some point, Karl came in, dropped a kiss on her forehead and said goodnight. At two A.M., when her eyes finally refused to focus on the screen, she reluctantly powered down and crawled into bed, with the glimmer of an idea but no real progress.

Once again, Karl was downstairs before her. She joined him at the table and poured herself a cup of coffee.

"Game day," he reminded her. "I have to spend the morning at the department, unfortunately, so I'll have to meet you at the game. I don't know if I'll make the kickoff, but I'll be there well before halftime."

"You'd better be. You're the star turn, remember?"

"Right. That's me. Karl Genesko, Superstar." The words were accompanied by a smile, but his voice sounded almost weary. He looks tired, Anneke thought; this one is beginning to wear him down.

"Hasn't there been *any* progress?" she asked.

"Not yet." He shook his head. "This is one of the one percent."

"What do you mean?"

"Ninety-nine percent of all crimes are solved by ordinary, slogging police routine. Then there are the ones like this, where the routine procedures don't seem to apply."

“What do you do then?”

“Oh, you still play it by the numbers,” he said. “You interview people, and you go over the crime scene with a microscope, and then you pray for a miracle.” He took a last drink of coffee and stood up. “I’ll see you at the stadium.”

THIRTY-NINE

"What would you like?" Richard Killian asked, gesturing at the crowded buffet table. "Name your heart's desire and I'll make it yours."

"Turkey sandwich and a diamond necklace, hold the emeralds," Zoe retorted, holding out her plate.

"Here's your sandwich, but they seem to be out of diamond necklaces. Will German potato salad do for a substitute?" Richard filled her plate and his own, and led the way out of the serving tent to one of the tables scattered across the grass. Zoe, carrying their drinks, squinted against the brilliant sunlight as they crunched across a carpet of multicolored leaves. On the other side of the field the president stood and chatted with alumni, conversing easily with the shifting group around him. She'd had Richard introduce her to him, first thing, as soon as they arrived—that was why she was here in the first place. Richard had called her minutes after she'd reached her dorm room the night before, and after only a brief hesitation she'd agreed to accompany him. The president's pregame brunch was a nice, informal event; she figured the prez was a lot more likely to remember her from an introduction here than from one of those dorky student receptions.

She was wearing makeup again, and her hair was once more piled on top of her head, but she wore the common game-day outfit of blue jeans and Michigan sweatshirt, and of necessity she carried her bookbag. She'd also inked out the name "Berniece" on her name tag and replaced it with a large, bold "Zoe," the Z a slash of black marker. This time, she'd wanted the prez to know who she was.

"How would you like to drive out to the cider mill after lunch?" Richard asked.

"Aren't you going to the game?"

"I'd rather spend the day with you." He reached across the table and stroked her hair.

"I can't." Zoe shook her head. Richard was no longer affecting the faint Irish lilt, she noted. Its absence made him sound uncommonly serious, and alarm bells rang in her head. Careful, she thought; he probably plans it that way. "I have to be at the *Daily* this afternoon," she told him, taking a bite of her sandwich.

"All right." He sounded disappointed but not insistent. "However, even you, dedicated as you are, can't have to work tonight. There's a fine victory party I insist you go to."

"I think probably not, thanks." Zoe concentrated ostentatiously on her food.

"Please, Zoe. I'm leaving tomorrow. I don't know how soon I can get back to Ann Arbor. Besides," he said, with a note of grim amusement in his voice, "I do believe Marta Wentworth will be there."

"Wentworth? Are you sure?" She looked up from her plate. She couldn't turn down a chance to meet Marta Wentworth, the Michigan alum who'd just signed a two-million-dollar contract as a network news anchor.

"Not a hundred percent positive, but she's supposed to be there." Richard sighed. "If you won't come to be with me, at least let me introduce you to Marta."

"You know her?"

"Yes, I know her." Richard didn't expand on his flat response, and Zoe wavered. But before she could make up her mind, a figure emerging from the buffet tent caught her eye.

"Anneke!" She stood up and waved, relieved at the excuse to put off deciding about the party. Anneke caught her eye and carried her plate toward their table.

"I didn't expect to see you here," she said to Zoe, sliding into an empty chair. She wore blue jeans and a blue denim jacket cut like a blazer over a pale yellow silk turtleneck.

"No student ever turns down a free meal. You look great. Is Genesko here?" Zoe craned her neck, looking around.

"No, he couldn't make it." Anneke bit into her sandwich a trifle savagely.

"I don't suppose you came up with anything on the Confer rumor?" Zoe asked.

"Well, not exactly."

"You did, didn't you?" Zoe bounced in her chair excitedly. "Come on, what'd you find?"

"Did you track down the person responsible for the Farmer rumor?" Richard had turned sulkily silent when Anneke joined them, but now he looked at her sharply.

"No." Anneke shook her head. "I just . . . well, I don't know *who*, but I think I may know *how*."

"Well, how? Come on, give." Zoe dug her pad and pen out of her bookbag, but Anneke shook her head again, firmly.

"No, sorry. There's no way I'd want to go into print with what I've got so far. It's too tenuous. And besides," she pursed her lips, "it really doesn't lead anywhere. It could still have been done by anyone with access to a computer."

"Well, could that *eliminate* anyone?" Zoe suggested. "Like some of the visiting alumni, at least? I mean, like Richard here wouldn't have access to a computer, would you?" she asked him.

But to her surprise, he hesitated, then smiled and shrugged. "Unfortunately for me, I brought a laptop along with me."

"Jeffrey Person had one in his hotel room, too," Zoe recalled.

"Well, so much for that idea." She reached for her Coke and took a drink. "I guess everyone has a laptop these days."

"I'm afraid so." Anneke took a last bit of her sandwich and rose. "I think it's time to go." Around them, the crowd was drifting away, all in the same direction, like a maize-and-blue river.

"Yeah, me too." Zoe stood up with her. "I've got to get back to the *Daily*. See you."

"Zoe—" Richard jumped to his feet but she gave him a sketchy wave and dashed away. "Six o'clock at your dorm," he shouted as she was swallowed up in the crowd.

Well, I'll handle the Richard thing later, she thought as she hurried toward the *Daily*, fighting her way through the crowds. It was less than half an hour to kickoff, and Game Day rules prevailed—chiefly, that anyone heading toward the stadium had right of way. The sidewalks were a solid mass of maize-and-blue-clad pedestrians, filling the pavements from building to curb and forcing everything out of its path. Going up State Street was like swimming upstream after a six-inch rainfall; Zoe swore briefly as the press of chattering, shouting humanity forced her off the curb into the street. The street, of course, was a parking lot, unmoving but not inactive—horns honked, people shouted, pennants waved from car windows, sudden choruses of "The Victors" periodically erupted from one group of excited throats and was rapidly picked up and amplified by others.

"Jeez, what a zoo." Zoe panted up the steps of the *Daily* and waved to Jeannie Franklin, a plump, normally cheerful news reporter pounding away on one of the Macs with furious concentration. Zoe dropped her bookbag on a nearby desk and peered over Jeannie's shoulder. "Big story?"

"Term paper," the other girl said briefly from between clenched teeth.

"Bummer." Zoe grimaced sympathetically and retreated to the desk. She was thankful to have the whole sports desk to herself—as sports editor, Gabriel was covering the game, of course, and pretty much everyone else was either at the stadium or watching it on television somewhere. She pulled papers and notebooks from her bookbag and tried to make sense out of her scrawls. First she separated notes on the murder from notes on the players' union, no easy task in itself—there was an awful lot of interlocking. In some cases she'd scribbled notes about both stories on a single page, forcing her now to transcribe one or the other onto a separate sheet of paper.

It was nearly two o'clock when she finally finished the task of sorting. Occasional play calls from the stadium loudspeaker drifted through the open window behind her. Maybe she'd still have time to catch some of the game, she thought, if Russ Blake would ever show up. She looked at the clock with annoyance—for sure she wasn't going to hang around all day waiting for him.

"Anyone seen Russ Blake?" she called out to the half-dozen or so people scattered around the city room. The ones who bothered to look up shook their heads. Grumbling down the aisle to the Coke machine, Zoe decided she'd give him another half hour and then split.

Back at the desk, she popped the tab on the Coke and riffled through the set of notes she'd gathered together for Blake. Anneke's printout was on top of the stack, and Zoe realized she hadn't actually read the thing through—it was just a report of what she'd already heard, after all. But, scanning it, she realized that Anneke had put organization into what had seemed like random, unfocused meanderings. It was a kind of blueprint for the investigation, Zoe decided, a list of questions that offered a new, clean approach. Just questions, of course, not answers. Well, there's a possible answer to one of the questions, she thought, drinking Coke.

A possible . . . She sat up straighter and stared at the printout, then shook her head. That's silly, she told herself. In fact, it's stone dumb . . .

Five minutes later she stood up, stuffed everything back into her bookbag and called out again. "Anybody here got a football ticket?"

"I do," a tall, good-looking blond guy called back from the business staff area across the room. "I don't know why I bother to buy student tickets every year," he complained, holding out the ticket to Zoe. "I'm always too busy to go, only I never admit it to myself until it's too late to sell them."

"Thanks, Will." Zoe snatched the ticket out of his hand and trotted toward the stairs.

"Hey, Kaplan, ready to go over those notes with me?" Russ Blake materialized at the head of the stairs.

"Sorry, Russ, gotta go." Zoe paused just long enough to shake her head at him, ignoring his outraged expression. "Catch you later," she called over her shoulder, racing down the stairs.

FORTY

He still looks like he could run down anybody on the field, Anneke thought with a little splash of pride. Karl walked out onto the field, in his impeccable dark blue suit and Michigan-striped tie, to an appreciative roll of cheers and applause from the stands, and waved to the crowd from the Block M on the fifty-yard line. From her plush seat in the President's Box, Anneke watched the ceremony unfold below and wished she were down in the stands. The box, set under the press box between the forty-yard lines, was carpeted, furnished like an expensive living room in soft velvet-upholstered sofas and chairs, and encased behind a wall of plate glass. Football, Anneke decided, particularly college football, was part sports event, part communal experience. Up here, carefully sequestered from the masses, she might as well have been home watching on television.

On the field, the Michigan Marching Band, spaced out from end zone to end zone in rigid precision, stood at attention. Russell Truhorne held aloft the dark blue Michigan football jersey with the bright yellow number 54, and announced its retirement in honor of Karl Genesko. The crowd cheered happily. The band swung its instruments, dipped flags, and burst into "The Victors," brass-heavy and high-tempo. The hundred and four thousand people in the stands stood and bawled the fight song along with them, pumping the air with their fists on each "Hail!" Karl smiled and waved, the band high-stepped to the sideline, and the small ceremony was over.

Behind her, as the teams poured back out onto the field to warm up for the second half, she heard Jeffrey Person say, "Lot of character out there."

"Character," Daniel Najarian snorted. "Where's the 'character' in being a hired gun? It isn't character if you're merely working for your own personal aggrandizement."

"Ain't it amazing how the white power structure defines morality as that which benefits the white power structure," Jeffrey drawled. "As I recall, Henry Ford said pretty much the same thing, back when the UAW was first formed—that 'his' workers were being 'disloyal.' "

"If you can't see the difference between a university and an auto plant, we obviously didn't teach you much," Najarian retorted.

"What do you mean 'we,' white man?" Jeffrey said, laughing. "Hot damn, I always wanted to say that." When Najarian didn't reply, he went on, "I'm assuming, by the way, that I'm off your committee, now that I'm a badass union organizer."

"There isn't going to *be* a scholarship committee," Najarian snapped. "Even Richard here can't be naive enough to believe we can ignore a scandal of this proportion."

"You're a nasty SOB when things don't go your way, aren't you?" Richard's voice held amusement, but there was an edge to it that made Anneke turn around.

"That's the money talking," Jeffrey commented. " 'The very rich are different from you and me,' " he quoted. "Among other things, they have the luxury of believing that institutions are more important than people—other people, that is."

"Sometimes they are," Najarian replied. "Some institutions improve the lot of *all* people."

“ ‘The greatest good for the greatest number,’ you mean?” Jeffrey laughed again. “Daniel, I never figured you for a Communist.”

“You know perfectly well what I mean.” Najarian’s face darkened with anger. “A great university offers a unique value to a society.”

“God, Daniel, you’re such a fucking elitist.” Eleanor Sullivan dropped into the chair next to Jeffrey.

“I wouldn’t have put it quite so elegantly, Eleanor.” Najarian inclined his head, his self-control restored. “But yes, I don’t deny the accusation. Is it such a terrible thing, to believe in the value of great institutions?”

“It is if you value them above the people they’re supposed to serve,” Jeffrey responded. “Those kids out there matter a lot more than some overpaid professor writing another book about some dead white guy.”

“That’s about what I would have expected from one of you people,” Najarian snapped.

Jeffrey jumped to his feet, his face twisted with rage. “You racist motherfucker,” he said in an almost conversational tone that Anneke found more threatening than any shout would have been. “I’m almost glad to hear you say that, because now we have the truth out in the open. That’s really what this is all about, isn’t it?”

“Don’t be ridiculous.” Najarian’s lip curled in contempt. “I wasn’t referring to *race*. I was talking about *athletes.*”

It was Eleanor’s whoop of laughter that broke up the argument. Richard laughed with her, and after a moment even Jeffrey smiled. Only Daniel Najarian remained grim-faced.

Anneke returned her attention to the field, considering whether she could leave. The game, after all, was already a Michigan blowout. Kyle Farmer, playing with a kind of controlled fury that seemed to resonate throughout the stadium, had blasted out 112 yards and three touchdowns in the first half, and seemed good for similar numbers in the second. “A Heisman Trophy performance,” the television announcers were calling it. An exercise in pride, Anneke thought. Kyle Farmer was ramming the football down the throats of his accusers, whoever they were.

The self-anointed college football expert who held forth on ESPN Friday evening had picked Wisconsin to win. The Michigan team, he pontificated, would be so unnerved by all the uproar in Ann Arbor that they'd be unable to focus on the game itself. It could have gone that way, of course. Only, Kyle Farmer didn't let it. Even from the distant box, Anneke could feel Farmer's intensity; the other Michigan players seemed to absorb energy from him like microchips feeding off a titanic motherboard. At the half, Michigan led 35-7, and the game was essentially over.

Still, she couldn't really get up and leave. It would seem insulting, probably, although she couldn't imagine who would care. Or even notice. She stood up and wandered over to the bar, where she poured herself half a glass of beer and thought about Kyle Farmer. A gutsy kid. She wished she could solve the Flash Rumor puzzle, if only for his sake, but discovering the how, as she'd told Zoe, didn't reveal the who. As Zoe had said . . .

"Please, will you just ask her?" The voice, muffled through the door, was certainly Zoe's. Anneke set down her glass, went to the door, and pushed it open. The security guard outside turned and looked at her sourly.

"Something you said," Anneke blurted, looking at Zoe wide-eyed. "I think . . ."

"Anneke, thank heaven," Zoe interrupted. "Can I talk to you?"

"Yes. Wait, don't come in. I'll come out." She ducked back into the glass enclosure, snatched up her purse, and hurried back outside. The other guests, as she'd suspected, didn't seem to notice. "Come on," she said to Zoe. "Let's go out to the walkway where we can hear ourselves."

They fought their way through the crowds milling around under the stands, past the long lines waiting for hot dogs or beer or the ladies' room, and finally emerged outside on the apron around the stadium.

"Now," Anneke said when they were finally more or less clear of the worst of the crowds, "what did you want to talk to me about?"

But now that she finally had Anneke's full attention, Zoe seemed hesitant. "It's going to sound stupid," she said with uncharacteristic diffidence.

"So is the idea I just came up with," Anneke admitted. "But if they're the same kind of stupid . . . Well, go ahead and let's find out."

"Okay," Zoe capitulated. "See, I was reading through that printout you did, of the discussion Wednesday night, and I suddenly realized I could answer one of your questions." As she explained, Anneke stared at her.

"It's the same kind of stupid, all right." Quickly Anneke sketched out her own deduction and saw amazed comprehension on the girl's face.

"If you're right . . ."

"If *we're* right. You realize it's preposterous."

"I know." Zoe gave a shaky laugh. "What do we do now?"

"We find Karl," Anneke declared. He wasn't planning to return to the President's Box until later in the game, she recalled. Ro had asked him to join the team on the bench for the second half. "We'll have to catch up with him on the sidelines," she said. "Come on."

They were, of course and inevitably, on the very farthest side from the Michigan bench. Anneke headed swiftly around the outside perimeter of the stadium, dodging spectators and vendors and racketing children, with Zoe racing to keep up.

"We still just have a weird theory," Zoe panted. "Couldn't we wait until after the game?"

"The longer we wait, the less likely it is that there'll be any evidence left," Anneke replied grimly. "If it isn't already too late." From inside the stadium, a gathering roar signaled that the teams were taking the field. People hurried past them, laden with cardboard trays of food and drink, rushing to their seats for the second-half kickoff.

"In here." Zoe made a hard right and headed toward an opening. "This is the closest aisle to the bench." Anneke followed behind, and shortly they emerged into the stands to the right of the tunnel, directly behind the Michigan bench. Anneke squinted in the sudden bright sunlight, trying to pick out Karl's huge frame from among the milling crowd on the field. The trouble was, she realized with a gulp of inward laughter, this is the only place where Karl is only a little more than normal size.

"There he is." She spotted him finally next to the bench, with Charlie Cassovoy beside him. Even from a distance Anneke could discern the controlled impatience in Karl's demeanor. God, she thought, what a time for an interview.

"How the hell did Cassovoy get a sideline pass?" Zoe asked angrily. "Come on, let's go down this way." They worked their way down the concrete steps, forcing their way past people milling around, searching for their seats, shouting at friends. They were still a dozen rows up when all movement came to a halt and all one hundred and four thousand spectators leaped to their feet cheering. On the field the Michigan football team charged forward, the kicker sent the ball aloft (badly, Anneke noted with one part of her brain), and the second half was officially under way.

There was a security guard at the foot of the aisle, as there was at every aisle all the way around the stadium. She could see Karl less than twenty feet away from her, Charlie Cassovoy still beside him, but both of them had their backs to the stands.

"I need to speak to Lieutenant Genesko," Anneke said to the security guard, hoping the use of Karl's police title might suggest official business. But if it did, it clearly made no difference.

"Sorry, ma'am," the guard replied, his face impassive. "No one's allowed on the field without a pass."

"Let me." Zoe leaned forward against the low brick wall and shouted at the top of her lungs, "Hey, Cantwell!" On the field, a chubby figure draped with cameras turned toward the sound, saw Zoe's pinwheeling arms and trotted in their direction.

"What's going on?" he yelled.

"Tell Genesko his lady needs to talk to him!" Zoe bellowed, causing the security guard and several rows of fans to turn and look at Anneke curiously. She felt her face redden, but she stood her ground and a minute or so later Karl was standing at the barricade. Charlie Cassovoy, to Anneke's dismay, was right behind him.

"It's all right." Karl flashed his police ID, and the security guard shrugged and stepped away from the gate.

"We need to talk to you," Anneke said as soon as they had stepped out onto the field, keeping her voice as low as she could manage.

"All right." He didn't ask any questions, just looked around quickly. Anneke followed his gaze. Out on the field, the Wolverine defense had Wisconsin pinned down, its back to the north end zone. Karl led them swiftly in the other direction, remaining silent until they were out of the main crush of television cameras, sound equipment, reporters, officials, and the various anonymous people who litter the sidelines at football games.

"All right," he said when they finally achieved a bubble of relatively open space, "what have you got?"

Anneke began to talk, keeping her back to the Michigan bench, conscious of Charlie Cassovoy's eyes on them even from a distance. It took nearly five minutes to tell it all, Zoe's moment of realization and her own chain of deduction. When she finished, Karl stared out at the field for what seemed like a long time before saying anything.

"The logic is impeccable," he said at last. "Only . . . well, we can confirm your first premise, anyway." Turning, he strode back toward the Michigan bench.

"You got something?" Charlie Cassovoy was waiting for them behind the bench, his pale, bloodshot eyes bright with suspicion.

"Mr. Cassovoy," Karl said, "you have your laptop computer with you, I believe?"

"Yeah." Charlie hesitated an instant too long, his eyes flicking down to the briefcase at his feet. "Why? You lose another file?"

"May I have your permission to examine the computer, please?" Karl asked, ignoring Charlie's sarcasm.

"No chance," Charlie snapped immediately. "I'm a reporter. My files are privileged, remember? Just like hers." He jerked his head at Zoe.

"I'm not asking to see your files," Karl said. "In fact, you needn't even open the computer. I only want to make a note of the make and serial number."

"The serial number!" Charlie looked nonplussed.

"Yes." Karl nodded easily. "We merely want to confirm your ownership of it. I assume," he phrased the statement carefully, "that you sent in the registration card when you purchased it."

Charlie stood perfectly still. So did the others. On the field, out of the corner of her eye, Anneke saw the Michigan offense lining up on the Wisconsin forty-yard line. The quarterback took the snap from center and dropped back. A wide receiver broke out of the backfield and cut downfield, pursued by a red-clad Wisconsin cornerback. The crowd roared with anticipation.

Charlie Cassovoy bolted.

He ran more or less straight across the field, his spindly legs pumping, briefcase clutched in his right hand. When he reached midfield he cut toward the north end zone, caroming off a Wisconsin linebacker and narrowly missing getting cut down by the safety.

By which time, Karl was already in pursuit. He didn't run Charlie's route; instead, he made the moves that Anneke recognized were the utterly instinctive act of a natural linebacker, picking up the angle on the runner as he raced downfield, vaulting a downed Michigan lineman at the thirty-five and weaving through the Wisconsin secondary. At the fifteen, Charlie turned and looked over his shoulder, eyes staring, mouth open and gasping for breath.

Karl brought him down on the three, just short of the end zone.

The crowd was on its feet, but the sound was more rumble than roar as they tried to process what they had just witnessed. Then the field announcer's voice boomed out over the loudspeaker:

"Tackle at the three-yard line, number fifty-four, Karl Genesko."

In the deafening thunder of cheering that greeted the announcement, Zoe breathed, "I wouldn't have missed that for a Pulitzer and a ride in the space shuttle."

FORTY-ONE

"It's not going to be enough, is it?" Anneke asked.

They were having a quick dinner at a restaurant on the west side of town, as far from the TV crews as they could get, at the end of an afternoon filled with confusion. After the surreal drama at the stadium, Karl had placed Charlie Cassovoy under arrest, handcuffed him, and hustled him away, with cameras and microphones and screaming reporters baying at their heels. He had made no acknowledgment of the thundering cheers from a hundred thousand throats reverberating across the huge bowl as he half-led, half-dragged Cassovoy through the mobs along the sidelines and out through the tunnel. But the expression on his face, compounded of grim anger mixed with exasperated amusement, would, Anneke knew, be shown on every newscast in the country. So would the grass stains on his trousers and the rip in the sleeve of his jacket; he had looked, she thought, trying unsuccessfully not to laugh, exactly like a man who had been playing football in a business suit.

"Not without more evidence than just the laptop," Karl answered her question. "And not without a *motive.*" He took a savage bite of his hamburger in a rare show of frustration.

"He's at least admitting he knew who Greenaway was, isn't he?" Zoe waved a french fry in the air. She was there, at Karl's invitation, after five minutes of negotiations during which the words "off the record" had been spoken at least five times. Anneke, feeling unaccountably ravenous, had virtuously ordered only a tuna sandwich and a diet Coke, and was nibbling the sandwich as slowly as she could to make it last.

"He couldn't very well deny it. The NCAA confirmed that Greenaway was the investigator in charge of the Eastern Michigan investigation last year." Karl nodded to her. "That was a good guess on your part."

"Well, it was Anneke's question," Zoe admitted. "She was the one who asked how anyone knew who Greenaway was. When Charlie mentioned to me that his last major story was about an NCAA investigation, I just thought maybe he could have connected with Greenaway over that." She took a bite of her hamburger. "Anneke was the one who made the big deduction," she added with determined honesty.

"Actually, it was a couple of things you said that triggered it." Anneke was happy to indulge in their mutual admiration society. "Remember when we were talking about the Flash Rumor? You commented that everyone has a laptop these days. It took a while for it to register, but I suddenly realized that the one person in this case who apparently *didn't* have one was Alvin Greenaway himself. And yet you said Greenaway's daughter made a big point about her father liking all the latest toys. Well, someone like that, especially someone who's on the road a lot, would *have* to have a laptop. And one more thing—something that Richard Killian said." She hesitated. "I hope I'm not getting him into trouble, but he talked to the maid at the Carlton." She glanced over at Karl, who smiled slightly. "Richard said Greenaway had some sort of special room for business travelers, although he couldn't see anything particularly special about it. Well, nowadays that usually means a room that's designed for computer use." She finished the last corner of her tuna sandwich and washed it down with diet Coke.

"Anyway," she concluded, "as far as I could tell, there was only one laptop in the stadium, and that was the one in Charlie Cassovoy's briefcase. I know, I know." She held up a hand, forestalling an imaginary protest. "The murderer could have taken the laptop and been long gone. But remember, we were hypothesizing that the murderer was meeting Greenaway at the stadium in the first place because he was there for some other reason. So it was a reasonable hunch. And once Charlie panicked and ran, of course, it was a lock." She reached across the table and snared one of Karl's french fries. "Did you get hold of the company?"

"Yes. The serial number matched. It was Greenaway's, all right." He turned his plate so that the french fries were closer to her. "Would you like some dessert?"

"No. What I really want is an order of french fries for my very own. But what I'd better do is fill myself up with more Coke."

"Is Cassovoy still sticking to his story?" Zoe asked.

"Yes." Karl grimaced. "He says that he found the body, saw the computer lying next to it, and took it because he wanted information about the investigation."

"Nonsense."

"Bullshit."

Anneke and Zoe spoke together.

"Well, yes." Karl looked from one to the other of them. "But there's no way to prove he's lying."

"But consider the scenario," Anneke protested. "The police find Greenaway's briefcase next to his body. Not only has the briefcase been rifled, there's also a notebook nearby with several pages ripped out. Now, if Charlie found the computer as he says he did, it would have to mean that someone killed Greenaway, carefully searched for and removed incriminating evidence, and *left his computer behind.*" She shook her head, irritated as always by illogic. "It's ridiculous."

"Well, what about the computer itself?" Zoe asked. "Are you sure there wasn't anything on it to show what Greenaway was investigating?"

"Not a thing." Anneke shook her head. "Greenaway had his hard drive partitioned into two virtual drives, the way a lot of people do—all his applications on C drive and all his data files on D. And by the time we got hold of it, the D drive had been wiped clean. There weren't any data files on it at all."

"Isn't there some way to undelete files that've been deleted?" Zoe persisted.

"Not in this case. The files weren't deleted; they were wiped. That means every sector on the partition was overwritten with a zero. Everything there is absolutely gone."

"Shit." Zoe took a bite of pickle. "Hey," she said suddenly, "isn't there such a thing as a hidden file? Could there be something like that?"

"Actually, there really isn't any such thing as a hidden file anymore," Anneke replied. "There used to be, but nowadays, with graphical interfaces like Windows, it doesn't work. You can't hide a file from a graphical program, because it displays every file on every sector of your hard drive, even if the filename contains characters DOS doesn't recognize." She stared into the brown depths of her Coke. "Believe me, I searched."

"Shit," Zoe said again. "Well, but look—isn't the fact that he wiped everything at least proof that he had something to cover up?"

"Yes, but not *what* he was covering up." It was Karl who answered. "At best, it only proves he might have been trying to cover the theft of the computer, not the murder. In fact," he said tightly, "as far as the murder is concerned, Charlie just keeps repeating the same thing over and over: That he had no motive and that in fact he *wanted* to see Greenaway get Michigan." His voice remained level, but Anneke could see his hands tighten on the handle of his coffee cup.

"Y'know, I can't come up with any motive for him, either," Zoe said. "I mean, he's not a Michigan alum, so he can't have been the one being investigated. Why *would* he kill Greenaway?"

"He could have been Greenaway's informant," Anneke pointed out.

"So?" Zoe spread her hands. "Hell, he'd be more likely to brag about that than kill over it." She picked up her last french fry and dunked it liberally in ketchup before putting it in her mouth. "Are we really sure Cassovoy did kill him?"

"What we're sure of," Karl replied, "is that whoever stole Alvin Greenaway's computer killed him to get it. What we don't know is why."

"I read somewhere that you don't need to prove motive to convict," Anneke commented.

"In theory, that's true," Karl said. "In practice, you aren't likely to sell a case to a jury if you can't at least suggest a motive. And here, we have to struggle even to document the barest connection."

They finished their meal in gloomy silence. "Zoe, do you want to be dropped off at the dorm or at the *Daily*?" Karl asked as they left the restaurant and walked through the starry darkness of the parking lot toward the Land Rover.

"The dorm, I guess," she said grumpily. "There's no *Daily* tomorrow, so there's no point writing up anything yet. And by the time I do get into print, the TV guys'll have done it all. It'll just be yesterday's news." She paused. "If we could just come up with *some*thing," she said fretfully. "Okay, look, what about the attack on Anneke? You know, Wednesday night? It has to be tied in, right?"

"I'd say probably so," Karl agreed, turning the car onto the unlighted stretch of Jackson Road, "but that's a professional judgment, not a fact. And since Charlie Cassovoy isn't talking about it, you have nothing to print in any case."

"It *was* the floppy disk," Anneke said abruptly. She felt a sudden chill of realization; the darkness outside the car seemed to press itself against the windows. "Remember, the disk in my purse was one I found in the computer's floppy drive. I'm willing to bet that

Charlie didn't even know it was in there until I mentioned it. Which would mean he didn't know if there was anything incriminating on it or not. He *had* to get it back."

"Oh, shit," Zoe groaned. "I bet you're right. So we could have had it in our hands without ever knowing it."

"We did have it in our hands," Anneke pointed out. "I was working on that computer for more than an hour Wednesday night, and we don't even know if Charlie had wiped the drive yet."

"How come he didn't freak when he saw you with it?"

"Probably because he didn't realize it *was* Greenaway's, until I gave it back to him." Anneke would have laughed at the irony of it if she hadn't felt so cold. "You pulled it out of his briefcase while he was off getting drinks, remember? When he got back to the table, all he saw was a computer consultant working on a computer. I think it just never occurred to him until it was too late."

"Jeez." Zoe did laugh. "He must have just about lost it when he realized it was the one he stole. Damn," she said more soberly, "I bet that floppy disk was Greenaway's backup, too."

"Yes." Anneke leaned back against the headrest and watched lighted storefronts whirl past, appearing and disappearing in the darkness. On a laptop, you didn't have the luxury of a tape drive. If you wanted to back up important files, you dumped them to a floppy disk; then when you got home you could link up to your desktop machine and download everything. She sat up abruptly. "What if . . . Karl, I just thought of something."

"What?" he asked quickly, not taking his eyes off the road.

"What if . . ." she began again, then stopped. "Can I take another look at the laptop?" she asked, unwilling to commit herself without evidence.

"All right." He said nothing more, but Anneke felt the Land Rover's speed increase.

"You're on to something, aren't you?" Zoe bounced forward in the backseat. "What is it?"

"If anything turns up, I promise you'll be the first to know," Karl said, turning right onto Division.

"Uh-uh, I'm in on this, too. C'mon," she wheedled, "let me come along, please? I can't print anything before Monday anyway, remember?"

Instead of replying, Karl swung the car right onto Huron instead of left toward East Quad. He turned right twice more, then made a final turn into the driveway that led to the underground police parking area. As they ducked underneath City Hall, Anneke saw a dozen or more people, many of them carrying television cameras, rush futilely toward them.

FORTY-TWO

They detoured to the evidence room, where Karl signed out the laptop. When they were safely behind the closed door of his office, he cleared a space on the big gray metal desk, moving stacks of paper into higher piles to make room for it.

"I figured you'd rate a bigger office," Zoe said, looking around the cramped room with bright-eyed curiosity.

"This *is* a bigger office," Karl replied with a smile. "Two visitor's chairs represent luxury around here."

Anneke pulled her chair closer to the desk, opened the lid of the laptop, and powered it up. Once Windows was loaded she sat for a moment examining Greenaway's layout.

"There!" She turned the computer slightly so Karl could see the screen and pointed to an icon within the Communications program group.

"What is it?" he asked.

"PcAnywhere. It's a remote program." Anneke felt both satisfaction and relief.

"The telephone call." Karl looked from the screen to Anneke and back. "So that's what he was doing."

"Yes." She nodded. "He was accessing his home computer."

"Remember, the Overland Park police checked his computer, and they didn't find anything relating to Michigan. The likelihood is that there's nothing there," he warned.

"There *has* to be," she insisted. "If he spent all that time on-line from Ann Arbor, what else would he be working on?"

"Oy! Hey!" Zoe broke in, craning forward to see the small screen. "You want to translate any of this for us techno-illiterates?"

"This is a program that allows you to control one computer from another," Anneke explained, pointing to the icon. "With this, Greenaway could connect this laptop to his home computer. Which means he could have uploaded information he got here in Ann Arbor directly to his machine in Overland Park."

"That's why he made a twenty-minute phone call to his home even though he lived alone!" Zoe exclaimed.

"Possibly." Karl's voice held a cautionary note. "But even if he did, we don't know that he uploaded anything that will help us."

"Can't you call in yourself and find out?" Zoe appealed to Anneke.

"Yes, I suppose so." She looked at Karl questioningly.

"Go ahead. Do you need the phone number?"

"I don't think so. It should be configured for it. But I will need a phone cord."

A sense of urgency seemed to crackle through the cramped office. Without a word, Karl unplugged the cord from the phone on his desk and handed it to her. She plugged it into the port at the back of the laptop. Double-clicked on the icon. Waited impatiently for PcAnywhere to load. Clicked on Dial.

"There it is." She leaned back and sighed. "That's Alvin Greenaway's home computer." It hit her then for the first time—she was looking at a dead man's computer screen. It was uncomfortably like confronting a ghost; but if so, she told herself, this was a ghost coming back to settle the score with his murderer.

"Now what?" Zoe asked, her voice almost a whisper, as if she too were conscious of the ghost within the machine.

"Let's see what's on here." Anneke clicked on File Manager and examined the directory tree. "Very nice," she murmured to herself.

"What is?" Karl asked.

"His hard drive. Organized as neatly as his laptop was." She pointed to the screen. "Two partitions—applications on C, data on D. Subdirectories on D organized by function—see here? 'Investigations,' with subdirectories under it for 'Pending' and 'Closed.' And separate subdirectories underneath for each school." They looked at the list of schools which had been under NCAA scrutiny; Michigan was not among them.

"What about that one?" Zoe pointed to a subdirectory labeled "Office." Anneke double-clicked to bring up a list of filenames.

"I don't think so," she said. "This seems to be for office routine—organization charts, minutes of staff meetings, that sort of thing." She stared at the Windows screen. "Unless we want to read through every word of five hundred megs of files . . . Wait a minute." She moved the mouse cursor to a small green-and-black square labeled Ecco. She double-clicked again, and a representation of a Day-Timer calendar page appeared, open to the current week.

Monday 10-14-96
10:00a-11:00a Staff meeting
New regulations update
Vacation schedules
Tuesday 10-15-96
6:00p-7:00p Pack for trip
Wednesday 10-16-96
9:00a-11:30a To Ann Arbor
Lv 8:15am, Arr 11:05am, NW #214
Thursday 10-17-96

Friday 10-18-96
Saturday 10-19-96
12:00p-4:00p Football game
Sunday 10-20-96
10:00a-12:30p Return home
Lv 10:35am, Arr 12:20pm, NW #705

"Nothing," Anneke said. "Well, Ecco's also an outliner—maybe there's something in one of the outlines." She clicked on the Outlines icon on the toolbar and read the list that dropped down. "New Regulations. Sports Agents. Meetings." She shook her head. "Still nothing," she said with a sick feeling of disappointment.

"But there has to be something on there *somewhere*," Zoe said angrily. "He spent nearly half an hour connected to this computer from his hotel room. What the shit was he *doing*?"

"I don't *know*." Anneke minimized Ecco, reopened File Manager, and glared at the directory tree in frustration.

"Weird," Zoe said, peering over her shoulder. "How can PC people survive with those dorky eight-letter filenames?"

"Actually, they have their uses," Anneke replied. "With the extensions, each filename gives you information about the file itself."

"What do you mean?"

"Take a look." Anneke clicked on the Investig subdirectory and pointed to the file list. "There's a file named Proced.doc. 'Proced' probably means 'procedures,' and the .doc extension tells you it's a Microsoft Word file. And that one—'logo.tif.' The .tif not only tells you that it's a graphics file, it also tells you what graphics format it is, so you know what sort of program you need to work with it. And this one." She pointed again. " 'Blue.exe.' An .exe extension means it's an executable file."

"You mean, like a program?"

"Right." She paused. "A program. But . . ."

"What is it?" Karl asked.

"He has his hard drive organized with all his applications on C. Why would he have a program file here, in a data directory? And it's named Blue . . ." They stared at each other for a moment. She quickly shelled out to DOS, but then paused for a second at the D:\INVESTIG prompt, her hands above the keyboard. Finally, with an inward prayer, she typed: BLUE.

"What the hell is all that?" Zoe asked, watching lines of text scroll down the screen. "Is that a program running?"

"No." Anneke laughed shakily. "I said .exe means an executable program, and it does. But it means one other thing—a self-extracting zip file."

"You got a translation for that?"

"A zip file is a file that's been compressed to save hard-drive space, using a utility called Pkzip. Usually, you need the other half of the utility, called Pkunzip, to decompress it. But a self-extracting zip file is one that unzips itself when you type the filename, and it always has an .exe extension. That's what this is. No wonder the Overland Park police didn't catch it. They were looking for data files."

"Now that it's unzipped, what is it?" Karl asked.

"An Ecco file." She pointed to the white letters on the black DOS screen. "See the .eco extension?"

"Well, let's see what's in it," Zoe demanded. Anneke typed EXIT to return to Windows, then reopened Ecco and opened the file named Blue.eco.

"There!" Zoe leaned forward, bouncing with excitement. "There's Cassovoy's name!"

Monday 10-14-96
10:00a-11:00a Staff meeting
New regulations update
Vacation schedules
Tuesday 10-15-96
6:00p-7:00p Pack for trip
Wednesday 10-16-96
9:00a-11:30a To Ann Arbor
Lv 9:15am, Arr 12:20am, NW #402

2:30p-3:00p Charles Cassovoy—Host Bar, DTW
7:30p-8:00p Russell Truhorne—Univ. Club

Thursday 10-17-96

10:30a-11:00a Cassovoy—Michigan Stadium, Gate 12
6:00p-8:00p Melissa—dinner

Friday 10-18-96

Saturday 10-19-96

12:00p-4:00p Football game

Sunday 10-20-96

10:00a-12:30p Return home
Lv 10:35am, Arr 11:50pm, NW #735

"*Got* the bastard," Zoe crowed.

"Not necessarily." Karl spoke finally, his eyes still on the computer screen.

"But this proves Cassovoy was the one who was meeting Greenaway at the stadium," Zoe maintained. "And look!" She pointed to the earlier entry. "He met with Cassovoy at the airport on Wednesday, too. So Cassovoy *has* to be the informant!"

"Probably—assuming he actually entered every one of his appointments," Karl conceded. "But that still doesn't prove Cassovoy is the murderer."

"But . . ." Zoe's voice trailed off. "Isn't there anything else on there?" she demanded of Anneke.

"Let's see what's under the Outlines menu." Once more she clicked on the toolbar.

And Alvin Greenaway told them what they wanted to know.

FORTY-THREE

• • • • • •

Wednesday, October 16, 1996, 2:30 P.M.: Report of Conversation with Charles H. Cassovoy

1. Mr. Cassovoy was known to me as a reporter for the *Detroit News*, from previous contact during last year's investigation of Eastern Michigan University.
2. Mr. Cassovoy called me at my home on the evening of Monday, October 14. He told me that he was doing a "wrap-up story" on that investigation and asked if he could speak to me about it. He asked me when I would next be in the Michigan area, and I informed him that I would be in Ann Arbor October 16 through October 20. He then asked if he could meet me at the airport when I arrived, and I agreed.
3. At the Host Bar in the Detroit Metropolitan Airport, Mr. Cassovoy made the following statements:
   a. That he had information regarding "a pattern of violation" of NCAA regulations among members of the University of Michigan football team.

b. That "a whole crew of" Michigan football players had received sums of money from more than one Michigan alumnus.
c. That sums of money had been given both at the time of their signing Letters of Intent, and subsequently.
d. That payments had continued after these players were enrolled.
e. That the father of at least one player is employed by a Michigan alumnus in a western state for a salary "about triple what the other guys in the same office are getting," and that the father of another player is currently being carried on the books of a company owned by a Michigan alumnus, and being paid a full salary by that company, while at the same time holding a full-time job elsewhere.
f. That "a couple of guys" were given free trips to Hawaii and elsewhere on private planes owned by Michigan alumni.

4. Mr. Cassovoy stated that his purpose in bringing this information to the NCAA was not altruistic but rather for personal gain. He stated that "this is going to be one huge mother of a story when it breaks, and I want to be the one to break it." He further demanded a guarantee that I would keep this confidential until he had published it in his newspaper.
5. Despite questioning, Mr. Cassovoy refused to reveal the names of specific players or alumni at this time. He stated that he wanted to confirm certain elements of his information for himself, but he said that names and other information would be forthcoming.
6. Note: Mr. Cassovoy's frequent contacts with Michigan football players through his job suggests that this information is likely to have sufficient basis in fact to warrant investigation. In the past, several major violations have come to light through the offices of the media.

"Jeez." Zoe reached the bottom of the outline and shook her head. "Talk about your anal retentives," she joked, then looked embarrassed. "Sorry. I forgot there for a minute."

"It may be stiff and choppy, but it's certainly complete," Anneke said.

"That's because he was trained to create an exhaustive paper trail," Karl pointed out. There was respect in his voice. "It's a good report."

Anneke closed the outline and clicked to bring up the next one.

Wednesday, October 16, 1996, 7:30 P.M.: Report of Conversation with Russell M. Truhorne

1. I met with Russell Truhorne, University of Michigan athletic director, in a private room off the University Club in the Michigan Union. The meeting was at my own request.
2. I informed Mr. Truhorne that a major investigation of the University was likely to be instituted by the NCAA. I told him that the investigation was likely to center around the football team, but I did not give him any further details.
3. I informed him that, since I am myself a Michigan alumnus, I would not be the principal investigator.
4. I suggested that full cooperation on the part of the University would go a long way to mitigate whatever penalties might be incurred, but I also warned him that the accusations were serious ones, including the possibility of a "pattern of violations."

"That would really have torn it," Zoe commented. "If they can document what they call a 'pattern of violations,' it could have meant the Death Penalty."

Thursday, October 17, 1996, 8:30 A.M.: Report of Conversation with Charles H. Cassovoy

1. Mr. Cassovoy called me by telephone in my hotel room in Ann Arbor.
2. He informed me that a report of my meeting Wednesday

evening, Oct. 17, with Russell Truhorne had been printed in this morning's *Michigan Daily*, the University of Michigan student newspaper.

3. Mr. Cassovoy demanded to know how this information had become known to the *Daily*. It was clear from this conversation that Mr. Cassovoy himself knew nothing about the source of this revelation.
4. I informed Mr. Cassovoy that I needed to see the *Daily* report before I could determine how to proceed. Since the *Daily* is distributed only in the campus area, I told him I would drive to campus and call him at the *Detroit News* once I had read it.

"So that's why there's no record of a phone call to Cassovoy from Greenaway's hotel room," Anneke commented as she clicked open the next outline.

Thursday, October 17, 1996, 9:15 A.M.: Report of Conversation with Charles H. Cassovoy

1. I called Mr. Cassovoy at the *Detroit News* after having read in the *Michigan Daily* (October 18, 1996, page 1) a report of my conversation with Russell Truhorne. The *Daily* report was an accurate rendering of that conversation.
2. Mr. Cassovoy was extremely angry and began by accusing me of "breaking our agreement."
3. I informed him that I was not responsible for giving this information to the *Daily* and pointed out that its publication was far more damaging to me than it could possibly be to him. I further insisted that he give me the names and other information he said he had.
4. Mr. Cassovoy, who was extremely angry and abusive, said the following: "Who gives a shit anymore? You want names? How about, okay, let's say Norville Jefferson. Sure, why not? He comes outa Brewster-Douglas, no father, coupla younger brothers, mother on welfare—you can't tell me he isn't on the take.

Or how about Jimmy Munson? Chicago slums, father in prison, you know damn well he wouldn't of signed on if there hadn't been something in it for him. Yeah, you start with those two, see what you come up with."

After pages of rigid bureaucratese, Charlie Cassovoy's words seemed to leap off the screen. The three people gathered around the computer stared at each other in dawning amazement before reading further.

5. I asked Mr. Cassovoy if he had any evidence that either of these players had in fact accepted illegal financial inducements to attend Michigan.
6. Mr. Cassovoy replied: "Shit, finding evidence is your job. If you can't come up with any dirt on those two, try some of the others. You know goddam well some of them'll be on the take."
7. I asked Mr. Cassovoy if he had any evidence of any kind against any member of the Michigan football team or against any Michigan alumnus.
8. He replied again that finding evidence was my job. He further stated that "if you run a full-scale investigation of a school like Michigan, you know you're gonna find something."
9. It became clear that Mr. Cassovoy did not in fact have any evidence of misdeeds at Michigan, but that he simply expected that an investigation would uncover some infractions.
10. I informed Mr. Cassovoy that he had seriously compromised both the reputation of the NCAA and my own personal integrity. I told him that it would be necessary to issue a public statement explaining the entire situation.
11. Mr. Cassovoy told me that if I did so, "your ass will be in that sling right along with mine," and said further that "the only way either of us is gonna get out of this mess is to play out the hand."
12. I informed him that my conversation with Mr. Truhorne was itself a sufficiently serious breach of ethics on my part that

nothing could cause me any greater damage than I had already caused myself. I further informed him that it was my firm intention to announce my resignation from the NCAA at the same time that I issued a statement exonerating the University of Michigan.

Anneke felt her eyes swimming. Even through the stilted language, Alvin Greenaway seemed to shine through.

"I told you he was a straight-up kind of guy," Zoe muttered.

13. At this point, Mr. Cassovoy became even more agitated and insisted on a face-to-face meeting. I told him that there would be no purpose to such a meeting, but he persisted. He claimed that he had information which he felt would cause me to change my mind.
14. I asked him if this information related to NCAA violations by University of Michigan athletes or alumni, and he said he would "have something" for me, and that I should not act hastily before he had a chance to show it to me.
15. Although I did not particularly believe him, I agreed to a meeting. He informed me that he had to meet other people at Michigan Stadium later in the morning, and pointed out that the stadium is customarily deserted on weekday mornings. I therefore agreed to meet with him there.

"My God," Anneke whispered. "It's like a voice from the dead."

"That's exactly what it is," Karl pointed out.

"There's more." Anneke clicked the pointer once more and opened the final outline.

October 17, 1996: Draft Press Statement—Alvin Greenaway

1. Ladies and Gentlemen: I've called this press conference for the purpose of announcing that there will not be an investigation of the University of Michigan football program by the National Collegiate Athletic Association.

2. The original intent to investigate was based on statements given me by Charles H. Cassovoy, a writer for the *Detroit News.* Mr. Cassovoy has since admitted to me that these statements were utterly and entirely false.
3. I originally believed Mr. Cassovoy to be telling the truth, and for that reason I told Russell Truhorne, Michigan athletic director, that an investigation was imminent. I am fully aware that my actions in so doing were a violation of NCAA practice.
4. I wish to make the following statements:
   a. First, I wish to offer my sincerest apologies to the University of Michigan.
   b. Second, I am hereby tendering my resignation to the National Collegiate Athletic Association, effective immediately.
   c. Finally, I urge the University of Michigan and the NCAA to pursue any and all legal remedies against Charles

Cassovoy and his employers, including the possibility of a lawsuit for defamation and/or prosecution for malicious mischief. I stand ready to testify in any such action.

"Y'know, he could've stonewalled. Just announced that my story was a crock, and that would've been it." Zoe kept her eyes fixed on the screen. "It would've been my word against his, and who'd have believed me?"

"Yes, but that would have meant a collusive lie with Charlie Cassovoy, and with Russ Truhorne, plus anyone else Russ might have told," Karl pointed out. "And all of it with you insisting you'd heard it, other media sniffing around it, and the players themselves caught in the middle. That sort of thing isn't as easy to pull off as it sounds."

"Look at Watergate," Anneke commented.

"Yeah, I guess you're right," Zoe agreed. "But I still think most people would've gone that route." She looked up finally, and her coppery eyes were bright with unshed tears.

"Will you copy those files to a floppy disk?" Karl asked Anneke, speaking more briskly than usual. "And print out copies of them, too, if you would."

"Yes, of course." She quickly downloaded the file and logged off the computer in Kansas. While she hooked the laptop to Karl's printer, he reconnected his telephone and she heard him calling the Overland Park police.

"They'll impound Greenaway's computer and ship it to us," he said after he hung up.

"What happens next?" Zoe asked.

"Next we turn everything over to the prosecutor's office," Karl told her.

"And I bet he releases it to the media the minute it hits his desk," she said gloomily.

"Probably so," Karl agreed. "After all, the prosecutor is also a Michigan man."

"Great." Zoe wrinkled her nose in disgust. "Oh, well." She stood up. "I guess I'm outa here."

"You understand," Karl warned her, "that nothing you've seen or heard here is to see print until we tell you so."

"Yeah, I know." She shrugged broadly. "It's not like I have anywhere to publish it anyway, with no *Daily* till Monday. And I'm sure as hell not going to give it away as gossip. I guess," she said reflectively, "I'll go to the victory party."

"Victory party?" Anneke clicked on Print and looked up from the computer.

"Yeah. Richard's going to introduce me to Marta Wentworth."

"Oh?" Anneke must have put more meaning into the monosyllable than she'd intended, because Zoe laughed and shook her head.

"Not to worry," she said, picking up her bookbag. "It's under control."

FORTY-FOUR

The Sunday morning President's Club breakfast, the weekend's closing event, was a lot more crowded than usual. At least according to Richard. Zoe queued up behind him at the buffet in the University Club dining room and allowed him to fill her plate with onion bagel, cream cheese and lox, rugalach and a large helping of fresh fruit salad. She was going to be sorry when Richard left and she had to go back to eating dorm food. On the other hand, it was probably just as well that he'd be leaving this afternoon. Things were getting a little too heavy.

The victory party had been fun for a while—although Marta Wentworth never did show—but she'd felt heavy with the burden of unrevealed secrets. At eleven o'clock someone turned on a television newscast, and she'd been unsurprised but still depressed to see the entire Greenaway story reported in full.

"Did you know about it?" Richard had asked.

"Yeah."

"And no *Daily* tomorrow." At least he understood the cause of her gloom. "Come on, let's get you out of here."

But once they were outside, instead of turning the ugly rental car toward East Quad, he'd headed in the opposite direction.

"Wrong way, Richard."

"I thought we'd drive out along the river." He reached over and took her hand.

"Uh-uh, sorry. I'd like to go back to the dorm, please."

"Just for a short ride." He stroked her fingers, running his thumb along the inside of her wrist.

"No, sorry. I want to go home, please."

"Zoe, I'm leaving tomorrow. Please come with me, for a little while at least."

"*No*, Richard." She removed her hand from his grasp. "Home. Now." Had she miscalculated him? Casually, she reached into her bookbag on the floor by her feet. She located her key ring by touch and wrapped her fingers around it.

"One stop," Richard said. "One kiss."

"One kiss," she agreed. "In front of the dorm."

"Like an undergraduate?" He sounded offended.

"I *am* an undergraduate."

"Some people have mature souls," he said, but when Zoe burst out laughing he had the grace to grin sheepishly. "All right, to the dorm it is. But you'll remember that kiss, I promise you."

Well, probably she would. It was one hell of a kiss, but that was as far as she was going to go. She sure wasn't about to screw with some guy she'd only just met—and married besides. Should she tell him she'd looked him up in the alumni directory? Nah, why bother?

She looked around for an empty table, then spotted Anneke in conversation with Eleanor Sullivan and steered Richard in their direction.

"I didn't expect to see you here," she said to Anneke after being invited to join them.

"Well, one way or another Karl missed most of the weekend, so he thought he should at least make an appearance." She gestured with her bagel toward the far end of the room, where Genesko stood with the president and Russell Truhorne.

"Did Cassovoy confess?" Zoe asked.

"You'll have to ask the appropriate authorities about that," Anneke replied primly, then laughed at herself. "Hell, I sound like some sort of assistant dean, don't I? No, as far as I know he hasn't."

"If he's got the brains God gave a gnat, he'll dummy up and yell for a lawyer." Jeffrey Person dropped into a chair and leaned back, stretching out his long legs and clasping his hands behind his neck in an attitude of easy relaxation. "I'll have a current union update for you this afternoon," he told Zoe.

"And maybe I'll have something for you, too," Eleanor said, waving an arm in the air. Across the dining room, Daniel Najarian shrugged and nodded at her and came toward them.

"Good morning, Eleanor." He set his coffee cup on the table and nodded to the others, his eyes resting sharply on Zoe for a moment as he slid into an empty chair. "I suppose you think you're entitled to gloat?"

"Damn right I am. I've got a whole batch of I-told-you-so's ready, and I plan to use all of them. The most important of which is that there *was no* recruiting violation at Michigan."

"A statement that neatly illustrates your customary disregard for logic." Najarian sighed rather theatrically. "The only statement you can make with accuracy, Eleanor, is that a single reporter, namely Charles Cassovoy, had no *evidence* of any violation."

"Oh, come on, Daniel." Eleanor snorted. "The whole thing was a scam, beginning to end, invented out of absolute thin air. There *wasn't anything there*, period, outside of Cassovoy's malicious imagination."

"Yes, there was something there," Najarian contradicted her, "and that is, the positive knowledge we all share, that if you investigate any college athletic program thoroughly enough, you can be sure you'll find illegalities somewhere."

"Well, sure. Any time you have a set of laws that are sufficiently unclear, inequitable, and badly and unfairly enforced, you'll have people who resist them."

"In other words, if people break the law, it's the law's fault?"

"Yes!" Eleanor snapped. "If enough people break a law, there's something wrong with the law."

"And of course, working to change the law is too much trouble, when simply ignoring it is so much easier."

"Working to change the law," Jeffrey interjected, "is precisely what the players' union is for. How come you won't support that?"

"Because," Najarian retorted, "I've never seen a union yet that didn't result in the tail wagging the dog. And the notion of unions *preventing* corruption is positively laughable."

"Excuse me?" Zoe interrupted hotly, but Richard's voice overrode hers.

"What I don't understand," he said, more loudly than necessary, "is why Cassovoy ran this scam in the first place."

"Because he hated Michigan," Eleanor replied. "You only had to read his columns to see it. I guess he figured he'd found a way to pull us down."

"Actually, I don't think that was really the point," Zoe said, then hesitated as the others turned to stare at her. "I think," she continued slowly, "that he was after the high."

"What do you mean?" Eleanor asked curiously.

"Well, you know he won a Pulitzer for investigative reporting years and years ago, but he really hasn't done anything much since except, you know, the same old same old. He was talking to me yesterday, and he sounded, I don't know, kind of weird, all about how it was all going to be downhill from here. I think what he was really after was another great story."

"Surely you're not suggesting that he murdered Alvin Greenaway just so he could write about it?" Najarian asked.

"No, of course not. But he didn't start out planning to kill anyone. At the beginning, he was just after a big exposé. He thought the same way you do, that if you investigate any program completely, you're going to find something. Like I said, I think he was after the high."

"That's ridiculous," Najarian said contemptuously.

"Is it?" Zoe looked directly at him. "Have you ever watched a

Super Bowl postgame celebration? Some of the guys are whooping and yelling and stuff, but some of them are just standing around with this amazing look on their faces, like they've died and gone to heaven. Not many people get moments like that, but breaking a really enormous story comes close to that kind of high. And I think when it happens to you once, sometimes you can spend the whole rest of your life wanting to relive it. I think that's what Charlie was after."

"Murder by midlife crisis," Najarian said, but his tone was less sarcastic than thoughtful.

"He had it all set up, and then I came along and blew him out of the water." Zoe felt a shiver go through her.

"In any case, Daniel," Eleanor said into the silence that followed, "I assume we're going ahead, now that you're sure none of us is a murderer?"

"Or worse, an NCAA rule breaker," Jeffrey added sardonically.

"Yes, we'll go ahead. But we can talk about it later, in private." Najarian looked openly at Zoe, avoiding Jeffrey's gaze.

"In other words, you're going ahead without me." Jeffrey nodded. "It's okay, Daniel. You go find yourself some brother who isn't involved in anything as socially reprehensible as an athletes' union. Maybe a corporate raider." He sipped coffee. "This has been one hell of a weekend." He didn't pursue the subject; well, either Eleanor Sullivan will give it to me, Zoe thought, or I'll pry it out of Richard. Whatever these guys are up to, it's got to be worth going after, or why bother to keep it a secret?

"Jeffrey, we need to go over the text for tomorrow's press release." Kyle Farmer approached the table. He was wearing a Michigan T-shirt under a shabby tweed sports jacket that strained across his broad shoulders.

"Right." Jeffrey nodded and started to rise, then paused. "You know, that reminds me—why did Cassovoy plant that rumor about Kyle? Just because he was the most famous player on the team?"

Most of the others shrugged in ignorance, but Zoe noted that

Anneke sat very still. Apparently, Jeffrey noticed it, too. "Do you know something?" he asked her.

"Not exactly."

"You do, don't you?" Jeffrey pressed.

"I think the young man has a right to know," Najarian said. "*If* you've really found out anything."

"Do you?" Anneke looked at him. "All right. Charlie Cassovoy didn't plant that rumor—he didn't have the computer knowledge to do what was done. I think you did it."

"What? Why on earth would I want to frame a Michigan student for murder?"

"You didn't. The murder wasn't the issue, was it? I think you wanted to discredit him because of the union."

"But my dear woman," Najarian said, offensively reasonable, "the rumor began Thursday night, before the union story even became public. How could I wish to discredit something I knew nothing about?"

"I think you did know about it." Anneke turned to Jeffrey. "Remember at the stadium, while you were waiting for Frank Novak, you said something about an appointment, and about 'social goals,' and Dr. Najarian asked if you were planning some sort of student protest. I think," she returned to Najarian, "that you were a bit worried about what Mr. Person was up to. So you decided to find out just what business here at Michigan he thought was so important—after all, he was going to be on your scholarship committee."

Scholarship committee? Zoe filed the words away in the back of her head even as she listened in fascination to Anneke's accusation.

"I think," Anneke continued, "that you hacked into his computer account to find out, and you discovered the union business. Were you," she asked Jeffrey, "using e-mail to communicate to all your athletes?" When he nodded dumbly, she said to Najarian, "After that, it was simple for you to plant the rumor anonymously."

"And just how," Najarian asked easily, "did you come up with this quaint notion?"

"It wasn't easy," Anneke replied. "You were very careful. You didn't even post the rumor yourself, did you? Instead, you sent e-mail to three or four people on Confer who were already involved in a discussion of the NCAA investigation, telling them that Kyle Farmer had accepted money to stay at Michigan."

"And you know this because you found an e-mail message signed Daniel Najarian?" Daniel asked sarcastically.

"Obviously not." Anneke shook her head. "You were careful there, too. Only," she looked at him, "you were unlucky. One of your targets saved your message in his online mailbox."

"Are you saying you broke into someone else's files?" Najarian all but pounced on her words.

"Let's just say it was there." Anneke forged ahead quickly. "Even there, you were careful—just not quite careful enough. Or maybe you aren't familiar with the anonymous sites you could have pathed it through. You edited the Sender line—the message came from someone who called himself MaizeFan—but you didn't edit the Path."

"What do you mean?" Zoe asked, her forehead furrowed in concentration.

"E-mail isn't sent directly from one computer to another," Anneke explained. "It's moved through the Internet from one physical machine to another depending on a number of different variables. And each message includes a Path statement which shows the route the message took. This particular message came through a small UNIX site in Florida, identified as glade.law.com."

"What?" Jeffrey Person leaned forward, staring. "That's our system—my law firm."

"Yes, I know." Anneke nodded. "And you were the one person I was sure wouldn't have planted a rumor discrediting Kyle Farmer. That's one of the reasons I think Dr. Najarian hacked into your computer, too—because, you see, the message that went through your system *originated* at a site in Chicago, identified as chem-one.rsch.org."

"Did it indeed." Najarian sat very still. "An elegant job," he said finally, inclining his head toward her. "My congratulations." He bestowed the word like an accolade.

"You . . . " Kyle Farmer grabbed Najarian by the arm and started to haul him to his feet, but Jeffrey was there first.

"Kyle, he isn't worth it." Jeffrey grabbed Kyle's arm in turn, struggling to pull his hand loose. After a second, Kyle released his hold on Najarian.

"Y'know, you're right." Kyle sounded almost surprised, and his mouth twisted into something resembling a smile. "We've got more important business than him, don't we?" He stepped back a pace and folded his arms, staring down at Najarian, who turned away.

"You do know," he said to Zoe, his face immobile, "that printing a single word of this fantasy would constitute absolute libel?"

"Maybe." Zoe contrived to look thoughtful. "And of course I will be pretty busy next week. Especially," she added, "if I'm doing a story on your scholarship committee."

"Eleanor, give her what she wants." Najarian's face was a mask as he stood and stalked away.

FORTY-FIVE

Thank God it was over—the murder, President's Weekend, all of it. Anneke crossed through the Arcade at double time, nearly scuttling in her haste to reach her office. She opened the door with such a gust of relief she felt almost giddy. Since it was Sunday, the office was more crowded than usual, her student programmers squeezing in hours when and as they had them.

"Is it true, Ms. Haagen?" Marcia Rosenthal asked, reaching down to pick up the pencil she dropped. "There really weren't any Michigan players on the take?" The others clustered around, and Anneke answered their questions and confirmed reports, calculating that they'd all get back to work more quickly that way—including herself.

"Was Charlie Cassovoy the one who started the on-line rumor about Kyle Farmer?" Calvin asked.

"We'll probably never know for sure who was responsible," Anneke equivocated.

"Oh, great. A hit-and-run on the information superhighway," Carol Coburn joked.

Instantly there were whoops of joy. "Pay up, Coburn," Marcia said, holding out a plastic diskette box labeled "Superhighway Metaphor Fund." Carol, red-faced but grinning, dug into the pocket of her jeans and dropped a dollar bill into the box.

Marcia poked a finger experimentally into the box. "Not bad. Pretty soon we'll have enough for a real Christmas bash."

"I don't know," Ken Scheede said dubiously. "We're all so careful now we may not collect much more. Maybe we should add in fines for draining the battery pack on the Powerbook."

"Not fair," Carol protested at once. "I use it twice as much as anyone else."

Anneke left them to their cheerful squabbling and sank gratefully into the chair behind her desk, looking fondly at her Compaq. Computers, she concluded, were a good deal easier to cope with than people.

Saturday's mail was still on her desk, unread. When she opened it, there were two more requests for bids—a local restaurant wanted to establish an on-line lunch ordering system, and a writer of fantasies wanted to set up a home page on the World Wide Web for her fans. Neither of them was technically difficult, but the writer was going to want something flashy in the way of graphics. Animation would work well. . . . Anneke clicked open her project management file. Max could do the restaurant project. Calvin had demonstrated a growing skill with graphics and sound, but he was already working on the Webster Packing Company network. Well she could work with him on the Web project—shove back the Marfield Realty deadline . . .

"Anneke?" Zoe's voice interrupted her as she was moving the Webster project line for the third time. "Got a minute?"

"Yes." She swiveled from the computer. "Pull up a chair, if you can find an empty one." When Zoe had commandeered a battered wooden chair from across the room, Anneke asked, "What can I do for you?"

"I just wanted to confirm a couple of things about the Kyle Farmer rumor. Don't worry—" she held up a hand "—I'm not going to mention Najarian. But can you say for the record that the rumor was started by someone from *outside* Confer?"

"Not really." Anneke shook her head, smiling at Zoe's crestfallen expression. "What you can say," she chose her words carefully, "is that the earliest identifiable references to Kyle Farmer were entered onto Confer from an outside source."

"Doesn't have nearly as much journalistic sex appeal," Zoe grumbled, scribbling in her omnipresent notebook. "The worst part of it is, readers'll think it was Cassovoy."

"You can say something like, 'authorities don't believe it was started by Charles Cassovoy,' can't you?"

"Yeah, I guess." Zoe scribbled further, then jumped to her feet. "Thanks. Gotta go—Richard's taking me to lunch at the Greenery before he leaves."

"Oh?" Anneke tried to keep her voice nonjudgmental, but Zoe caught the edge in her tone.

"Don't worry, it's strictly for the food. Well, okay, not strictly," she admitted, grinning. "Richard's kind of fun. But believe me, that's as far as it goes. Totally wrong category."

"Wrong category?"

"Sure. See, I figure men come in two basic categories. There are the ones you take seriously, and then there are the other kind. Richard's the kind of guy you keep as a pet." When Anneke laughed aloud she laughed as well, then became more serious. "You're lucky," she said. "The one you've got is a real keeper."

When Zoe was gone Anneke turned back to the project manager, still trying to shoehorn eighty hours of work into a forty-hour week. Her work, after all, was the real constant in her life, the one thing she had held onto. Besides Karl, of course.

Karl, in fact, was the one who'd pointed it out to her—that she'd lost so much in the last year it was natural for her to cling to her work. Well, wasn't it the natural thing to do, when you've lost everything, to hang on to what's left? To be afraid of losing even more?

Afraid. The word tasted bitter in her mouth. Clinging to what she had left, afraid to let go. Afraid.

She shut down the project manager and tossed the new proposals into her Hold box. Looking around the office, she decided they could get along without her for the rest of the day, and after a quick consultation with Ken, she picked up her briefcase and headed out the door. Carol, she noted, was already commandeering the Compaq.

She did what she always did when she needed to think—got in her car and drove. The Firebird purred its way out Dexter Road under flame-colored trees that seemed to impart a glow to the roadway. When she reached the tiny village of Dexter she turned north to Huron River Drive and then back toward Ann Arbor, following the bright ribbon of water framed in the brilliant reds and golds of fall.

When she arrived home late in the afternoon, bearing a grocery bag that contained two thick steaks, potatoes for baking, and a large Styrofoam container of salad, Karl was already there. He was stretched out on the long sofa with a book in his lap, and Anneke was struck once more by how well the room suited him.

"Is it all over, then?" she asked him when she'd stowed the food in the kitchen.

"Well, there's still investigative work to do," he replied, "but in general, yes, the rough part is pretty well over." He set his book on the coffee table and reached out a hand to her. She started to sit next to him, but somehow she found herself horizontal and thoroughly entangled.

"The drapes are wide open," she pointed out when she could finally speak.

"So they are." He stood, picking her up with him in one smooth motion. "Have you ever," he asked with a wicked grin, "seen my Rhett Butler imitation?"

The bedroom drapes were open as well, but upstairs it didn't matter; no one was near enough to see in. Afterward, she lay curled beside him and looked at the gold of the big maple outside the window, and beyond it, the sky darkening into twilight.

"What are you thinking?" Karl asked.

"That I absolutely hate those drapes," she blurted.

He laughed aloud. "There's an ego check if I ever heard one."

"I'm sorry." She laughed with him, embarrassed. "It's not . . . I don't *hate* them, really, I just . . ."

". . . can't stand them," he finished for her. "I know."

"You know?"

"You make a face every time you open or close them."

"Do I? I'm sorry," she said again.

"Sorry for what? For not liking the drapes?" He looked down at her. "Don't you think it's time you took charge of your home life just as you do your work life?"

"You sound just like Michael Rappoport," she said crossly.

"An intelligent man, even if he does occasionally look like an overaged Ken doll."

"Not fair," she said, laughing. "All right, all right." She threw up her hands. "I'll think about it. It's just that our styles are so different." Charcoal gray carpeting, she thought, with silvery drapes. Touches of the burnt orange that Karl liked, to add brightness and color. "I'm hungry," she announced.

They dressed and went downstairs, where they rummaged in the refrigerator, pulling out chunks of cheese and tiny carrots and dark rye bread.

"Are the steaks for tonight?" Karl asked, pointing to the package. "I thought Marianne left a casserole Friday."

"Yes, she did, but I thought I'd save it." Anneke took a deep breath. "I fired her."

"Thank God," he said in a voice filled with relief.

"But . . . You mean you're glad?"

"I'm absolutely delighted." He smiled slightly at her confusion. "I know how much trouble she's been giving you. I've been waiting for you to fire her for some time."

"But if you wanted to get rid of her, why didn't *you* fire her?"

"Because it was something you had to do," he said quietly.

"Yes, I suppose it was." She picked up the plate of food and carried it to the living room, while Karl brought glasses of soda. When they were seated on the sofa, she turned to him and asked, "Why did you want to marry me?"

He looked at her quizzically. "I take it 'because I love you' isn't going to be a sufficient answer."

"Let's stipulate that." She smiled. "But why marriage?"

"Isn't that what people do when they fall in love?"

"Not necessarily. Especially nowadays, and especially at our stage of life. Think about this—during all those years after your divorce, you must have met other women you could have fallen in love with."

"I suppose I could have, but I didn't. Is all this leading somewhere?"

"I think there's a reason you didn't fall in love until you came back to Ann Arbor. You said yourself, you had the feeling you wanted to come home. You were *ready* to come home."

"And you think I simply looked around for someone who fit into the mental image of home I'd constructed in my head."

"Not exactly, but . . . Don't misunderstand me," she said anxiously. "I don't doubt that you do love me. But I think, where women decide to marry after they fall in love, men fall in love after they decide to marry."

"So you think that if it hadn't been you, it would have been someone else."

"I think," she said directly, "that you were looking for someone to 'settle down' with. Which is one reason you wanted someone in your own age range."

"Instead of a twenty-year-old football groupie, you mean?" He laughed aloud. "I can think of fifteen better reasons than that. As Zoe might say: Been there, done that." He looked at her more seriously. "It's not like you to be insecure."

"Oh, insecure." She waved the word away. "That's not it at all." She hesitated. "Ken Scheede is finishing his M.A. this semester."

"Oh?" He waited for her to expand on the apparently irrelevant statement.

"I'm going to offer him a partnership."

"So that you don't lose him? Good idea."

"Not so I don't lose him. So that I don't lose myself." He had been expecting her to say: So that I don't lose you. He looked both surprised and oddly gratified, and Anneke felt her heart expand.

"Zoe was right," she said. "You are a keeper. I guess," she declared, "that I will have to marry you. Eventually," she added.